Life
After
Wren

Verona Anne VanderVen

WINTERS
PUBLISHING

winterspublishing.com

Life After Wren

Copyright © 2023 by Verona Anne VanderVen

Published by Winters Publishing
www.winterspublishing.com
812-663-4948

Printed in the United States of America

Library of Congress Control Number: 2023935558

ISBN: 978-1-954116-19-1

Table of Contents

Cast of Characters

Carrie - Leading Character: Wife of Matt and mother to Anna, Durinda, and Tim

Matt - Carrie's husband and father of Anna, Durinda, and Tim

Adam and Anna - Parents of Anton and grandparents of Carrie

Anton - Carrie's father

Maria I - Carrie's mother and first wife to Anton

Maria II - Carrie's stepmother and second wife to Anton

Maria III - Carrie's Aunt Mary and younger sister of Anton

Jan - Husband of Maria III and uncle to Carrie, father of Carrie's cousin

Jan - Son of Adam and Anna, brother to Maria III, Anton, and young Adam

Adam and Eve - Uncle and aunt to Carrie. Adam is brother of Anton. They are godparents to Carrie and parents of Lynn, Ed, and Lena

Betka - Sister to Carrie and Milka, and half-sister to Ria

Milka - Sister to Carrie and Betka, and half-sister to Ria

Grandma and Grandpa Fisher - Carrie's great-aunt and great-uncle; aunt and uncle to Maria I

Durinda Hansen - Carrie's high school teacher whose influence was strong

Pastor B - Carrie's confirmation pastor and mentor

Doctor Munson - Carrie's physician after Timmy's birth and mentor to Carrie

Irene - Carrie's hairdresser and close friend

Professor Tschirhy - From Switzerland, Carrie's second Russian professor

Thelma - Matt's adopted sister and wife of Larry; in the U.S. Army

Polly - Matt's youngest adopted sister.

Oma - Wren's sitter (Oma is Dutch for grandmother)

Chuck Anion - Carrie's favorite high school principal

Cathy and Harry - Matt's Dutch cousin and her husband, who lived in Canada and were frequent hosts to Matt and Carrie

Reta - Cathy's sister and first cousin to Matt

Jonathan Cates - Extended cousin to Carrie

Chapter III contains Yedinka/Edith and other Latvian friends; Yedinka's sister, Elsa.

LIFE AFTER WREN

The child is father (or mother) of the man (or woman)
And I would wish my days to be bound each to each
In endless piety.

(To paraphrase Wordsworth)

Chapter 1

Word Warriors of the Cold War

They were all there at the railroad station—her sisters, Betka, Milka, and their mother's cousins, Anna, Sue, and Steve. The cousins were always there for Carrie, and now, at this important moment of departure, again they were there. Anna was sad; her son was suffering from leukemia. When Carrie asked her about him, she merely shrugged her shoulders and the look on her face said more than words could explain.

Milka, however, announced some happy news. "Betka has something to tell you."

It took some prodding to get Betka to finally spill it out—"I just won a thousand dollars." Earlier, while shopping at the local grocer's, she had participated in Customer Bingo, and she won.

Only hours before, Carrie had boarded the train, which was to take her from the town in western Michigan to Chicago. Matt was there, holding the two-year-old Wren, who reached for her mother. With a divided heart, Carrie held her close before returning her to her father's waiting arms, and hearing the reassuring words he gave his departing wife. "You're going to do something positive for your baby's future. It's okay, hon, she'll be fine."

On the previous weekend, they had celebrated the birthdays of all three daughters together at the restaurant that supplied cakes to dining families. The three birthdays fell on dates within three weeks, so their claims fell well within the guidelines of the restaurant policy; but Matt still admitted feeling like an *oink-oink* in accepting all three chocolate cakes, though the manager insisted. It was more than a birthday celebration, it was a farewell party, to which a few close friends had been invited.

Carrie reminisced. So much had occurred since the birth of little Wren two years before. Matt graduated with a degree in Education and a major in Geography, his favorite subject. He had been assigned to an inner city elementary school with a very empathetic principal, who showed much interest in the unique learning difficulties their son, Timmy, had encountered. She confided to Matt her own son's difficulties with learning. Her empathy proved to be helpful during Matt's first years of teaching.

Carrie graduated from the Christian college and immediately found employment teaching both English and Russian at a suburban high school. Now, after a year there, she was eligible to participate in a special NDEA graduate program for teachers of Russian from all over the United States. There were forty-four in all, and the university selected was located in San Francisco, ideal because of the many Russian émigrés who had settled there. These immigrants had been recruited to share their knowledge of the Russian language and enhance the skills of the students, who were actually teachers of Russian in high schools and colleges from all over the country.

Bidding everyone farewell, Carrie boarded the train with all three suitcases, plus a small carry-on. Given a choice, she had chosen San Francisco above New Hampshire, when selected to attend the NDEA graduate programs for Russian instructors. This would be her first visit to California. She had never been farther west than Missouri, and was looking forward to viewing the scenery across the country. Besides, she felt the need of a change. This first year of teaching had proved grueling. Matt always pitched in to help with the cooking, some of the home chores, and attention to the children. Anna was almost fifteen when Wren was born and Durinda had become a teenager. Timmy, disappointed that his sister was not a boy, soon became reconciled to the new baby. He presented her with little gifts he had collected—a small doll and a styrofoam snowman rescued from the discard pile of a neighboring variety store.

The family had experienced several tragedies shortly after Wren was born. The first was when Timmy, eager to find caterpillars in a friend's yard, climbed a tree from which he fell and broke his leg. Durinda insisted on accompanying her father when he took Timmy to the hospital. Surgery was required and crutches were needed for about six weeks. Then, before his recovery was complete, Anna, who had been a guest at the cottage of a friend, suffered another tragedy.

The phone call came from the director of the camp where the cottage was located. It was a Saturday morning, and Matt did not waken Carrie. Aware that she had been up to nurse little Wren during the night, he wanted her to sleep in. Now he also wanted to protect her from the sad news. It was Durinda's voice that Carrie heard first.

"Aren't you going to tell Mom what happened to Annie's hand?"

Her words roused Carrie, who was gradually waking from her early morning nap. "What happened to Anna?"

Matt hesitantly explained. "It seems she had an accident with a fan and cut off her finger. The man who called promised to pray for her. Since there is no hospital close by, they're bringing her here to the one in Grand Rapids."

They were instructed to meet her with the cottage owners in the Emergency Ward at the same hospital where Wren was born.

Frightened, Carrie entered the bathroom, and raising her eyes to the sky she could see through the window high above the tub, she prayed the first personal prayer she had offered in a very long time. "Please, God, don't let this be, please help my daughter."

Experts at microsurgery were not yet available at this hospital. When the industrial surgeon arrived, he advised removing the portion of the left index finger, attached by a thin shred of skin, to avoid further problems. Infection was one. Carrie questioned him, "What would you do if this were your daughter?"

His gesture indicated a slice. "Exactly what I would advise you to have done."

This wonderful, beautiful daughter of ours, Carrie thought. When she reentered Anna's room, she kissed her and told her how sorry she was to have let her go to the cottage. *I felt something was wrong*, she thought, *for all did not go as planned.* The friends had come very late to get Anna, who walked little Wren to sleep earlier that evening. It seemed Carrie was experiencing a premonition. Premonitions were not uncommon in her mother's family, for she could recall Grandma Fisher had premonitions when something was happening to a family member, though that person might be far away. Matt, however, persuaded her to allow Anna to have this weekend visit with her young friend and her family, reminding her that this family had driven to their cottage many times late at night, and knew the way there very well. Also, Anna promised to wear a life jacket if they went boating.

Was it guilt that Carrie felt when she told Anna how sorry she was that she had allowed her to go?

"No, Mom, this is not your fault. I am fifteen now. I have to take care of myself."

Anna proceeded to tell how she and her friend were relaxing and chatting. Anna was still in bed when she stretched out her hand to feel the breeze emitted by the fan placed parallel to her bed. There was no guard, and suddenly, Anna was struck by one of the fan blades. Looking at her bleeding hand, she realized that most of her index finger had been sliced off. She quickly advised her friend to get a cold wet washcloth and to call her mother.

Carrie wished it had been her own finger instead of her daughter's. *A typical maternal reaction,* one close friend and advisor responded. There were other reactions. One, Carrie clearly recalled, occurred while shopping for school shoes with Anna. Startled, one elderly clerk, upon noting the bandage around her index finger, excitedly asked Anna, "My goodness, girlie, what did you do to yourself?"

Before Anna could answer, Carrie interceded, "We had an accident in our family."

Later, after Anna returned from school, the tears came. Hugging her daughter, Carrie listened as she told how badly her hand hurt during pep assembly, when the students were clapping for the football team about to have their first game of the season. So Carrie planned a strategy to revive her spirits.

"Let's make an appointment for that haircut you've been wanting." There was still a limited budget, for Carrie had to finish the last year of college. Maybe next year there would be a teaching job. Matt had just completed his degree and was assigned to a school in the inner city. This would reduce the repayment of the NDEA loan that covered his tuition. But a hairdo and maybe a new outfit could be squeezed into their carefully-planned budget. Carrie phoned her friend with the beauty shop in her basement. Her prices were the most modest, yet her personal care was unique. Irina was a saint!

That appointment made, she also planned to scan the clothing stores to check on the sales items. Anna favored colorful fabrics, liked traditional styles, and much of what she chose would be similar to what Carrie also liked. Carrie recalled how she and Anna once shopped at two separate stores, but both purchased the exact same sweater for themselves. They chuckled over this experience for a long time. Yet when Carrie learned that Anna had paid a dollar less for the very same article, she returned to the store of her purchase, and explaining the difference, was reimbursed the dollar.

Another challenge had to be faced for Anna. For the first time since attending high school she missed being placed on the Honor Roll. Typing proved to be difficult with her left index finger partially gone, and the grade given was a D. Intervening for Anna was her best friend, Marie, who approached the senior advisor and explained Anna's plight to her. It was decided to waive this grade when computing the others, for Typing was only a minor subject and an optional course, not a required one. Anna's major subject was Art. She was destined to major in Art from the time she was a youngster in kindergarten.

"It's because I can never keep my hands still," she once confided to Carrie. "They always need to be doing something." She seemed to want to record all that her eyes could see. Some of her talent was used when writing for the high school newsletter, both in drawing and in writing. Working closely with the editor, who was in the class one year ahead of her, she succeeded in becoming the editor during her senior year. She also won prizes for a picture she sketched of her brother, and another which revealed her depth of interest in the command given by Jesus to His disciples, that Anna entitled *The Great Command.* Carrie always managed somehow to pay the tuition fees for art classes Anna attended at the city's gallery on Saturday mornings. Recalling her own childhood interests in art, she was determined to provide this experience for Anna.

Carrie managed to finish college this last year, earning her AB. She had a babysitter for the afternoon classes at the college, which included more Literature and Philosophy. She studied when little Wren slept, sometimes late into the night. Mornings kept her busy making certain the older children all had their lunches ready for school. Timmy was now attending a school for children with special needs. Anna was a high school sophomore, and Durinda in middle school. This was the year that Durinda seemed to clam up. Anna, out of habit since infancy, shared all her thoughts and concerns with Carrie, as did Timmy. Durinda had expressed fondness for the nun who taught her reading class in summer school, telling Carrie, "Sister is like a mother." Carrie did wonder, *Was Durinda unconsciously sending a message to Carrie?*

That summer when Wren was born, both Timmy and Durinda attended reading classes at the Catholic College. It was reported that Timmy had advanced six months in his reading ability. The kind sister directing the school had arranged for him to have the same teacher he had at the private Catholic academy the summer before. His growth was evident in many ways. That fall, however, he returned to the private school affiliated with the mental hospital south of the city. It was not long before he complained to Carrie, "Mom, you know what? I need *harder* work. We're doing all the same stuff we had last year."

Carrie and Matt realized that, due to the diversity of growth pattern of the children in his class, the tempo was very slow to accommodate all of the children, many of whom were much slower learners than Timmy. This school had been his fifth school placement;

he had repeated kindergarten at the private church school; then he was placed in a special needs class at the public school where he did not feel comfortable, and at Carrie and Matt's request, he was transferred to a regular classroom in their district elementary school. When, after a year, the school district's administrators decided to exclude him from the district's public school, in spite of the intercession of the tutor Matt and Carrie had hired to instruct Timmy privately, they tried a private parochial school. All of these changes had to be puzzling for the young boy, but he tried to assimilate as best he could. It was still the early sixties, and schools did not offer the resource rooms that were to be later available for students with dyslexia. Their present school was located on the south side of the city and meant that he and Durinda both traveled there by bus. The placement lasted only six months. It was then decided to enroll Timmy at a school for special needs children, affiliated with the psychiatric hospital south of the city. Needs were diversified: children with Down syndrome; a few were emotionally disturbed, some suffered from epilepsy, or were diagnosed as aphasic. Timmy developed a unique level of compassion. He told of one classmate who experienced an epileptic seizure while there.

"I felt so bad for her," his tone was almost mournful.

He described how one little girl had difficulty walking because of her palsy. Timmy drew the name of this palsied youngster for a gift exchange at their Christmas party. When Matt took him shopping, he showed particular interest in selecting two items he had learned the little girl would like as gifts, leading Matt through several departments at the store until he found exactly what he was looking for.

Probably the class most appealing to Timmy was the woodshop. If his progress in reading and academics were wanting, he did learn something about woodworking. He also learned the Bible stories told in a very slow manner, with many illustrations to aid the children with handicaps. Transportation was provided, which eased the burden on Carrie and Matt during this last year, for they only had one car. Often, Matt rode the bus to his school, less than three miles from home. Anna usually rode with Matt, for the high school was close by. Durinda was enrolled at the new junior high, located a short two blocks away from home.

These were busy days for the family. Carrie recalled how Matt would bake three meat loaves on Sunday afternoon and place two in the freezer, to ease cooking chores during the week. There always was something to do. Their only luxury was to send out the ironing, that a kind lady was willing to do in her home for a modest cost. Anna helped Carrie with the housework. Somehow, they got through the year. Carrie graduated.

Matt's aunt and his cousin's wife, Etta, accompanied him to the graduation ceremony. The tender look on Matt's face was imprinted in Carrie's mind. He had truly been her helper and encourager to finish her college training. Her last task had been the completion of her English lit paper, a project that had tied her up for three whole days. Again, Matt shouldered household tasks—cooking and supervising the children, so Carrie could write. She had received an extension of time from the English professor, and arranged to deliver her essay to him personally, at the end of the weekend.

"May I now congratulate you for your completion of your college degree?" he prompted encouragingly, as she delivered her paper.

Russian classes at the other college were taught by an exchange professor from Switzerland. His family had accompanied him and joined them for dinner one Sunday. The Swiss professor gave Carrie a different perspective on the Russians in the Cold War. When asked about the Soviets' capturing first place in space, he commended them, reminding his American students, "In your country you have everything, beautiful books, many consumer goods, lovely homes, which many Soviet citizens lacked, but now the Russians have something of which they can be proud." Carrie noted his appreciation for American books. He had traveled with his Swiss college students to the Soviet Union a number of times, and was able to compare and contrast the cultures very vividly. This European professor's outlook expanded her horizons. Credits for Russian classes transferred and her foreign language requirement was completed for graduation.

Fortunately, Carrie found employment almost immediately at a suburban high school. The Latin teacher had left, and their principal and administration were anxious to fill the foreign language slot to compete with the city's system, which now had also opened a class in Russian for its high school students. The principal was most cordial. Having taught Spanish at a high school in another state, before becoming an administrator, he expressed much empathy for the needs of foreign language teachers. Carrie found him easy to work with, and as the school year went on, he also was considerate when special family needs had to be met.

Babysitters had to be interviewed. One that had proven satisfactory for the one-year-old Wren suddenly gave notice about a change of residence, for her husband was being transferred to another town. So a last-minute decision was made with a couple living close to their home. However, just before Christmas, Wren became ill with what appeared to be mumps. Misdiagnosing, the pediatrician administered a shot, which did not help. After nursing Wren for a whole night, they met the doctor at the hospital. Tests proved that her condition was a staph infection. A pediatric surgeon was called in to remove a lymph node. A week later, the same surgical procedure was done to remove the lymph node on the other side of her neck. Both times, Wren spent the night at the hospital, following surgery. The second time, when the eighteen-month-old saw her parents come to get her at the hospital, she very vividly showed her annoyance at Matt. When asked if she was mad at Daddy because he left her there at the hospital overnight, she nodded, so that Carrie and Matt knew her feelings.

In spite of busy circumstances, Carrie and Matt enjoyed their youngest daughter, being helped much by both Anna and Durinda, who seemed quite thrilled with this baby sister. The first week after Wren was released from the hospital, each took turns being excused from school—Carrie, then Matt, then each of Wren's older sisters. Looking back, Christmas week with Wren's illness seemed like a nightmare.

The Swiss professor had given each of the children a copy of *Tri Medveda*. Carrie loved to read stories to her young daughter, and she practiced using her Russian by reading this one. One Saturday morning, after looking through several other books, the child chose this storybook. Later, eager to demonstrate the eighteen-month-old's ability at distinguishing to Matt, she suggested that he read to her. He began to ad lib an English version of *The Three Bears*. Wren, who was used to having the Russian version read to her, took the book out of his hands, and went to her mother, expecting it to be read in Russian. Both Carrie and Matt chuckled, as they realized that their little daughter was so verbally acute that she could distinguish the same story in two languages, although she was only eighteen months old.

Carrie spread herself thin this first year of teaching high school. Attempting to continue her Russian studies, she approached a professor at Michigan State, a refugee from the Soviet Union, for studying an advanced course. What she did not realize was the difference in accents between her childhood exposure to Slovak and that of the modern Russian. The content was not difficult to absorb. Reiterating it verbally in the native language was something else. Was it merely lack of experience, or were her childhood fears resulting from the forced memorization of Slovak Bible studies returning to haunt her, so that she could not memorize and reproduce the content in Russian orally? She had difficulty with the final exam, and though she passed the course, she was disappointed. How could she continue?

The kind professor gave her a suggestion, which led to her application to attend one of the NDEA institutes the Federal government provided for teachers of Russian. The victory of landing in space by the Soviets had spurred the President and Congress to assess the educational needs of American children. It was from their assessment that the National Defense Education Act was created by Congress. Carrie applied, and when two options were offered, Carrie decided on the program in San Francisco, rather than the one in New Hampshire. Matt, always encouraging, urged her not to be concerned, for he wanted her to continue her studies. Besides, Anna, now seventeen, had a summer job. Durinda willingly would help care for Wren. Timmy would attend classes at the same school where Matt would be teaching this summer. Matt's plan was that if Timmy had a successful summer, he would seek to have him enrolled at the same elementary school in which he was assigned to teach, in the fall. In that way, he would have direct personal contact with his teachers and be able to monitor his progress.

Knowing all this, Carrie set about to pack for the two-month stay away from her family. Their friends, Gale and Dale, came to say farewell, and Gale gifted her with some stunning earrings. When Carrie, who still had some misgivings about leaving her youngest daughter for so long, confided her concern to Gale, she was reassured by her friend's prompting. "You go. This baby has two other mothers to dote on her. She'll be fine." Her husband, Dale, emphasized, "We're proud of you."

And so it was that Carrie set off for San Francisco, where for eight weeks she would be immersed in the Russian language, with forty-four other instructors, whom she termed as Language Warriors of the Cold War. This experience proved to be a valuable one for her entire academic career. What she was not prepared for were the various personalities she encountered at the Institute.

There were a few native speakers, émigrés who really did not need the intensive instruction given. One, named Olga, spoke in a derogative manner when referring to the lecturer on culture. Olga made it plain that attending this Institute was a *free paid vacation* for her. Her parents were refugees from the Bolshevik Revolution, who were first given asylum in China, before finally arriving in the United States.

"There is nothing here they can teach me about the language," she asserted, "and as for the lectures on culture, they're boring."

The American-born teachers of Russian came from all over the U.S.: New Yorkers; Ohioans; a Kansas native who spoke Russian with a western drawl; a teacher from Butte who was planning to move to Oregon to escape the limited stratification he was experiencing; a priest and a nun who were teaching in private Catholic schools in New York. All expected to acquire stronger language skills than they had when they arrived in San Francisco.

San Francisco itself was like a magic town with its many sights and cultural highlights. To introduce the participants to their environment, a tour was arranged on Saturday of the first weekend after their arrival. There were the trolley cars, holding their own on steep narrow streets; then the tour around Hippy-land with its tents and lean-tos, inhabited by longhaired, bearded young men and their families. Mimi, one of Carrie's closer colleagues accompanying her on the tour, commented at the sight of couples with their infants and youngsters. Childless, but happily married to a history professor, she uttered half prayerfully, "I wonder how these children will grow up normally. Why, oh why, won't the dear Lord give one of them to me?"

Classes began Monday morning. The dorm was about a half-mile's walk away from the building with the language lab and classrooms. Breakfast was served in the commons, just a short distance away from the dorm. Time was at a premium, so notebooks and texts were carried to the dining hall from where students continued their stroll to the classes. Levels were assigned to each according to one's command or lack of command of the language. Carrie's expectations differed from the reality in which she found herself. Until now, much of her studies in the language were written and silent. Here, emphasis was placed on oral training and usage. Small groups of nine met for forty-five minutes with oral drills. Following a brief break, students were ushered into the language laboratory, where rote repetition in words and sentences took place. This was followed by a lecture in Soviet and Russian culture. The speakers were seasoned travelers to the Soviet Union, and had much to offer in the way of social and political information. The afternoon sessions included more small group drills, and language lab assignments. At times, Carrie found it difficult to focus, which made it necessary for the instructor to redirect her attention back to the oral exercise he was leading. Only her regular letters from Matt consoled her homesickness. How faithful he was!

In the evenings, films were provided. Carrie found herself in tears after observing Sholokov's story, *Fate of a Man*. Others, like *The Cranes are Flying*, revealed the great sacrifices the Russian people made during World War II. This should have balanced some of the very negative propaganda issued during the Cold War. Music and drama, and dance instruction all occupied the students after hours. About ten per cent of San Francisco was inhabited by Russian refugees. It was these native speakers of Russian who were lunch and dinner partners, providing the students with opportunity to speak the language they had been drilled for earlier in the day. Many had been refugees from the 1917 Bolshevik Revolution, who had sought asylum in France, China, Korea, and wherever a country opened its doors to them. From there, many finally settled in San Francisco, where they were welcomed to attend services at a beautiful Orthodox cathedral.

As for San Francisco itself, the images of the town that remained with Carrie for years to come included her visit to that Orthodox Cathedral with its beautiful gold-domed roof. Delicious *piroshky* were available at the Russian restaurant on Geary Street. The unique shops, art exhibits, the opera in the grove, and the waterfront all held Carrie's enchantment.

Among the students there was much discussion on the difference between what was happening in the U. S. and the Soviet Union. The Vietnam War was raging. Meetings were being held on the campus with protestors advising young men who were draft age on how to avoid being sent to war. The problem did not seem to be resolvable. Some believed it was necessary to stop the spread of communism. Others, particularly the professors and leaders at

The Golden Gate Bridge in San Francisco.

the college, believed Americans needed to learn much more about the history and culture of the Russian people before rushing into judgment.

Carrie was too tired and too eager to review her lessons of each day to join the group that preferred to socialize at late hours. Besides, she wrote to Matt and the family frequently. Letters arrived from Matt almost every day. He went into much detail on all the activities of the children: Anna was enrolled in two summer classes at the high school; Durinda was selected to attend training classes for teaching swimming; and Tim was enrolled in summer school. Wren was cared for by Durinda, but all took turns at caregiving for their youngest sister. Carrie was surprised, amused, and comforted by Matt's letters. His details kept her informed of all their activities, social visits, and the learning progress of each child in their individual commitments, including those of little Wren. He even shared what foods and menus he planned. Matt had earned their livelihood selling *Wear-ever* pans in *the early* years of their marriage, so cooking was second nature for him. She felt very secure that Matt was fully in charge. What amused her were the various ways he would address her in his letters, as well as his sign-offs. Ever the creative thinker, he might begin with *Dear wife, Dearest, Darling, Dear Sweetie, or Dear Bunny* and close with something like *Daddy Rabbit & the Bunnies, Dad and the noodles, or enumerate with all, Love and kisses, Matthew, Anna, Durinda, Tim, and Wren.* At the close of one letter, Matt told of reading Luke, Chapter 12 in Scripture, and advised her to read it, as well.

Wishing to share, she opened her Bible. Luke writes of Jesus' teaching that includes both a warning and assurance of God's care, not only for the sparrows and the ravens, but even more so for His people. He tells the story of the foolish rich man who placed more faith in the accumulation of his crops, yet when God's timing called him from the earth, his hoarding proved unnecessary. Jesus cautioned, *Do not worry.* Worry cannot add time to one's life. Jesus also advised watchfulness. Be prepared for the arrival of the Master. As Carrie read through this long chapter, she felt a thankfulness that her husband had faith and shared it with her. She was sure it was this faith that directed his responsible, thorough care for his children in her absence, and for her. In spite of loneliness for her family, the efforts of her husband sustained her.

Carrie was subjected to learn other lessons than Russian conversation. When you place several dozen persons together, with their dozens of backgrounds and personal values for each to contend with, a conflict can be aroused. Maybe the word *misunderstanding of a situation* would prove to be a better description than the word *conflict*. A young man who surprised her was one she had met on the train to San Francisco. He was married, yet now he was keeping company with one of the single students, to console and reassure her. When Carrie made a surprised comment about the matter to someone, it was misinterpreted and created some misunderstanding. Actually, it proved to be an innocent friendship, but another was not so innocent in appearance. One of the men students had begun dating the young intern instructor, who was a native Russian speaker. According to Mimi, who had become a close friend of Carrie's, it was not unusual in an Institute. *Summer school affair*, Mimi termed it. But when homesickness overtook Carrie at one point, the young man made a derogatory remark to Carrie, insinuating she had been a troublemaker because of her questioning statement about the first couple. It was then that the tears erupted.

Mimi, who came to the rescue, arranged for Carrie to be excused from all the afternoon classes. Then she made her an appointment for the hair stylist. A stylish cut, followed by a manicure, did much for her morale, as well as for her appearance. Mimi advised her to use teabags for the puffiness under her eyes.

That evening, they were all invited to the home of the director and his wife, another Russian professor at a neighboring university. Traveling to their home with one of the leaders meant crossing the huge bridge between San Francisco and Oakland. Situated upon a very high hilly section, from which one could view the lights of the city at night, this was a magical transformation from the routine daily classroom drilling Carrie had been experiencing. When one of the men asked her to dance, he spoke in Russian to inform her he felt empathy for her flight in tears, earlier that day. He, too, was homesick, he confided, missing his wife and children. There was a consensus between him and some of the other more serious students that the native speakers who had bragged about knowing as much Russian as the instructors should have been placed in a separate group with more sophisticated assignments. Their assignment could require them to write a *doklad*; that is, a term paper, one requiring research, perhaps on one of Russia's world-renowned authors or composers.

Later, one of the group leaders approached Carrie. "Can we talk?"

Alone in an alcove, off the kitchen area, he expressed his concern about Carrie's upset. "Why were you so unhappy this morning?"

It was then that Carrie was able to verbalize the pent-up feelings accumulating during the past weeks at the Institute. She reminded him that he had previously asked her about remarks made about the first couple having an illicit affair.

"I never said that," she explained. "I only expressed surprise because I remembered all the thoughtful things he said about his wife, as we visited on the train while traveling here. Besides, how do you suppose I feel when people make untrue statements? I came to study, so I can teach much better next fall, and my husband is working his head off back home, taking care of our four kids, all by himself, including our little two-year-old daughter."

"Well, by now, we know that a certain woman has a big mouth, and perhaps we erred in not keeping her and a couple of the others busier so they would have no time for gossip or trivia."

Carrie knew without his identifying her that he meant Olga. After chatting a few minutes longer, both returned to the party. The hostess had taken advantage of the lovely bakeshops on Geary Street to provide her guests with delicious *pirozhki* and pastries, appetizers, and other delicacies, Russian style. Unknown in the western Michigan town where Carrie and Matt made their home, the foods proved to be a unique treat.

Carrie was overjoyed to see Matt and the children when they arrived from their journey across the country, for a visit. She had inquired and learned of the location of the restaurant where the

Matt, with 2-year-old Wren on his lap, while driving to join Mom in San Francisco.

special Russian cuisine was served. That was the first place Carrie directed them to eat lunch when Matt arrived in San Francisco. They loved the *pirozhki,* and Durinda announced that if she ever came back to San Francisco, this would be her first stop, the restaurant on Geary Street. Wren, who had been in the close personal care of her older sister, Durinda, was reintroduced to her mother.

"Here's Mommy," and shyly smiling, Wren approached her mom. *How much does she remember me, after eight weeks away,* Carrie wondered. As for Timmy, he was happy to be with his mom again. Several times during her absence from the family, she spoke with him by phone. Each time, he asked, "When are you coming home, Mom?" Anna, who was now seventeen, had taken an independent stance and worked on a factory assembly line as a temp, to earn money she needed for college next year. She wanted to share all her experiences with her mother. Happily, Carrie joined them in the motel where Matt had made reservations.

Waking early in the crib provided for her, little Wren enumerated all the family members: "Dada's here, and Timmy, and Rindy, and Anna, and Mama's here, too!"

"One more day, our graduation from Russian School, and then we'll be on our way to see Aunt Beth. Did you know she and Uncle Louie came to see me last month?"

Relating the visit with Matt's sister and her husband, she told them about the delicious dinner they had at Chinatown, and promised they would eat there before they left San Francisco. They had joined Louie's brother, who was employed and living there.

"*Oo vas kharawshaya cemya,*" a colleague from Butte, Montana told Carrie. Their level of conversation had been improved in their eight weeks of intensive study, so he spoke confidently when he complimented her on her fine family. She had opportunity to introduce them at lunch. With them present, Carrie now felt a sense of wholeness she lacked when alone. Graduation was over, certificates received, and farewells given.

After eating dinner in Chinatown, where their servings were superfluous, they took away *doggy bags* filled with enough food for another meal. Storing it in the cooler filled with ice, they traveled north of San Francisco, until they arrived at a Best Western in Mount Shasta. The next day they continued on to Washington. Their plan was to visit Beth and Louie, with their family, for about ten days before traveling eastward and home.

Each had something to relate about their trip westward. They had camped in a number of state parks along the way. Matt had invested in a tent and folding cots, which the girls helped him put up. Their stops included Grand Canyon and a visit to cousin Pauline in Omaha, Nebraska. In Omaha, little Wren became ill with an earache that kept her in tears until Matt arranged to take her into the local hospital's emergency ward. Not familiar with the city, he was offered an escort by the police, as arranged by the motel manager there. Cousin Lena expressed surprise when she learned of Matt's aid, during breakfast at her home the following morning.

"Why, I doubt they would offer to do that for us, the people who live here!" she declared.

A shot and a prescription to be administered until gone healed Wren. The last spoonful was fed to her when they arrived in

California. Matt described their trip through New Mexico, where they visited his sister Tammy. While there, they viewed an annual Native American celebration. The girls took pictures of their parade. Matt had planned their trip to include, not only scenic places across the U. S., but also visits to the family members living in towns en route from their home in Michigan to California.

Arriving at Beth's home in the Seattle suburb, they received a warm welcome and opportunity to visit with cousins, as well as many of Beth's neighbors and friends. Attending Beth's reception were Louie's law partners and their wives, and the Dutch friends whose nephew was visiting them from the Netherlands. He loved to swim and when he learned Durinda did, as well, he eagerly persuaded his aunt and uncle to invite her to their home so they could be company for each other. Matt, ever protective of his daughters, emphasized his social standards to the uncle before granting his approval for the visit.

Beth arranged for Carrie to meet with one special neighbor who was Russian and who served as a deacon at his Orthodox church. Carrie found him and his wife to be very hospitable. She practiced some of her Russian conversation with him. He invited her to attend the worship service, and later, gave Matt directions to the church.

The visit to the Orthodox church was a new and unique experience. Meeting them at the door was a young priest.

"Interested in becoming Orthodox?" he asked.

"No, but we are ecumenical," Carrie announced.

"Well, we're not!"

"We're from out of town, and we've been invited here by your deacon," Carrie explained.

"Then let me welcome you."

In further conversation, Carrie explained that they were Lutheran. The priest countered that he, too, was once a Lutheran, but had converted to Orthodoxy. He did not explain his reasons.

A little later, the young priest brought Carrie and Matt a hymn

The Orthodox Cathedral in Seattle.

book, which contained the liturgy, with Old Church Slovanic on the left page and the English translation on the right page. Everyone stood during the service. Carrie followed the pages, noting that much was like the Slovak language which she had learned in childhood. She noted that the deacon began the service by waving the incense holder and chanting, declaring the presence of the Holy Spirit.

When they had been at the worship service for almost two hours, Matt whispered that his back was sore from standing so long. As the congregation members approached the altar for Holy Communion, the visitors slipped out the door.

This had been Carrie's first experience at worship in an Orthodox church. She had only one opportunity to visit and tour the one in Lansing, Michigan during their International Fair. While in San Francisco, she had visited the beautiful gold-domed cathedral, but other than a wedding in a Ukrainian Orthodox church in Chicago during her teen years, her experience at Eastern Orthodox churches was limited. She recalled the wedding. It was the godchild of her Aunt Mary who was the bride, and the wedding was during Lent, which met with the disapproval of certain Lutheran friends. However, it was still during World War II, and the groom was slated to be sent overseas, so the decision to set an earlier date met with the approval of the priest performing the ceremony, regardless of the Lenten timing. Carrie had been given the history of the Orthodox church when attending the International Fair at the church in Lansing, Michigan. Carrie recalled, when seeing a copy of the contents in the Orthodox liturgy, she had exclaimed, "Why, your liturgy is like ours, in the Lutheran Church!"

She was countered by the history teller, "But your church is less than five hundred years old! It is rather, that your liturgy emulates ours, which dates back to the early Christian church, probably even before the third century!"

This insight led Carrie to study more when she returned home and had time to read. Fedotov's book at the library of her alma mater proved to be an invaluable resource. She learned of the introduction to Christianity brought by the brothers Cyril and Methodius from the Byzantine Church. Added to this, was the information that they had been invited by Prince Pribina in Nitra to bring the gospel to his people in Slovakia around the seventh century, B.C. But archaelogical evidence revealed that Czechs were Christians long before this fact had been historically recognized. The archival museum displayed crosses worn and used along with the everyday utensils and artifacts uncovered on the grounds in Michalčice. When two adventurous youths made the discovery, word was sent on to the professors at the university in Brno. Even during communist times, when funds for excavation were not available, loving citizens who appreciated their historical heritage, volunteered to excavate the area by hand. They discovered the remaining foundations of three basilicas that had been buried for many centuries. They also dug up many items that proved their culture and civilization to be far more advanced than credited by their enemies. There were spurs, belt buckles, plates and cups, buttons and clasps, and many items used in everyday living. And there were crosses. These served as evidence of their exposure to Christian faith.

After ten days of being hosted by Beth and Louie, farewells were given, and the family was homeward bound. As they crossed the state of Idaho, Matt stopped at a state park, but was not encouraged to put up the tent and stay the night. A native explained why. "I love this forest, but it is so dry, that a fire can evolve any time," so, referring to the drought that was currently being experienced, she urged them to travel on.

By the time they reached Montana, Timmy had become ill, and stopping at a clinic near Butte, it was learned he had pneumonia. Because they were traveling, the doctor administered a shot rather than a liquid antibiotic prescription. He was to be given as much liquid as possible—water, ginger ale, and kept resting. So it was decided when they reached Yellowstone Park, and Matt and the girls had set up their tent, that Timmy would remain in the car to sleep through the night. However, their night's rest was interrupted by the intrusion of one of the bears that walked freely throughout the camp, and Matt, who hardly slept, kept a "weapon" handy. It was an old table leg.

"I doubt that it would be adequate protection," Carrie cautioned.

"Better than nothing," Matt retorted.

Earlier they learned from one family in a motor home that their window had been broken by an intruding bear who was looking for food. That was the problem. Many campers and visitors, contrary to the advice of the park rangers, fed the bears and interfered with the park's program. A neighboring pair of campers, grilling hot dogs on their site, were invaded and lost their meal by another furry intruder.

Sensing danger led Matt to pack up earlier than they intended the following morning and leave the park without waiting to view Old Faithful. On they traveled to Minnesota, where they met and visited with cousin John Fisher and his wife, Dagmar. They had not seen each other for several years, so it was fun catching up on family news, and Dagmar's warm hospitality added to their pleasant visit. John Fisher was the older brother of his three siblings that were present at the railroad station, when Carrie boarded the train leaving Chicago.

John had lived in Minnesota, where he had found work as a young man. Then having met, courted, and married his sweetheart, Dagmar, Minneapolis became his permanent home. Absent from his Slovak family, John, nevertheless, strove to recall his training in both language and religion as a youth, and to follow the Christian teachings which his father, Michael Fisher, so strongly upheld. Mike had been quite strict with his children, having them gather at the kitchen table on Sunday afternoons and reviewing Martin Luther's catechism with them. John recalled an incident when his father had been assumed to be asleep during part of a Slovak church service. It was Mrs. Klebeta who called his attention, "Ty spal, Mishko?" Mike retorted, asking her what were the Bible passages read during the service and the gospel for that morning. She could not remember, but he was able to recite them, though accused of dozing during the readings.

Once, John told them when he was visiting his father, he spoke quite openly, "You know, Dad, you were *too hard* on us." His words brought tears to the elder man's eyes. He attempted to explain. "We were here, in this new country. I wanted so much for my children to grow in the faith and to become good citizens."

After bidding their hosts farewell, Matt drove on, crossing northern Wisconsin and driving into Michigan's Upper Peninsula. The girls kissed the ground, they were so happy to be in their home state after weeks of travel. What Durinda did not realize was that her purse fell out of the car, and it contained her medication. So when it was time for her to take her prescription, as they neared home, she realized her loss. However, upon phoning the state police in the border area, Carrie was able to direct them to the spot where they had stopped, and the purse was retrieved and sent to Durinda a few days later.

The family's travel adventures ended, all prepared to enter a new school year. Timmy would now attend Matt's elementary school. If Timmy was able to assimilate well, Matt would be able to have close contact with his teachers and the classroom activities. The plan worked well, and that fall Timmy accompanied his dad to school each morning. The entire experience was to open a whole new world for Timmy, leading Carrie to take notes about his progress and experiences. Anna and Durinda were both in high school, and the very best of child care was arranged for Wren. A native of the Netherlands, *Oma*, as the family all called her, proved to be one of the other saints in Carrie's life. Johanna, as she was named, was a woman of deep faith. She knew how to be firm, yet thoughtful of young children's needs. Later in the school year, she also had Tim visit with her on afternoons when the school day ended. Carrie was thankful for the genuine care her younger two children received from Johanna. She was like a second mother to Wren, who in later years was to name her own daughter Johanna, after her.

Both Carrie and Matt returned to their schools, and the fall, winter, and spring all proved to form a successful year. Anna continued her art classes. She also assisted the editor of the school newspaper. Durinda, two years behind her sister, seemed glad to be away from the middle school she had attended close to their north-end home. There were changes in the high school that affected her in a way that did not seem to trouble her older sister.

The former high school on the south end had been closed. This resulted in an influx of students being transferred from that end of town to the centrally-located high school now attended by the two older girls. This added attendance changed the culture of the school. One had to understand the personality of a teenager like Durinda to realize the challenges she was facing. Influenced by the music, she found herself playing the popular records favored by the incoming group. Carrie, who all her life, preferred the music of the classical composers, found herself dreading the extreme difference of the tunes her daughter played. What she did not realize was her daughter was trying very hard to understand and identify with this new group of students, some of whom became her friends. Unfortunately, there were also those who, because of lack in their own background, did not appreciate the kindness Durinda offered with her friendship. Rather, they considered kindness to be a weakness and took advantage of the opportunity. There would be a tragic event brought to the attention of Durinda's parents before they became aware of their daughter's plight.

Chapter II

Teaching or Writing?

Carrie loved teaching. Yet her other ambition had always been to write. She kept journals and articles of interest until her accumulation was difficult to store in a way that was convenient. Matt teased her. When an elderly neighbor died, her heirs rented a huge dumpster to toss away many of her belongings—magazines, papers stored for years, and other items. "That's what will happen to your collection," Matt predicted. Carrie pondered sometimes, wondering when she would be free to write to publish some day.

Which way should I go? Carrie's thoughts pondered a while. When she returned from San Francisco with Matt and the children, she was happy for a school that was a home base. Her principal, Chuck Anion, bless his heart, was genuinely happy to see her. The summer studies gave her the confidence she had lacked the previous year. Her teaching had been merely imitative. Everything she had learned from Dr. Mudry was applied to her ten students. Now she would have fifteen, two of which had remained with her to study Russian a second year. Good. They had completed half the text, the very same one she had used at the fledgling college where she was studying while expecting Wren, two years ago. Now they could continue and complete their studies from this same text. The brightest in the first year's group, they could also be helpful with the new beginners.

After all her experiences in the Institute, Carrie felt like she had become a unique person in history. There had been people from all over the nation, yet they totaled only forty-four. From the

Carrie's first high school Russian class.

population of this vast country, it was only they and a few more who could adequately begin to understand the lives and struggles of the Russian and Slavic peoples throughout the centuries. The native speakers contributed, for they were able to share their plight—the changes in government from tsarist to totalitarianism when the Bolshevik Revolution took place in 1917. The confiscation of private property, the collectivization of farms, the exiles and executions of any who had opposed the new regime, all these and more formed the history told to the Institute students by the refugees who had lived and suffered through the process, and who had now, as exiles, made their home in San Francisco. The refugees came from many places; some from China, others from European countries, Italy or France. Most came from France, although many had remained in France, because the French citizens had always shown hospitality to Russians. Perhaps it was because the Russian nobility that made up the military administration had admired the French, ever since they participated in the European occupation after the defeat of Napoleon.

History repeats itself. When one nation conquers another, those

Two students enjoying Russian foods at an open house.

who have been subjected to the victor often conquer their victor in culture and style, and sometimes in theology. Consider the Romans who admired and often emulated Greek thought and custom. Russian military leadership stationed in France became acquainted with French culture and European mannerisms. They admired the slogan *Liberty, Equality, Fraternity.* The military leaders, gleaned from the nobility, longed to bring these ideas back to their own country. Hence they imported French governesses and housekeepers that would share their homes and tutor their children in French language and culture.

How much there was to learn, how much Carrie wanted to teach to her students! Chuck was supportive and Carrie thanked her lucky stars that her principal had been a language teacher before he became an administrator. Of Italian descent, he remained in the Romance language group and taught Spanish. Perhaps some of Carrie's own background made it easy for her to relate to him. After all, she had spent her early years living in an Italian neighborhood in Chicago. Later, as a high school student, she had majored in

Spanish. Besides, this man possessed some of the gentility that the exposure to the liberal arts shaped and molded in people. Or was it his faith? A devout Catholic, he spoke of Sunday mornings with his children.

"First, we all go to church. Then we come home and have a good breakfast. After that, they can do what they want for recreation— ride their bikes, watch a movie, or whatever!"

Certain faculty members unfortunately took his gentility to be a sign of weakness, for he had followed a rather didactic administrator who had "kept things in line." Carrie was ashamed of the colleagues who had written some derogatory remarks on the blackboard in the teachers' lounge. What was it? Something like a "Deygo goes wop, wop, wop!" She hoped she was the only one to read it, and disgusted, she erased the entire message. *They do not really know this man*, she thought. What a disappointment in her fellow professionals! Not only that crudeness, but also the absence of intellectual interest; for each time Carrie had attempted to cultivate a conversation when she accompanied them in the lounge, she was rebuffed. And upon her evaluation was the complaint that she *wanted to talk shop* when others were *relaxing, away from the classroom*.

Recalling the dedication she had observed during her own high school days, Carrie wondered, *Why are these people teaching?* Don't they love learning, themselves? Don't they enjoy the exchange of ideas? When one referred to Carrie's Russian students as *commies,* she wondered, *Am I in the wrong place for me?*

Was it being a Pollyanna to believe she could make a difference in the future, in her country, perhaps even in the world by teaching the youngsters Russian language and culture?

Sometimes Carrie thought about alternatives. She had always loved to write. Before accepting her first teaching position, after she had completed her college degree, she had applied for a writing/ editing position for a large food distributor. Their personnel office had given her a psychology test. During that same week, she had applied for and been accepted as a fourth-grade teacher in a suburban elementary school. When given a choice, she decided on the teaching contract. The writing job looked interesting, but it was mostly journalistic and limited to the structure in which she would be employed. She recalled that, during the years when Matt sold pots and pans, she had written his weekly newsletter, doing this very same thing—commended the sales reps for their successes, gave information on births, engagements, anniversaries, and other personal events. Besides that, how did she feel about being under corporate control? Influenced by Matt's experiences in the business world, she decided, enough of that!

Yet, something way back in her psyche created a desire to write, to record experiences, how her life was tied into historical and global events. She might never be a Tolstoy or Solzhenitsyn, but that was the type of writing she wanted to emulate. So she kept journals. Her training in English lit at the colleges helped. Maybe someday there would be time …

"Remember, your time will come to do this," her Ed prof had reminded her when she expressed the desire to research, to learn, and then share what she had acquired by writing. He was one of the few people she had ever met who seemed to understand her mind.

However, Carrie never regretted her decision to teach. Teachers are right there, in the firing line. One could never know in advance what had formed and shaped a student's thoughts, and by teaching them to write, she was able to know them better and learn how to direct them. There were a number of unforgettable incidents she recalled, particularly during her very first teaching assignment at the northern suburban school, before Wren was born. She was excited when the superintendent offered her a contract to teach the fourth graders.

Eager to become acquainted with her would-be students, she arrived at the school two weeks before classes were to begin and studied the files of each. By the time she met them on the first day of school, she felt somewhat prepared. Her approach to the young Barbara, considered slow, was to encourage her. She soon learned the child was quite an avid reader, who wore glasses for near-sightedness, and was somewhat shy. But slow, never! Neither was Billy, in spite of the fact that his cumulative record indicated that he was "slow." Carrie was forewarned that he had a slight hearing problem when his mother accompanied him to class.

"Billy needs to sit in front so he can hear you better," she advised Carrie before exiting.

Carrie found her experiences with Timmy had made her sensitive to other children's needs, particularly those she had been given the responsibility to teach. She took a firm stance with Billy, who had a tendency to dawdle. One noon, he had not finished his assigned lesson, in spite of Carrie's gentle prodding. He seemed to be daydreaming. So, the solution? When the other students were dismissed for lunch, Carrie had him remain.

"You have to finish before you can leave," she spoke with firmness.

"You're mean," Billy retorted, but tearfully and hurriedly finished in minutes what had to be completed.

When he returned, Carrie asked him, "How was your lunch?"

"Well it was good, but kind of short," he replied, grinning at his teacher.

Later, she conferred with his mother, who completely endorsed the idea that Billy needed to finish his assignment, but asked that Carrie have the school secretary phone her so that she could keep his lunch warm. Actually, it did not happen again. At another time, Carrie was rewarded with one of those precious intangible results teaching offers by a response from Billy.

Carrie's enthusiasm for literature and history carried over in her efforts with her fourth graders. One afternoon after recess, she decided to read a story, *The Emperor's New Clothes*. Her voice carried well, and all thirty-six appeared to be listening very intently. When she finished, Carrie raised the question, "What do you think about this story; what did you learn from it?"

Some of the children from whom she expected a response merely shrugged their shoulders. One or two raised their hands and said it was a good story. But it was Billy who waved his hand eagerly to reply,

"I think, always tell the truth, yeah, tell the truth," and hesitantly, he added, "and never, never *trust* a weaver!"

There were many intangible rewards with teaching. Carrie's very first assignment at the suburban school was a fourth-grade class, which held thirty-five students. The thirty-sixth arrived later in the semester. Her parents had moved from Matt's school district in the inner city to the suburb. The little girl was thrilled that she could transfer from Matt's fourth grade class to Carrie's. Her family was a refugee family from Indonesia. Several girls in the class welcomed her warmly, and soon they were skipping rope together at recess time.

Lots of things happened that fall. Some made memorable history. Carrie had four Stephens in her class. Their personalities stood out for different reasons. One was quiet, almost sleepy, and the slowest in the class to complete his assignments. Carrie wondered, *Is he getting enough sleep at night?* A parent/teacher conference helped somewhat, for the boy seemed to rally, with prompt seatwork in class.

Another Stephen was rather shy. During the school year, he was involved in a car accident. The result was injuries to his face that required treatment from a specialist. When his mother phoned Carrie, it was a mother-to-mother response that Carrie felt. That afternoon, after Stephen's treatment, which the mother called "planing," he had come home and having looked in a mirror, declared, "I can't go to school Monday. I look like a monster." After hearing the problem, Carrie advised her to just send him. "We'll handle it."

When the class convened on Monday morning, Carrie offered her usual morning prayer with the group. Then she called Stephen up to the front of the class. "Tell us, Stephen, about your treatment for the injury you had with the accident." Shyly, but confidently, the boy responded, smiling and concluding, "It will take a while to heal."

"But, here he is, he's still our Steve!" The matter grabbed the sympathy of his classmates, and there was never a fear of derogatory remarks or further anxiety for their classmate. Nor was there any more concern expressed by either Steve or his mother.

The other two Stephens proved to be more vociferous. One was the son of a lawyer, and quick with answers. Carrie looked back with some regret at the punishment she gave him when he made some vulgar remarks in class. As teacher, she felt the situation called for discipline. She isolated him for half the morning by sending him to the empty gymnasium, "to think about his statements." During recess, she met with him and asked him if he had thought about his unacceptable language. When she asked, "You don't want to be separated from your classmates again, do you?" Shrugging his shoulders, he replied, "Well, that's up to you."

The fourth Stephen proved to be the greatest challenge of all. Very quick to learn and consume all the material that was covered in the class, he was constantly looking for more to do. Early in November, as Thanksgiving Day approached, he came up with a plan that would involve the entire class—a play on the life of George Washington, with a song that all would sing. Costumes and wigs were made, and the toy rifles brought to school were carefully closeted in the teacher's cloakroom. Stephen directed the group with the parts they played and the final song, giving tribute to George Washington. He even engaged the music teacher to help

Students participating in a play about George Washington during Carrie's first year of teaching fourth grade. This scene shows the marriage of George and Martha.

Young George chops down the cherry tree during the play about George Washington.

them learn to sing it properly. The day that the play was to be put on for the school, assembling in the large gymnasium, was to forever commemorate another important historic event.

At lunch time, the teachers gathered in the little lounge, to eat, to smoke, as was still permitted in 1961, and to visit; some to gossip. On this day as they gathered, the teachers had already been informed of ominous news. Turning on the small black and white TV in the lounge, they surveyed the news from Dallas. President John Kennedy had been shot and was now hospitalized. As yet the final medical results had not been announced. A brief glimpse of Jackie Kennedy brought the remark from the second-grade teacher, "I bet she's shook!"

When the bell rang at the end of the lunch period, the principal decided all classes would continue as usual, and advised Carrie to have her class put on their play. It was during the middle of the performance that Carrie looked up to see the other fourth-grade teacher signal her with a thumb pointing down. Now the principal was outdoors, lowering the school flag to half-mast.

After the play, and the children's recess ended, Carrie gathered all in the class to tell the tragic event. "I want you to know that something very sad has happened in our country. Our president has been shot and has died." After a few minutes, Carrie asked, "Does someone want to offer a prayer?" Darcy spoke, "I will, but it's a Catholic prayer." "That's okay," Carrie allowed, for she knew the child spoke her *Hail Mary* from her heart. Not to be undone, another classmate, Gary, whose parents were Methodist, offered *The Lord's Prayer*. School was to be closed for the remainder of the week.

"I miss him already," Matt voiced his personal grief for the president to Carrie when she arrived home. Neither spouse had voted for Kennedy, believing he needed more experience for the high office. Yet the attitude toward John Kennedy had become warm, as they had observed his activities during his time in office. The entire week brought all the details of the nation's response—the flight home from Dallas, the coffin lying in state in the rotunda, Jackie's funeral plans carried out in stately fashion, the three-year-old John-John's salute to his fallen father, and Caroline's declaration: "I only cried once." All events were to stay on their minds forever. It has been said that memory is aided by emotion, and the nation was to respond with feelings; though the election and Kennedy's win had been a close one, with rumors that Papa Kennedy had *bought* the election.

When Carrie began teaching in the high school, she found herself becoming attached to the students in much the same way as her former high school teacher, Durinda Hansen, had been to her and the classmates in her homeroom group and English classes. The first year's assignment included three freshman English classes, in addition to her Russian class, as well as a study hall during the last hour. Study hall was her greatest challenge. Her advisor believed this would be helpful for lesson planning, grading papers, and other duties. However, some students had a different idea. Instead of quietly working on their homework, studies and reading, they wanted to talk. This disturbed the serious students. Complaints were voiced. Finally, one brave student addressed Carrie with an ultimatum.

"You're not like our last study hall teacher. She came around to see us, and help us with our homework."

True, Carrie knew some Geometry. Physics? No. As for Chemistry, she had been fortunate to earn a C+ in college. The school year would end with Carrie's request to teach a fourth English class, rather than have a study hall during the following year.

Carrie wrote her experiences in her journal. Life had always provided the material. Someday she hoped to share these with others. It was part of her nature to tell. When she was in elementary school, she was often tagged as the class tattletale. Teachers leaving the classroom alone knew they could rely on Carrie to relate the happenings, such as Frank Ricci's jokes and tales, bringing about giggles and noisy haws from his sixth-grade audience. Other incidents were recalled and Carrie noted them.

What happens when we write? We not only record; we create. We recreate. We learn. One recalls tidbits stored in one's memories. We see connections otherwise not realized. Carrie often wondered about the ties between her father, Anton and husband, Matt. In recalling her relationships with each, she saw the similarities in character and personality of each. She wondered, is this what led her to fall in love with Matt? Although both men were born in different parts of the world, they were both "country boys," products of rural areas in their homelands—Anton in old Austria–Hungary before World War I and Matt in the rural hamlet in western Michigan. Much of the outlook of each was from a natural, earthy setting, one without the façade of urban living. Looking back, she realized there was only one other man in her life with whom she would have ever considered marriage—H. J. in high school. He was an artist, very sensitive, and for a time, attracted to Carrie. But their friendship was diminished when his family moved away from Chicago because of a change in his father's employment. H. J. did correspond with her occasionally, but after a year or so, even that communication ended. In greater maturity, Carrie wondered, is it the Spirit of God that enlightens us, gives us vision, and prepares a path for us to follow?

Persons who knew Carrie considered her well-read. One young man she met from the college, who was dating Anna's close friend, Marie, shared a paper he wrote on the death of Jan Masaryk, son of the first president of Czechoslovakia. Carrie was so delighted to read his work, she began to recommend other books about Jan's father, as well as those written by him. "Whoa," was the twenty-one-year-old's reply. "Give me time to catch up with you; I'm just a young man yet."

What did Carrie read? Books abound. Her intense search for identity with her parents' homeland and the struggles of their people interested her immensely. She read all she could find by and about Masaryk. Another was Comenius, the exiled pastor of the Moravian Brethren. When she realized the ties with other Slavic countries, particularly Russia, and the similarities in their languages, she turned to them. Carrie could not escape the influence of the twentieth-century writer, Solzhenitsyn, who wrote in the same vein as Tolstoy and Dostoyevski; their religious influence compelled Solzhenitsyn to become the spokesman for Russian Christianity in the twentieth century. There was Pushkin, credited with fusing Old Church Slovanic with modern Russian; Goncharov and his *Oblomov*; Turgenev and his *Fathers and Sons* or *Gentle Folk*; the plays of Checkov; and modern authors who wrote of unhappy experiences under the Bolshevik regime. She assigned books to be read from a list that each of the students in her Russian class could choose for book reports. This was their opportunity to become acquainted with Russian literature and culture, past and present. She remembered the chuckle she felt when one girl who had read Tolstoy's famous novel, *Anna Karenina,* stated that it was "like a soap opera." When Carrie told this to her professor at the Russian School, he bristled with annoyance. (How dare this young American upstart reduce this novel to the level of a *soap opera?*)

Carrie decided that if she must bide her time before she could become a full-time writer, she was at least for now, fulfilling the ambition of acquainting a number of students with the Slavic world, in particular with Russia. Her small window of understanding just might contribute to building a bridge of peace. She was yet to realize in future times and experiences what teaching and the study of Russian language and culture would bring forth in her life, as well as in the lives of others. **

*** The author is here informing the reader that Carrie's teaching and studies in Russian and their results would be contained later in this book.*

Chapter III

The Other Saints in Carrie's Life

Was it chance or Providence that arranged for Carrie to meet these extraordinary people who played an important role in her life, and in Wren's? Returning from the intensive study of Russian and Soviet Culture at the NDEA Institute, she was determined to continue, not to lose the fluency in Russian she had gained during the summer graduate courses. Yet this small town was limited. She sought help from her colleague who was teaching an informal class in Russian at the high school on the south end of town. John and his family were Latvian émigrés. Familiar with Russian, he felt as Carrie had, that there was an obligation to familiarize the interested students with the language and culture. So he introduced her to a professor at the Catholic college who tutored students privately.

That was how she became acquainted with Yedinka. If it is hard for someone to imagine life in another world other than the U. S., the opportunity to share a life's experience from one who has lived a different life should never be overlooked. Yedinka, or Edith, as her English name would be, was gifted with languages. Other than her native Latvian, she knew Russian. In fact, she often claimed, "My culture is really Russian."

Born in St. Petersburg, she was raised in a family that was able to afford the best in that city's society. Her father was a chemical engineer, who was given favored assignments by the last Tsar. For

Yedinka Mezhaks, whose English name was Edith.

a time he served in Afghanistan. All three of his daughters had the advantage of a higher education. Yedinka excelled in languages. Not only did she already have a mastery of her native Latvian, but by the time she was a young student in her teens, she had studied English, French, and Spanish, as well as German. Her hobby was reading the classics in the various languages. Carrie chuckled, as she realized that Yedinka probably knew more about American literature than most Americans.

Carrie learned many anecdotes of Russian and Soviet history from Yedinka. One was the fierce attitude of Tsar Peter the Great, a leader who wanted so much for his native country to catch up to the progress of other European nations, France, Germany, England, and Holland. As a young man, Peter traveled to Holland and was so impressed by the canals and bridges, the ship-building and the many technical advances he observed, that he was determined to reproduce these in Russia. If he was successful building St. Petersburg, he was a failure at fatherhood. His son, Alexis, influenced by his mother who firmly preferred to preserve the old ways, using religion as a basis for rigidly conforming to them, was executed. His wife was retired to a convent. Peter also displayed cruelty and insensitivity with at least one particular mistress. Learning of her infidelity, he arranged for her execution. Although she wore her most appealing finery as she was led to the executioner's block, with the intent to entice Peter or perhaps appeal to his mercy, she was unsuccessful in moving him. By lowering his arm, he gave the motion to have her beheaded. Then, moving to where the decapitated body lay, he picked up the head of his fallen mistress, held it up to his face, and there where all his court could watch, he kissed her lips.

The barbarism which Yedinka and her family actually experienced took place during the Bolshevik Revolution. The fact that her father was a chemical engineer made his knowledge important to the communist regime. So his life was spared, yet his family was required to make certain sacrifices.

As many of their neighbors in St. Petersburg, they were forced to give up their lovely home. In its place they were given a log cabin beside the munitions plant where their father was assigned. Hunger permeated. Yedinka told of experiencing a fainting spell while a student at the university. It was during Lenin's administration that a deal was made with the United States to provide food. Interestingly, Lenin willingly compromised communism to obtain this food for the nation. (Carrie recalled a student in her Russian History class questioning the professor about the wisdom of dealing with Lenin in this way. The professor countered with his Christian belief, "Yes, one should feed one's neighbor when he is hungry.")

In 1926, nine years after the Bolshevik Revolution, Latvia became a free country. It was then that Yedinka, together with her family, returned to their native land. Here, they were to prosper and retrieve what they had lost under the communist regime in Russia. Here, they were to greet the German army as protectors from the spreading communist regime. After the initial occupation, the honeymoon ended. Yet when the Germans left at the close of World War II, the Treaty at Yalta forced another migration upon them.

However, Yedinka did relate a bit of humanism shown her family by the retreating Germans. One soldier, offering to take them in his vehicle with whatever possessions they could carry, observed Elsa's (Yedinka's sister) Singer sewing machine, destined to be left behind. (Today that very Singer sewing machine is in the possession of Elsa's granddaughter, who lives in the state of Michigan in the United States.)

"Frau, you will need this machine, wherever you go," he urged, and carried it into the truck that would take them away from their home.

"I was greedy," claimed Yedinka. "I saw our silver spoons, and could not bear to leave all of them behind, so I packed as many as I could carry in my pockets."

The refugees first were accommodated in a refugee camp in Austria. Yedinka, fluent in English, gave lessons to prepare them for living in America, where most of them were destined to go. Later, they were sponsored by the Amish, in Iowa, who arranged for their arrival and provided them with a home. In 1950, Yedinka, with about two thousand refugees, came to western Michigan. Here, they made every attempt to continue their culture and religious beliefs. Three churches were purchased, two Lutheran and one Catholic. A few years later, they built a Latvian Hall. It was here where Elsa planned and presented her ballet recitals and programs, and Wren participated in these events. At Christmastime, the young girls performed at the church. Wren was later to tell her mother how much her ballet training helped her with balance and confidence.

Elsa, Yedinka's sister, was an equal saint in Carrie's life. She was always a sympathetic listener, no matter what the situation was. Advice? Seldom given. Her listening proved to be gift enough, for when one related a problem to her, or shared a puzzling situation, one was somehow provided with a resolution, merely by the lending of a listening ear. Carrie recalled the words from a pastor's sermon—*Listening is spiritual hospitality.* Elsa was the spirit of hospitality. Seldom did Carrie leave her home without samples of Elsa's baking, particularly her ginger cookies, usually prepared at holiday time.

Another dear friend was Oma, as all the family came to know

her. She began by caring for Wren, when Carrie was teaching. Her home was an excellent environment that offered Wren both comfort and a consistent measure of discipline, with a grandmotherly love. She was to care for Wren until she was in the first grade and attended school all day. Wren was not deprived of social exposure, for Oma also cared for a little boy, Mikey, the son of a single working mom. Probably, he was the first little person that was influenced by Wren. She entered the household already toilet trained, and the boy, who was a few months older, had been hedging. When he saw Wren, knowing she no longer needed a diaper, he began taking the initiative to make toileting needs known, and soon was also fully trained. This lightened the load for both his mom and their caregiver.

For a time, when teachers were on strike and classes were cancelled, Tim also spent time in Oma's household. Her empathy led to fulfilling his social needs. Wren never forgot this lady's care, and later in life, she was to name her first daughter Johanna, after her beloved caregiver.

Another close friend of Carrie's was Raya. It was she and her husband, Jim, who became close friends and Canasta partners. Raya, who was born and raised in Finland, where she received nurse's training, married an American. They raised three sons. Matt and Carrie were to attend the weddings of all three young men, although it meant traveling out of town for two of them. The oldest married at a Catholic church on the eastern side of their state. At the reception, Carrie was to meet Raya's mother, who had traveled from Finland to attend her grandson's wedding. The reception was a deluxe affair, with dancing and serving gourmet foods at the wedding dinner. Carrie and Matt remained at their hotel overnight, deciding they, too, would have a special outing that weekend. When the youngest son of the three married, the ceremony took place in Atlanta, in an area called Buckhead. The Lutheran pastor proved to be very sociable and understanding. At the ceremony, the bridesmaid sang "Ave Maria." When Carrie encountered the pastor at the reception, she inquired, "You must be a very liberal minister to allow this to be sung in your church." His reply was that the bride had requested it; the words were sung in Latin which he did not know, and besides, he had more important issues to deal with.

One of the side benefits of traveling to Atlanta was a visit on Sunday, the day after the wedding, when Carrie and Matt were to meet her cousin and his wife. Jonathan actually was a "cousin once removed," Carrie explained to Matt. In Slovak, "*On rodilsa na druhich kolena,*" or literally, "born on someone else's knees."

"Jonathan's Aunt Mary is also my Aunt Mary, but from another side of the family. Aunt Mary, my father's sister, is married to Uncle Jan, the brother of Joseph, who is Jonathan's father. But they are all considered to be extended family. And I called his dad Uncle Joe, and he was instructed to call my dad Uncle Anton."

After breakfast, they attended the same church where the wedding had taken place the day before. Again, the pastor agreed, that though both couples were members of a different Lutheran synod, their declaration of faith was adequate for them to be served Holy Communion at his church. What a warm welcome the travelers received!

After church, Jon and Yvonne took them on a long tour of Atlanta and the area surrounding highlights—the King neighborhood and the home of Margaret Mitchell, where Jon took photos of Carrie standing at Margaret's desk, by her typewriter. They also went to

Carrie, standing beside the desk of Margaret Mitchell in Atlanta.

Carrie and Matt, guests of Jonathan Cates,
visiting Stone Mountain in Georgia.

Stone Mountain that Jon wanted them to see. Later, they enjoyed a dinner at a unique Chinese restaurant, and Matt and Carrie were presented with a bottle of plum wine to take home with them.

What was very special about Jonathan was their travels together in Czechoslovakia in former years. However, those visits and experiences await to be contained in a future writing.

Again, as often occurred during their travels, Carrie and Matt did some touring and sightseeing en route. Cumberland Falls and the university in Kentucky were enchanting and interesting. Carrie took turns driving and recalled an unusual experience while trying to maintain the speed limit in Knoxville, Tennessee. The sign allowed for 45 miles per hour, but caught in a third left lane, where cars exceeded this amount, she was stopped by a kindly state patrolman. She hardly had room to pull over to the left of the third left lane; when pulling over, behind her, the officer approached Carrie at the driver's side. "I'll probably get a ticket for going too fast, and I'm from out of state!"

However, her concerns proved otherwise. "Lady, you're going too *slow!*"

"But your sign back there said forty-five, and I was trying to respect your speed limit," she tried to explain.

"Never mind the speed limit. You have to go according to the speed of the traffic. Now, I am going to monitor your driving back into that left lane just as soon as there's a space, and you must speed up. I don't want you to get hurt because you're going too *slow*. I'll be right behind you."

What a switch, Carrie thought. Later, she related the incident to the manager at the bed and breakfast by Cumberland Falls. Shaking his head, he stated that, they are continually repairing that highway, and they're never done.

The hospitality was pleasing, and their last stop before returning home was in Ohio to visit Durinda and her family. Grandson Andrew was in a special musical event, so they got to listen to his soothing voice sing the hymn selected.

Thinking about certain of her friendships, Carrie realized how closely she felt a kinship to European friends, no matter which country they were from—Latvia, the Netherlands, Finland, and also the Dutch cousins. Particularly, Slavic people whose language she usually understood, welcomed her interest.

"I believe I am half-European," she sometimes explained to Matt.

"Perhaps that's why my dad likes you," he agreed.

Matt's father was born in Rotterdam. Only he and one brother, of nine, migrated to the United States as young men. The brother settled in California, but Matt's father made his home in Michigan. Carrie was very fond of her father-in-law. She felt the same affection toward him that she had for her own dad.

In the summer after Timmy was born, for the first time, Matt met his cousin from the Netherlands. She, together with her husband and her parents, were visiting in the States. They had learned English in their European school. The family had lived through the horrors of World War II and lost a young son. Cathy and Harry applied to come to the United States, but the quota for immigrants had been filled. However, they were welcomed into Canada. It was there that Harry eventually acquired his fortune in real estate development.

Matt was quite excited about meeting this cousin from his father's family. Both young couples enjoyed becoming acquainted. Harry invited them for a visit at their home in Toronto. The following year, when Timmy was a year old, Matt's Aunt Anna offered to stay with their children, so that Matt and Carrie were able to accept their invitation. It proved to be a splendid visit.

Harry took them on a tour of the city, and included the castle which Harry described "was built by a fool," for when the builder's funds ran out, the city of Toronto took over to make it a tourist venture. In the evenings, they met Harry's friends, who had joined them for dinner. They, too, had migrated to Canada and were members of the same church. The wife had opened a fabric store. Encouraged by Harry, her business grew prosperous. She described her hesitation, when the hope was still a plan, and somewhat scary at the beginning.

What if I don't get enough customers?

Ever the optimist, Harry, himself a businessman, advised, "Be patient, be honest and helpful, and people who appreciate your efforts will tell others, and the business will grow."

She followed his advice and within a short time they were able to purchase a home in Harry's neighborhood.

Harry, himself, was to live an immigrant's success story. When he related his experience to Matt, he declared, "People who live here do not see the opportunities." When he and his wife arrived in Toronto, he applied for a sales position with several large companies. After being interviewed by several, he was not hired. Told he was hindered by his English, spoken with a Dutch accent, he applied at a real estate firm. Happy to have him, they assigned him clients who were immigrants, to whom his accent created a kinship with their own. Houses sold and commissions paid the bills and the accumulation of a small bank account. He was to put it to good use and eventually build a fortune. During his assessment of properties for sale, he came across a large corner that had been on the market for months. It seemed to lack interest from buyers.

This is a good property, Harry decided. Since no one wants it right now, I shall buy it. He paid a small down payment, with agreement to continue payments and taxes. After three years, a large company approached him. This corner was exactly what its corporate was attracted to and the sale gave Harry one million dollars. He paid cash for his new home in a deluxe residential suburb of the big city, as well as a new Mercedes. Now his wife gave up her temporary job to supplement their income, in order to become a stay-at-home mom for their adopted baby son.

Along with these pleasant changes in their lives, was a transition in Harry's business interests. Instead of a focus on selling homes, he became a real estate developer. He would study locations in select neighborhoods and determine which areas would require unique sites for apartment and condo dwellings to accommodate an ever-growing population in this large city. Visiting the dwellers in a select area, he would approach them with offers to buy their properties, assuring them of allowing continual rent until all properties were purchased. Then he would await the right buyer, one ready to excavate, and build that dream apartment or condo facility.

The couple adopted two more children, daughters who became sisters to the older adopted son. After their successes in Canada, they decided to build the exact home in their native country, in a town bordered by the Atlantic Ocean. Here, young Harry went to school. Harry Senior tutored his son, so the boy would gain a mastery of the Dutch language. The family was to live in the Netherlands for six years before returning to Canada.

When Matt and Carrie planned to go abroad to celebrate their twenty-fifth wedding anniversary, Harry and Cathy arranged for them to be met by Cathy's sister Reta, whose hospitality knew no bounds.

After their return to Canada, Carrie and Matt were to visit the Dutch cousins a number of times. Once they took Beth, Matt's sister, with them. It was a real family-reunion type of visit.

However, Canada itself as a vacation get-away had always appealed to Matt and Carrie. Every year, they enjoyed the plays at Stratford. Matt particularly favored the musicals and many of the plays. He tolerated certain Shakespeare selections for Carrie's sake. Knowing this, she always included reservations for Gilbert and Sullivan's musicals, which Matt enjoyed. Except for the summers spent in Europe, Carrie and Matt enjoyed visits to Canada. During most visits, they were hosted by a lovely lady named Carmen, whose home was a haven for travelers. She seemed to enjoy her guests just as much as they enjoyed being with her.

Often, the couple would tell their friends, "If you cannot get to Europe, the next best place to vacation is Canada." Attending the plays was only *one* appealing feature. The atmosphere was relaxed. People were hospitable to their tourists. Food was tasty. Restaurants prepared entrees from scratch in their kitchens, thus serving meals with a homemade flavor. Clothing stores tended to offer styles that were traditional. Carrie found herself wearing her purchases for many years without discomfort. Matt helped with selections to be given as Christmas presents for the children. Canada, unlike the United States, at that time, accepted imports from China, so some became unique gifts for family and friends in the States.

After their excursion in the Stratford area and Kitchner, they often traveled the ninety miles to Toronto. There, they were hosted by cousins Cathy and Harry, and their close friends. Cathy always welcomed Carrie into her kitchen; each would prepare the specialty of her choice. Dining out was a favorite of Harry's. There were no boundaries for him. He was comfortable making friends with headwaiters and cooks. In one particular Chinese restaurant, he took Matt and Carrie on a tour of the kitchen. Harry had chosen, living in Toronto, his favorite eating places, selecting gourmet items such as lobster bisque or stuffed shrimp. A favorite pastime was games— Rummy Kube, a game they had to teach their guests. In turn, Matt and Carrie taught them Canasta, the game that was popular during their first year of marriage, a game they continued to play throughout their life together with friends and family. They even taught it to their children and grandchildren, something all looked forward to.

What is life without friends? How does one distinguish between an acquaintance and a friend? Carrie and Matt enjoyed their friends. Not many were merely acquaintances.

Chapter IV

Timmy's Challenges

After Matt was able to enroll Timmy at his own elementary school, he had the opportunity to have direct communication with his teachers. Because Tim was taller than his classmates, they nicknamed him *Biggy*. Here, the students totally accepted Timmy as a person. Unlike some of his previous academic settings, his teachers demonstrated an earnest desire to help him succeed. Tim's favorite subject was Social Studies, and he particularly enjoyed the movies presented with the various topics being covered in class. The results produced sometimes puzzled his teachers. Matt made a deal with him on his weekly spelling tests. Tim memorized each word carefully, to reach his goal of 100%, so he could earn the dollar that Matt offered him as an incentive. Although he earned a number of dollars, Matt noticed that, three weeks after a test was taken, Tim could not always spell the word correctly. Yet he was able to recognize the word when reading it in context and know its meaning.

Testing had been done and it was known that Tim had a hearing problem. The question was raised about the possibility of his suffering from dyslexia, as well. But Timmy and his teachers struggled along together, and progress in learning was noted. Tim was popular because when the boys were playing basketball, both teams wanted him on their team, knowing his height and power to make the baskets was greater than anyone else in their classes.

When he graduated with the sixth grade, and was scheduled to

(Above) Timmy at age 13.   *(Above) Doting big brother Timmy,*
holding Wren's hand.

(Above) Anna, Timmy, and Wren,   *(Above) Timmy enjoyed*
sitting on Timmy's shoulders.   *playing baseball.*

enroll in junior high the following fall, the school principal approached
Carrie and Matt with his suggestion. He strongly advocated Tim's
entry in the junior high on the west side of town, where expectations
for academic achievement were lower than that of the junior high on

the east side, a short walking distance from their home. However, Carrie was aware of reports that there were many social problems at the school on the west side. Her response to the principal was that she would rather have Tim struggling academically than to be caught up in a budding gang manipulation that might be difficult for Tim to handle. He had been exposed to a sheltered workshop, and his naivete and kind heart could be mistaken for being a sissy, a pushover for an aggressive street person.

Junior high did not prevent exposure to some meanness and bullying, as well as the expected struggles academically. Carrie had forewarned him about the bullies.

"You're a big guy, Tim, so if someone pushes you or acts like they want to start something, just move far away from him. Don't let him trap you into a fight and get you into trouble. Just avoid him."

This may have been too much good advice, for late in the school year, Tim was to be confronted with a situation that proved to be challenging. And the academics, as had been expected, did prove to be challenging. Yet, Tim's teachers were considerate of his needs. At parent/teacher conferences, they noted his cooperative behavior in class and his great desire to apply himself and learn. The most successful event, however, took place at the close of the school year, at the end of eighth grade. Tim won a letter for his achievement on the football team. The letter was presented at the eighth-grade dinner. His classmates honored him with a standing ovation.

Yet one of Tim's greatest drawbacks had not been overcome. Communications were difficult for him. He either was silent, keeping unhappy experiences bottled up, or acted out his behavior in an extreme fashion, by expressing his feelings with shouts of anger. Unfortunately, the latter often found him blamed for a circumstance brought upon him that usually was not initiated by him. Such was the incident that caused him to become expelled from school.

Tim told his dad that he had been expelled for fighting. That was all he would say. It was not until the second day of his forced absence from school that Carrie was finally able to get Tim to tell her what had happened.

"You told me not to fight, no matter what," Tim reminded his mother. "But this time I couldn't help it, I had it!"

This last incident bringing about the expelling of both boys from school was only the tip of the iceberg. It happened in the gym. At the close of the Phys Ed hour, the instructor asked Tim to carry the batch of soiled towels and place them in the laundry room next to the gym. Partway there, with his hands full, the culprit tripped Tim, who came close to falling. Tim dropped the huge bundle and went after him, grabbing his shirt with intent to shake him. Just then, the school counselor entered the gym. Viewing the conflict, he made the immediate decision to expel both boys. Tim felt he was not given a chance to explain and that he was treated unjustly. Why?

Throughout the school year, this same student had been taunting Tim in various ways. When the classes met for assembly, he had pulled Tim's chair out from under him, just as Tim was trying to get seated. He also resorted to name calling, referring to Tim as *the Ox,* fun-making at his physique. Finally, when he tripped Tim in the gym, the recourse was to go after him, as Tim did, only to be penalized for defending himself.

When Carrie related the entire situation to the school principal, his response was that he was glad that Tim acted in his own defense, and that maybe he might have done so sooner if Carrie had not advised him to avoid all fights. The other lad assumed that Tim was afraid, a *pushover*, and continued to antagonize him, believing he could get away with it. The principal termed it as the *junior high pecking order*. He asked that Tim return to school and come to his office. Later, the principal arranged for the two boys to meet with him together. He phoned Carrie to inform her that after this meeting, the boys agreed to reconcile and shake hands. There were no further hostile incidents.

High school was not easy for Tim. He attended classes and attempted to complete all assignments, but reading was difficult. Finally, a reading class was begun due to the efforts of the Superintendent, who told Carrie that at last it was realized that not only the little people in elementary needed help with reading skills, but also the big people in the high school. The reading class was considered by some students to be for "dummies," and Tim was in that class. Yet, he was accepted for training on the football team, of which he was very proud.

His naivete caused him to be taken off the football team, in spite of winning the six points for a touchdown in a game played against another high school in the city. His name was written in an article on the sports page of the local press, reporting the touchdown. Carrie always regretted that neither she nor Matt were present at this game. Both were tired from their week of teaching and decided to stay home and rest, not realizing that Tim would be a leading player at that Friday evening's game. What made Tim unhappy was that he was not invited to a party given on the following evening at the home of the coach, whose son was a member of the team. Most of the other team members were invited. Confronted with a rejection, Tim decided to celebrate with his friend, a neighborhood orphaned teen who was living with an older sibling. The two were going to show these players that they were big men, too. After attempting to buy beer at the local grocery, and being refused because they were under age, they persuaded another older man to buy the beer for them. They walked around the neighborhood, openly drinking from the bottles, showing off, as young guys can do. They stopped in a fast food store, only to be chastised by the clerk there. After some conversation, she decided to phone the police, who came immediately, and arrested both boys and placed them in the city jail. What a sad ending to Timmy's football success of the night before! When Matt went to arrange for Tim's release, he received an order to appear in court. When he returned to school on Monday morning, the coach informed him that he was no longer a member of the football team. A triple punishment—a night in jail, an appearance in court, and removal from the football team.

Carrie and Matt did meet with the coach to ask him to reconsider, but he refused, stating that none of the members on his team were allowed to drink. Yet it was later reported that there was liquor served at his son's party. The coach did suggest that Tim might be eligible for the wrestling team, but Tim was not interested.

The judge pronounced a fine, allowing for time so Tim could earn the money and pay it himself. Matt was angry at himself for not giving closer attention to Tim's needs, and he told Carrie he would prioritize his time to attempt to do this. The friend who was arrested with Tim was forbidden to meet with Tim for a time. Yet the two boys enjoyed many good experiences until other forces played into their lives.

Because of Tim's difficulty in communicating, he sometimes was blamed for things that he did not cause. One incident brought the city police to Carrie's door. The officer who spoke asked for Tim and stated he had a warrant for his arrest. When Carrie questioned him, he replied that Tim had broken a very expensive picture window at a home several blocks away. Chuck Green had reported to the officer that Tim had announced he was going to break this window because he was angry at the boy who lived there. Carrie was already familiar with Chuck's previous actions that had caused problems for Tim. Not too long ago, Chuck had joined another lad in the neighborhood to throw snowballs at a motorcycle rider. They were still in the process when Tim came upon the scene, just as the motorcyclist stopped his vehicle. The throwers ran away, leaving Tim alone to face the angry cyclist. He grabbed Tim and socked him in the mouth, causing damage to his upper front teeth. When Matt confronted the cyclist's father, he merely retorted that Matt should let his lawyer call their lawyer to settle the matter. It was Carrie who confronted the cyclist, scolding him for attacking Tim, who was not the person throwing the snowballs. Knowing the family were members of their sister church, she reminded the cyclist of his Christian training and responsibility. Then she phoned Chuck Green's father, who defended his son. "Boys will be boys, and they all throw snowballs." However, he did extend his sympathy for Tim's broken tooth and advised her to call the cyclist's parents to pay the dental bill.

Tim was not home when the officers approached. They stated, "We'll be back!" Carrie's friend, CeeCee, who was visiting, overheard the officer's words. She asked, *What proof does he have, this rookie gendarme?* But the whole matter caused concern for Carrie. When Tim came home, she questioned him. At first, he grinned when she asked him where he had been, and asked him where he was when the window was broken. It turned out he bashfully admitted he had been visiting a girl in his class who he wanted to date. Her name was Debbie. Carrie found out her address and phone number, so she could contact her and verify Tim's presence at the times when he visited her, and at the time the window was broken.

Not satisfied with the lack of evidence, Carrie walked the few blocks to the home with the broken window. No one was home, she learned upon ringing the doorbell. However, an elderly neighbor was outside, and when he saw Carrie approaching the house and observing the window, he apprised her of some facts. There had been a party and lots of noise. He thought the boys might have been drinking, because the boy's parents were away up north, and he had some of his friends over. Then Carrie scanned the window and saw that the broken glass around the hole pointed outward, as if it had been broken from the inside. Could it be that someone in the party had broken it, and now the homeowner's son needed an alibi, someone to blame? This led Carrie, with her resolve, to write a letter to the Chief of Police and report her observations, as well as the information gotten from the neighbor.

It was Chuck Green who was called back by the officer, and asked to report to the police station. Some days later, Tim received a letter stating he was *nolle prosequi* and the officer ultimately informed Carrie and Matt that, when called to repeat his claim, Chuck Green changed his story.

There were other incidents that Carrie was to look back on with regret. After high school graduation, she encouraged Tim to enroll in junior college. He enjoyed volleyball, in which he earned an A. He liked his art class, struggled through Math and was assigned reading. The reading teacher suggested he take at least one, maybe two courses in reading enrichment before attempting College-level English. Tim was interested in architecture. This interest should not have surprised Carrie or Matt, as their son wanted to build houses from the time he was a youngster. But now, the technical training required more academic training than he had been prepared for. For the first year, he enrolled for only two classes, plus Phys Ed, and was able to handle them. Then his counselor decided to give him a full load, fifteen class hours. Carrie tried to persuade him this was too much for Tim, but the counselor argued that Tim had to sink or swim.

When Tim realized this was too much, he confided to his friend, Dave, who persuaded him to just take off. And take off, they did. What Carrie was to learn later was that Dave's older brother suggested they do this. He no longer wanted to care for his younger orphaned sibling, now beyond the age of eighteen, and challenged him to take off and find work in another town. Prior to the boys' leaving, Carrie overheard their plan and warned them they could be placing themselves in danger. Who would try to attack Tim, Dave asked, with his height and strength? "A man with a gun," Carrie replied, not knowing that this was a prophecy about to be fulfilled.

A few days later, when Tim had been absent from home and school, the phone call came. It was from a sheriff in a small Kentucky town. The boys had been hitchhiking, forbidden by law in that area of the country. They were arrested for vagrancy. The sheriff explained to Matt that Tim could be released if he would send money for his bus fare home. The fine was just enough to pay for the meals served. The next day, Tim arrived home, leaving Dave behind. Tim worried about his friend.

"If something happens to him, I'll never forgive myself," he pleaded with Carrie. She and Matt had paid Tim's bus fare and fine money from his savings account. But Dave had no money to bail him out. Carrie suggested that maybe Tim would like to use more of his savings to help his friend.

"I think I'll phone Judy," Tim decided. But the news was favorable. Dave had been helped by the Salvation Army with bus fare and his meal payment, and was already on his way home.

The tragic result from this escapade was that Tim stopped attending college for good. However, he managed to become employed. During his first year of college, he worked in a local restaurant, one of a national chain. He was well respected as the favored busboy by all the waiters and waitresses, for he proved to be a willing worker. This experience prepared him to work at the local bar, where he served drinks, sandwiches, and also served as a door man, referred to as a *bouncer*. Acquainted with the people that came there regularly, he became quite popular. Young girls felt secure with him around, they told the owner. Unfortunately, this also had a sad ending. When Tim refused entry to a heavy drinker one night, he had no idea the man would avenge Tim's action. Several days later, when Tim was leaving for home, he was accosted by this man with two of his buddies, one a professional boxer. Severely beaten, he was left lying on the parking lot. An ambulance was called to take him to the hospital.

After a series of X-rays were taken, the emergency physician phoned. Matt went to bring Tim home. His nose had been broken, one eye had a black ring around it, and a number of bruises throughout his body caused him pain. Medication was administered to help. Matt led him to his bed, and quietly assured him, "We all love you; I love you, your mother loves you, and now, just go to sleep and rest."

A few hours later, another phone call came. It was Jerry, announcing to us the birth of Elizabeth, the daughter delivered by Anna at the same time her brother was being attended with his wounds at another hospital.

The family was happy at this happy ending to a sad morning. During the following months, Timmy was yet to face some other challenges. Refusing to return to the junior college, and not yet employed, he encountered another option—joining the Navy. The recruiting officer came to his home and discussed the possibility with Matt and Carrie. After consulting Tim themselves, they learned that he definitely wished to enter the Navy. For a short time, Carrie had arranged for private tutoring for Tim with a retired nun at the convent close by. Her goal was to help Tim advance with his reading skills. Carrie, hoping that Tim would make headway, questioned Tim about his choice. When he discussed his plan with the tutoring nun, she voiced a strong negative.

"No, I don't think this is a good move for him. They'll just put you down into the hole of the ship, and won't help you for your future!"

Although Tim never even got on a ship to find that hole, he did suffer some disappointments. After less than two months, it was decided by the commanding officer that the Navy was really not the right place for Tim. He received an honorable discharge, but what neither the officer nor Tim's parents could foresee were the aftereffects on Tim socially and emotionally. It was another *rejection* in the young man's life. He turned to companions and dates that were not preferable. One introduced him to a bar on the questionable side of town. Another to a young lady whose behavior was not in keeping with the standards that Tim had been raised in. The first led him to remove some expensive equipment "on loan" to his companions, who promised to return them in a couple of weeks. They were probably used to provide funds from a pawn shop, and of course, Tim never saw them again. He pleaded over the phone, to no avail.

"We're in trouble over this!"

"We not in trouble. You in trouble," was the reply.

As for the young lady, her demand was as much money as she could command from Tim. He had found a job at a local factory and moved into a rental room with a kind professor and his wife. But after paying his rent, he did not seem to have anything left for food, and he succumbed to walking the two and a half miles from his job each evening. Carrie, learning of the situation, prepared a large bag lunch for him, and met him on his walk. This went on for several months, until he finally cut loose from the girlfriend, and moved in with his friend who had been his runaway companion in Kentucky on a previous year.

After a few months, Tim asked to return home. His buddy had lost his job, and Tim could not carry all the expenses alone. Carrie and Matt eagerly agreed, seeing that their son appreciated his home much more than he had previously. But Tim, smiling, stated, "You gotta' admit, Dad, I *did* make it on my own," not taking into consideration the many handouts in food and needs his parents had provided.

Tim found himself doing a variety of jobs. He continued working at the local bar where he felt familiar. One daytime job was in landscaping during the summer. Friends from away from town also invited him to join them at events. One meeting introduced him to his first wife. She was from a small town about thirty miles away from his home. He brought her home to meet his parents.

He had decided to marry her. The wedding was planned in a very unconventional way. Somehow, however, the couple seemed close, in spite of a rocky beginning. When Matt and Carrie, together with Wren, decided to buy and share a home with Maria IV, they offered their present home to Tim and Tamara, to rent with the option to buy. Tim was happy to give up the tiny apartment in the town where Tamara's parents lived and come to the home that had been his since childhood. Tamara however, missed her parents, particularly her father, with whom she had a close relationship and some of her friends. Her phone calls became more expensive than Tim could handle financially. To avoid controversy, Matt provided the funds to pay the bills, exacting a promise from Tamara to repay him when she became employed. Most of it was never repaid. She also dipped into the rent money Tim had saved and most of it was gone before Matt was paid.

The most serious challenge to their marriage occurred during the second year, when Tim was diagnosed with testicular cancer. The surgery took place on Maundy Thursday. Tim suffered intense pain, from which he began to be relieved on Easter Sunday. What was most difficult for the young couple was the adjustment to their intimate relationship, enjoyed prior to Tim's surgery. Several months later, they moved away from the home belonging to Tim's parents at the advice of her parents, who arranged for them to rent the vacant home next door to them. Subsequently, Matt rented their house to two nursing students who signed a lease for one year.

During the following year, Carrie and Matt were to experience the illness of Maria IV that proved to be fatal. They had shared the home for almost two years, but the deadly cancer reared its ugly head again. For Wren, it was a tragic loss. Maria IV had been as close as a grandparent and her passing left a great void in Wren's life. Nine months later, Tim phoned Matt to ask him to bring him home. Tamara had asked him to leave. She wanted a separation, telling him she did not love him anymore. Matt brought him home, assigning him the bedroom in the lower level with its own bath.

With tears rolling down his cheeks, Tim tried to express his feelings to Carrie. "You don't understand, Mom; you've never been divorced. This is awful. It's like losing Marie (Maria IV)." Losing her was indeed a sadness for Carrie. She had learned only a short time before that Maria IV was born in the same year as her own mother, and she realized their friendship was like that of a daughter to her mother, without the hang-ups of having raised her.

How can those who have been blessed with living, caring mothers begin to understand the voice in the life of a motherless child? This was undoubtedly why Carrie was determined to fill in the gaps in her own childhood by helping her own children. One by one, she attempted to fill in those gaps. With Anna, the eldest, with whom she was aligned the closest, there were many events that opened opportunities to build a special closeness. Art work seemed to be a part of Anna's whole being. She was drawing constantly. While still in high school, she won two recognitions for pictures she had drawn. One was actually a portrait of her brother. The other was a picture of several robed figures walking together. Anna titled it *The Great Command*.

Mother and daughter also enjoyed shopping together. Interestingly, they often selected the same styles. Usually they were traditional, skirts or suits one could wear for a number of years, without concern for style changing. Neither was impressed by *fads*. Anna was always willing to help Carrie with household chores. She proved to have a talent at organization and orderliness. She was always willing to fill in gaps. When her younger sister was less orderly, she would take time to fold her clothes and place them in her dresser drawers. Carrie found her doing this for Durinda one day and asked Anna why she didn't let her sister take care of her own things.

"But, Mom, you don't understand Rindy, she has other things she can do real well," she defended her younger sister.

It was true, Rindy was not as bookish as her older sister. She was more action oriented. She learned to play the piano well. Carrie wanted her to have every advantage she herself had missed while growing up. Durinda had a lovely singing voice and music was a great interest. She also was an accomplished swimmer. Still in her teens, she was hired to teach the young children how to swim. What Carrie was to regret in later years were the changes in Durinda's life that came about as attempts were made to educate Timmy in his earlier years. Yet there was also a bit of the *cut-up* in her personality, expressions of humor— that Matt claimed she had inherited from her dad.

Both parents were awed and surprised by their son. If he made mistakes, was taken in by foul companions, whom he trusted though they might not be worthy of trust, one main characteristic remained with him, or maybe two. They emanated from his experience at the private school's Children's Workshop. He was right at home at woodworking. There he was, enrolled with an experienced woodworker, who taught him how to make things. Carrie was gifted with an attractive wooden shelf that housed the knick-knacks and items given to her on various occasions by her children and hung in their bathroom. He loved making things with wood. But long before the Workshop, even as a five or six-year-old, he loved being where houses were being built in his neighborhood. What was always considered *off-limits* for other youngsters in the neighborhood, was made welcome for Tim. He would sweep broken pieces and shingles for the builders, hand them tools, and make himself useful in any way possible. Sometimes at the end of the day, he would be given leftover wood pieces to take home. With these he would build a tree house next to the bottom of the weeping willow tree at the back of their yard. It was the envy of visiting cousins one day, whom he invited to come spend time with him there.

There was something else, a seed that was planted by the teacher who taught the handicapped children Bible stories at the Workshop. She would speak very slowly and clearly, so the young listeners would understand. Tim knew the story of the Creation, of King David's triumph over the Giant, the Teachings of Jesus, and he believed, literally, one must be kind and thoughtful of others. This he practiced even when someone had not been very considerate of him. He literally believed that *people may look on the outside, but God looks at the heart.*

Chapter V

Summer in the East

The year was 1969. Matt had begun his master's program in Geography, so the previous summer it had been his turn to study, and Carrie taught summer school. This summer she began a serious master's program in Russian at the invitation and limited financial assistance at the eastern college that specialized in teaching languages at an advanced level. Students who enrolled were serious, with careers that required a level of oral fluency. Standards were stricter than Carrie had experienced in the west two years before. Students were required to sign a pledge to use the Russian language exclusively. No radios or television sets were allowed in their rooms or in the dorm. There was only one exception—the Moon landing. For that particular event and that one only, a television set was brought into the dorm to observe the photos taken of this historical occasion. News included conversations with observers that brought about chuckles from the students whose oral training was far more advanced than one American who pronounced *thank you* with *spa-see-bow*.

Earlier, Matt had made the decision to drive Carrie east. There were so many things to pack that he arranged for a U-Haul to hold Carrie's clothes, books, tape recorder, and typewriter, as well as their tent for camping, to be hitched behind their Olds. En route, while camping in the Adirondacks, they met with a severe thunderstorm and lightening that interrupted their sleep. Carrie, who could not bear to part with Wren, had insisted on taking her along, and cuddled her close during the storm. But daylight brought wonderful

Middlebury College in Vermont.

sunshine and soon they were at the college grounds, unpacking and helping Carrie get settled in for this unusual adventure. Was it Masaryk who claimed when you learn another language, you live another life? Here, Carrie was to become exposed to a totally closed society of faculty members and students in a unique way. What proved to be helpful was one of the kind students who had studied with her in San Francisco was also enrolled. Carrie's roommate, Mary Anne, also had a fluency in the language, so she could speak to Carrie in Russian, yet was not unwilling to whisper in English when necessary. She had previously earned a master's degree in French that gave her a special advantage as she progressed through her Literature class conducted by Madame Volkanskaya, a cousin of Russia's Leo Tolstoy.

After hearing her speak, and eyeing her previous training in Russian, the native instructors placed Carrie in three classes— oral conversation; grammar and syntax; and Phonetics. It was the Phonetics class that came close to being her undoing. The instructor was a taskmaster and difficult to please. His total approach was European, aimed at drawing as much as possible from each student. Carrie read aloud when called upon. She also completed all assignments faithfully. Yet there was something about this instructor that caused her to recall the Mr. Nemudry of her early childhood lessons at the church school. His remarks were sarcastic. Once, when she did not understand a segment of the transliteration, she met with him privately, as he had advised. It was then that he told her she was strongly opinionated. What was worse, instead of addressing her as Carrie, he used the name Karla, with his Russian accent. When she couldn't stand it anymore, she "ran away." But she really did not quit. Carrie began her "tablitsa"—an assignment given to the students that was a preparation for acquainting them with words and sounds, a chart Carrie was to keep and use throughout her teaching career. She also went in to have a chat with the director, spilling her difficulties. He heard her out, then gave his response. "Our teachers have this deep zeal for their native language and some, like this professor, are perfectionists. They tend to come on rather strong."

"Okay, but do I also have to eat with him? Class is enough! You want us to mingle with the instructors, I know, but others in whose classes I'm not enrolled, might give me better digestion. Yet, I'm assigned to his table."

"Of course, pick wherever you wish to sit, you're free to do so."

When Carrie offered a brief outline of information on her previous stay in San Francisco, in Russian, in her Conversation Class, after a silence that spread out through several weeks, she astounded the professor, who was complimentary. "I can't believe this! You have spoken, Karolina, what has happened to you?"

It seemed that the childhood memories of having to memorize many pages of the Kralice Bible had come to haunt her, and at critical times, plagued free expression.

What only her roommate knew was that back in their shared dorm room, Carrie cried every day. In her letters to Matt, she told him how much she missed the family, and how hard it was to be there. Matt confided this to friends of theirs. They urged him, at no matter what the cost, to go there and see her.

And visit her, he did. Grabbing a flight to Toronto, then renting a car to take him to the eastern college, he arrived just as the group was gathering for a special reception. Carrie was wearing her rose colored dress, set for the party, when Matt appeared in the entrance to the reception hall. Surprised and happy, she ran toward him. Seeing their meeting, the wife of the Phonetics professor approached her and asked if she had been given permission to speak English, to which Carrie replied, "Nyet."

"Very well, I give it to you, now, while your husband is visiting."

Chuckling at her "permission to speak to each other," together they left for the motel Matt had already rented.

Their weekend was uplifting for both, but what neither was to know until many weeks later, there was a family price to pay because of Matt's absence from home.

****

Matt came for Carrie when her courses were completed. The ride through the Adirondacks was refreshing and Carrie was feeling the welcome release from the program that had required her to speak only in Russian. The car radio offered lovely music, and the freedom to have it played also added to the relaxation she now appreciated after the restricted program, aimed at perfecting the students' use of the language.

Wren was in good hands with the care of Durinda. It was almost as if the baby sister was her own child. Both younger and older sister were happy to see their mom. Durinda had perfected her chicken casserole to serve for her mother's first dinner home in more than eight weeks.

Later, Durinda was to confide her problem indirectly to Carrie. "Mom, I hope I'll be getting my period soon."

Carrie reassured her, drawing from her own experience that irregularity was not uncommon, and not to worry. Durinda loved to swim. Knowing this, Carrie dismissed the anxiety expressed.

But when Matt, together with the seventeen-year-old, returned from the family pediatrician's office a week later, the source of

Durinda's anxiety was revealed. Matt led his wife into their room and closed the door.

"I have something to tell you, now don't be alarmed. Durinda is pregnant."

In disbelief, perhaps in denial, Carrie shook her head. "How can this be possible?"

Carrie felt she had good open communications with her daughters, and had discussed sex with each of them and together. She even recalled Durinda saying something like, "Mom, I would never let anyone touch my body in that way."

What had happened?

It was several days later that Durinda offered her explanation. The conception took place on the very same evening that Matt had arrived at the eastern college to visit Carrie. A classmate of Durinda's had invited her to a party at his house. Anna tried to dissuade her from going, but Durinda had learned to drive, and assured her older sister she could find her way to Pedro's house. The home was located in a marginal area, but was well cared for and comfortably furnished, as Durinda noted. Pedro had previously asked Durinda for dates, but both parents agreed he was not the right person for her. However, the young man was a smooth persuader, and learning that Durinda's parents were not in town, convinced her she needed an evening of fun.

Arriving at Pedro's home, Durinda noted that she and the host were the only ones present. The party? "Well," Pedro explained, "I really wanted you all to myself!"

Tearfully, Durinda continued, "That's when I wish now that I had turned around and left. Pedro put his arms around me and began to kiss me. I felt overwhelmed, and before I knew it, he led me into his parents' bedroom and began making love to me. I couldn't seem to stop things. And now I'm going to have a baby, one that is half black and half white! How I wish this never happened. Yesterday I walked across the bridge over the river and wanted to jump in and drown!"

Matt shared his own guilt feelings with the pediatrician. "I wonder if we neglected to show our daughter attention; we have concentrated so much on our son's learning disability."

Aware of the family's concerns, the physician merely responded, "Well then, show her love and attention now."

Carrie hugged her daughter. On the following day, she phoned Matt's close friend, a social worker at one of the city's most conservative hospitals. Jason had many experiences with young girls with unwanted pregnancies, counseling them about their options. This was a time long before Planned Parenthood or abortion clinics. His sympathy was for Durinda; for during their friendship, Jason had gotten to know Matt's children quite well. When he was apprised of the girl's situation, his advice to Carrie was to make an appointment with Dr. Prompt and request that he perform the surgery. And, if he was unwilling to do so, ask him to advise of another physician who would.

Hearing Carrie's plight, Dr. Prompt contemplated the situation. Should he refuse help, endangering the young girl's mental health, and a possible suicide?

Finally, he offered a resolution. He had performed abortions before, but only in special situations. His advice was to have Carrie take Durinda to two psychiatrists and have them evaluate the young girl's situation. With their recommendations, he would approach the hospital board for their approval of the surgery. He gave Carrie the name of one psychiatrist, a Dr. Reckoning.

Matt and Carrie went together for this first appointment. He listened to their request and then gave his interpretation of the situation. Quizzing them, he asked why they had not allowed the boy to date their daughter, was it his skin color?

Carrie tried to explain that he was a couple of years older than Durinda, and they felt she was not ready for this type of relationship.

"Why didn't you let her find that out for herself?"

When Carrie pointed out that his motives and consequent action proved they were correct in withholding their permission, he replied, relating his own experience with his daughter.

"Ah, yes. But as you told me, your daughter had already made a decision long ago that she would not allow someone to invade her body. If you had allowed him to come to your home to hang out, she would have had your protection to maintain her earlier stance. Instead, she was thrown to the wolves, so to speak. I had an incident with our daughter who dated a black fellow for a number of months. He would come and hang around often."

"How did you feel about that?" Carrie wondered.

"Utterly helpless! My wife and I breathed a sigh of relief when, after a few months, our daughter politely and in her own way, told him that their relationship was ended."

Carrie and Matt both wondered had they been mistaken to refuse Durinda this type of experience? But then, Dr. Reckoning gave them more food for thought.

"Don't you think you have failed your daughter, and now you are trying to cover up with a situation that will affect her entire life. Why? I think I understand and feel sorry for Durinda. As for the abortion, I have to think this over after I talk with your daughter and then give you my answer."

Carrie made an appointment to have him meet with Durinda. Yet Carrie did not feel comfortable with this man. She still felt that withholding permission was acting in Durinda's best interest.

Surprisingly, Durinda held her own when being confronted. She related her experience with Pedro, accusing him of overpowering her, of virtual rape. After the appointment, Durinda confided to Carrie that she did not feel comfortable with this man. His questions and remarks seemed to blame Durinda for the affair.

Although the psychiatrist's parting words to Carrie were, "You'll be hearing from me," the only communication from his office was a hefty bill for his service.

"Now what do we do?" Matt asked Carrie. Two weeks had passed.

Carrie again phoned Jason, relating the results of their experience with the first psychiatrist. Jason strongly recommended a friend at the hospital where he was stationed. Dr. Michaelson proved to be sympathetic, and wrote a recommendation for the surgery. He also recommended another psychiatrist who was Jewish. Carrie recalled from her many studies that Hebrews believed life does not begin until birth takes place, so his view would, undoubtedly, be that of a strong ally. Kindly and sympathetic, he not only wrote the recommendation, but also indicated that Durinda be counseled after the surgery to put closure into this situation.

Closure? Just as the Japanese admiral declared after the attack on Pearl Harbor, that perhaps a sleeping giant had been awakened, thus it was with Carrie.

Dr. Prompt met with Carrie after the surgery was completed to advise her that Durinda had responded well and would be hospitalized for several days. Her sleeping giant was Carrie's conscience, as she questioned Dr. Prompt.

"This was the lesser of two evils, wasn't it?" she inquired.

Dr. Prompt replied without hesitation, "I don't know why you are questioning this now, but I did it for the psychological welfare of your daughter. We'll see you at my office in two weeks."

Disturbed by his statement, Carrie went to the nearest public telephone and dialed the pediatrician who had diagnosed Durinda's pregnancy. She told him about the surgery completion and her brief conversation with the obstetrician. Dr. Carly understood her feelings well, but then remarked, "It's over now. You have made a decision, and now you will have to live with it."

And live with it, she did. But she did phone the responsible young man's parents. The call was answered by the boy's mother. After Carrie told of Durinda's experience, how she went to her son's home, believing she was going to a party with other persons present, and finding the son home alone, the intimacy happened. Durinda had previously expressed empathy and friendship for her black classmates. Mornings would sound out from her record player the black music her friends enjoyed. At this time she tried to identify with their culture for want of friendship. One of her teachers at a parent conference termed it "over-identification."

The mother responded, "You'll be hearing from us." And so, that happened.

Carrie was teaching a night class in Russian on Thursday evenings. When she returned home the following class night, she found the parents of the young man, who was now about nineteen years old, visiting with Matt in their living room. An attractive pair, they introduced themselves, explaining they wanted to see both of Durinda's parents. The woman, proving to be the boy's stepmom, was beautiful. She told Carrie she worked as a nurse's aide in a local hospital. The father had been employed at a furniture factory for many years. He had three older sons, and spoke of their vocations: one was an Episcopal priest, another worked for the sheriff's department, and their third was studying to become a physician. He spoke with pride of their accomplishments and his disappointment at the behavior of this, his youngest son.

After Carrie and Matt discussed Durinda's surgery, and the emotional and financial experiences involved, the father acknowledged his son's responsibility. "He will pay for the medical treatment involved."

Departing, both parents thanked Matt for contacting them. A week later, the boy's stepmom phoned Carrie to tell her she would like to bring her the money as agreed. She arrived with two cashier's checks from the local credit union. They had deducted the money from the savings account they had, with the hope it would be for this youngest son's college education. Before leaving, the mother thanked Carrie for informing them. "You could have gotten him into a lot of trouble." Durinda was only seventeen, but the undesired lover was already nineteen, and the law would have undoubtedly favored Durinda.

Hearsay at school informed Durinda that the young man had left his father's home. "Kicked out!"

Concerned, Carrie phoned his mother. "Yes, he's gone, living with another relative, maybe with his grandmother. His father had confronted him, and the boy lied to his father, so his father felt he should leave for a while and consider what he has done.

Many years later, Carrie met the young man, now more fully grown—or matured—on an elevator in a downtown building and learned he had become a trained social worker. He did not recognize Carrie, though she claimed he looked familiar. He introduced himself and told her his office was in this building. Quietly, Carrie thought, *Ah, we do grow up!*

The young preacher who visited Durinda in the hospital was not advised of what type of surgery had taken place. Neither Matt nor Carrie wanted to talk with him about it. However, Carrie's conscience was troubled. She tried to discuss this with Matt, whose views differed. "We made a decision to help our daughter in a tough situation, and now it's over with. Let's put it out of our minds!" Matt felt God understood, but Carrie wondered. No one believes in abortion until their kid gets into trouble.

A personal call came from Dr. Michaelson, who headed the psychiatric hospital in the county. He expressed concern for Durinda. The doctor spoke reassuringly to Carrie, reminding her that this was not her decision alone, but a medical decision made by professionals. Learning that the pediatrician had referred Durinda to a counselor, he expressed approval.

The counselor was a nun trained for the local social agency. During her sessions, she firmly supported the belief in the sovereign power of God to create life, and wanted both Carrie and Durinda to realize how serious had been the decision that had been made, perhaps hoping it would never be repeated. It would be a long time before Carrie felt she was forgiven by God. Each time she participated in Holy Communion at church, she thought and prayed about it as she approached the communion rail.

Durinda, too, had thoughts about the aborted infant. Yet she was also relieved that she could return to school and continue her young life without the stigma of an unwanted pregnancy. She joined the cheerleaders' team. An exceptional swimmer, she became employed by the YWCA to teach youngsters to swim. And she graduated with her high school class, an important goal for her, as well as for her parents.

The restlessness, however, persisted. Carrie urged her to sign up for a Chemistry class at the junior college in the summer after graduation. She tried to concentrate, and with the help of a sympathetic classmate, she barely passed the course. Later, Carrie wished she had not pushed her, but thought this would be a good start toward her nursing program, for Durinda had always stated she wanted to become a nurse. Having done some special reading, it was Durinda who applied first aid and bandages as needed for injured members in the family. Even among her friends, it was believed she would become an RN.

A friend sent her to personnel at the local hospital and Durinda was hired to become a receptionist at the desk in the surgical unit. Her empathy for patients got her into difficulties with certain staff members, to whom nursing was merely a job to pay one's bills. They lacked the depth of feeling Durinda revealed, as she chided them for not being prompt with medication or attending to other needs.

"I guess my big mouth got me into trouble," she explained to Carrie and Matt the day she returned from work after being told she was fired.

Then she went to the eastern side of the state to stay with a young man she became acquainted with on a camping trip. His initial reaction when she confided her experience was one of understanding and sympathy. He wrote her a letter inviting her to visit at his home and meet with his parents, who admired Durinda's influence on their son, which seemed favorable at that time. He attended church with this girlfriend, something his parents had unsuccessfully attempted at their own church.

But living together did not work out. He phoned Matt to discuss the difficulties he was experiencing with Durinda "settling down." After discussing the situation with Carrie, it was decided they should drive to the eastern university town and bring Durinda home. Carrie found a letter written to her daughter by the exchange student from Guatemala she had met in college. Apparently she had written him. telling of her feelings of confusion and heartache, for he was attempting to console her. All of this convinced her parents she needed help.

"I don't want to go home," Durinda protested, "I'm not happy there!"

Matt would not be deterred in his decision. Gesturing to Carrie, he commanded, "Pack her things!"

"Oh, okay, I'll do it," Durinda agreed, and the two gathered all she had brought to Tom's apartment. Tom, himself, agreed with her parents, telling her he would be in touch with her.

The return home lasted three days. On the fourth morning, Durinda's bedroom was found empty and many of her clothes were gone. The note she left her parents explained that she left because she did not want to be a burden to them. No address was given.

It was two weeks later that Durinda phoned to ask if she could return home.

Relieved, Carrie answered, "Of course, you can. We'll start over again."

What neither parent was aware of and would be announced by their daughter several weeks later was that Durinda had become pregnant. This time, declaring she was now of age, at nineteen, she would keep this baby. Carrie and Matt found themselves in a new life's odyssey.

The weeks and months went by, as they waited. Matt's parents were told Durinda's news with accepting willingness to help. She was invited to make her home with them. They also financed a special course for her to complete that would aid her in getting a bookkeeping job. In the end, Durinda made the decision to allow the newborn son to become adopted. What had changed her mind? Two reasons.

The latest boyfriend, who wanted to marry her, claimed he would have difficulty because of his own background to become a father to another man's child. Durinda, herself, stated, "Every person should have *both, a father as well as a mother.*" Papers were signed. Durinda was ready to continue with her postpartum life.

Three weeks later, Matt's father died suddenly of a heart attack.

Other changes had taken place. Carrie, eager to expand Russian classes in her town, changed school districts. She was invited to become the instructor at a special centrally-located high school, offering classes not available in the existing high schools in the city, and decided to make the move. Matt warned her that this change might prove to be difficult. Matt's warning proved to be an unwelcome prophecy. After all, there was only one Russian class. Carrie was contracted for only one hour of teaching. In contrast to the situation at the suburban school, where she had been assigned a classroom with her own desk, file cabinet, and all the materials necessary for conducting a class successfully, here she was assigned a room for only one hour and shared with another teacher. Very reluctantly, her colleague allowed her one deep drawer to store materials in the desk. She was told by the director they would order another file cabinet, for the one in the classroom was already taken up with materials by the first teacher.

Carrie discovered that the Russian typewriter had been set upside down, in the closet. She had no space to prepare lesson plans or mark papers or record grades in her record book. It became necessary to carry all in her briefcase and take schoolwork home each day. Carrie also learned the lesson of being low person on the totem pole. She requested more classes for the following semester, perhaps English or History to add to her hours. Other colleagues who already had been promised teaching positions were given these assignments, though they lacked Carrie's background and experience.

Somehow, she finished the school year, hoping for a more suitable assignment in the coming fall. But it didn't happen. However, her contract received by mail indicated she was assigned to a half-time position. When she met with the director, he appeared furious. Someone had made a mistake; he felt Carrie was at fault. "You think you're unique, don't you? Well, I don't have more than one class of Russian for you."

"But I can teach a Lit class, then," Carrie offered.

"All are filled up by people who have more seniority in this district!"

"Let me take this up with Dan Schultz!"

Years before finishing college and starting her teaching career, Carrie had been Dan's secretary for a time. He had always proven thoughtful, so she was certain the situation would be resolved.

"Go ahead, maybe another school can use you!"

Dan was not in his office, but his secretary offered an appointment for the following day. Overnight, an idea struck her mind. Couldn't the Assistant Superintendent, in charge of foreign languages, use some assistance? His major was in French, and he had created such an attractive impression on the Superintendent that he was assigned the position of monitoring the curriculum and activities of all foreign language instructors in the district. Carrie had met him at a recent reception, and he indicated his job was quite complex, as it meant covering both middle school as well as high school programs. He also hinted at a desire to offer languages as an enrichment for students in the upper elementary grades. Born in Europe, he was familiar with programs wherein elementary students began studying languages of neighboring countries at an early age.

When she met with Dan the following day, she explained what had happened in the director's office. Then she proposed the possibility of filling up her contracted time by assisting the foreign language director. Before their meeting was concluded, the director of the special high school joined them. Now, he was somewhat submissive and almost apologetic to Carrie for his lashing out at her the previous day. When Dan told him about the proposal Carrie made, he spoke agreeably, complimenting her on the idea, which would enable her to use her language teaching background in a suitable way.

"We know your experience will be very helpful to him."

Dan, himself, phoned Fredrick to arrange an appointment for Carrie.

Fredrick seemed happy to receive administrative help. The interview was pleasant. He even asked Carrie to help him pronounce the name of the Russian author, *Solzhenitsyn*, whose book he was reading. They set up a plan for Carrie to appear at his office directly after teaching her Russian class. She was assigned an hour and a half with his department each day.

Most of the time, the errands and assignments were pleasant. It was not long after Carrie worked with him that he suggested she approach some of the elementary principals to arrange for enrichment classes in Beginning Russian for their students. She found the administrators were eager to have her arrange for classes. They seemed much more open than the high school principals. Of course, it meant Carrie would travel to the schools. There was no need for busing the elementary students. She also received an invitation from a couple of kindergarten instructors. It was fun teaching their students the Russian birthday song and pronouncing their names in Russian.

The fourth graders thought the alphabet was *cool.* They also enjoyed the *karavaj* and choosing favorites to replace them with, each singing session. The middle-schoolers enjoyed practicing short dialogs with each other, emulating Carrie's introductions to everyday phrases and greetings. The school personnel informed Carrie that many of the parents were pleasantly surprised and pleased that their children had this opportunity to learn an exotic language.

These changes in the Russian program brought additional teaching hours for Carrie. She was to experience a greater level of fulfillment, knowing many more students were becoming acquainted with Russian language and culture. On the following school year, she no longer accompanied Fredrick in his office. Her time was taken up teaching at two middle schools and two elementary schools, as well as continuing her high school classes. By the ninth year, she was contracted to 90 per cent teaching time.

Her studies in special government programs continued. She was able to exchange ideas and updated information on events in the Soviet Union from colleagues attending the sponsored events from other areas of the country. It was at one of these events that she received news that her teaching career would be subjected to changes.

Chapter VI

The Larger School District

What a contrast Carrie experienced from her former position in the suburban school district! Formerly, she was endowed with everything a teacher might need or wish to have to carry out her lesson plans. Primarily, she had an empathetic principal, who had been a foreign language teacher himself and wanted her to have all available tools to carry out her plans. Books, records, and other materials were at her fingertips for both her Russian and English classes. It was believed that this small school district was very prosperous, second only to one on the eastern side of Michigan, because there was a General Motors plant in the suburb, and revenue to the schools there was generous.

At the big city school, a specialized setting with special classes was required to be approved for federal funding. Carrie hoped to enroll far more Russian students than was possible in the much smaller suburban high school. She had given up much to make this transition. However, she did not expect the lacks that she encountered. For one thing, she had a smaller assignment in hours. She was only given one class of Russian students to teach. The teacher who shared the room was unwilling to share either her desk drawers or her file cabinet. Because she was teaching full time, she felt entitled to the space. After some searching, Carrie finally located the Russian typewriter. It had been placed upside down inside of the closet, underneath a pile of maps and bulletins, somewhat discarded. Carrie decided to make the best of the situation, and just focus on the students. She already had her background of experience to draw from, and found her resilience paid off as the students learned eagerly. Some of them had plans for their futures. Eventually, one lad became an Orthodox priest, whose career Carrie was to follow proudly. Another became a journalist. One was employed for a time by the Department of Commerce. Some became teachers of English to Russian students.

One student, Janey, practiced her conversation as well as devoted time for study so well, that when graduating high school, she entered a college that placed her with third-year Russian students. After receiving her bachelor's degree, she was given a scholarship to an eastern university, where she completed a master's degree. Janey also spent one summer studying at the same Russian school Carrie had attended years before. At the school where she completed her master's degree, she was invited to enter the doctoral program. But she phoned Carrie, and told her she had a calling for something different. She entered a mission training program sponsored by a Slavic Organization in the Midwest.

At that time 10,000 Russian émigrés were freed by the Soviet Union and came to Chicago. There, she was able, with her fluency in Russian, to help them in many ways—housing, food stamps, training in English, job placement, and as opportunity arose, to share her Christian faith. Because the Soviet Union discouraged or forbade the practice of faith, not only to Christians, but also to Jews, there was a void in their religious background and an openness to receiving Christianity was enjoyed by some. Her former student did no proselytizing; rather, she devoted herself to the refugees with a genuine willingness to help, armed with her strong faith. One refugee told her, after receiving counseling and help, "Now I know there is a God, because of what you have done for me."

When Carrie attended the special service at Janey's church, she had tears in her eyes, as she heard her greet the congregation with the words of the Apostle Paul in Russian. From the pulpit, she enumerated the various experiences she had working with the Russian newcomers in Chicago. What later occurred was this student would meet a young man from among the émigrés who would become her husband. They invited Carrie and Matt to attend their wedding in a church in Chicago, the town in which they would live in their first home together. What a happy memory for them and for Carrie to witness this outcome for her student.

Because the enrollment was small, Carrie had both beginners as well as advanced students in the Russian class. Two students stayed with her for three years and acquired quite a mastery of the language. One planned to enroll in the language in college. It required special planning for Carrie to meet all their needs.

Yet the class was not without humor. One student, who proved to be a "shutterbug," threw a pencil in the air, after Carrie had assigned quiet study of the following day's assignment. Carrie became aware of this distraction and watched with vigilance. When the third pencil was thrown in the air, she frowned disapproval, only to have the shutterbug snap her grimace with his readied camera. His parents were of Ukrainian heritage, and he had learned some of the language from home. The accents of some words were quite different, so Russian was challenging to him.

This shutterbug proved to be helpful to Carrie privately. He agreed to have copies of a dated wedding photo of Carrie's parents made up, so she could have them for her sisters and children to share.

As time went on, Carrie's school experienced a change in administration. The new principal was a harsher person and moody. One never knew what to expect from him, or how he would respond to a request. Because this school was isolated from the other major high schools, with their own physical settings, students who elected to enroll in its special classes had to be bused in. A greater problem evolved. The desire for these special classes created a rivalry between the staffs and principals of the regular high schools and the special school. Enrollment in Carrie's classes was usually smaller than others, so the threat of discontinuing the Russian courses constantly existed. It was the parents' support that helped them to continue.

In addition, some adults asked to be included for enrollment. One had aged parents to care for, who knew more Russian than English. Another had traveled in the Soviet Union and wanted to learn the language for personal reasons. There were four or five who added to the class of high school students, which rounded out, made a respectable total. The principal, in a moody frame of mind, warned Carrie that in the following year, there were not to be any adults included. When they showed up, Carrie informed them of his decision. However, when these adult students approached the principal, he consented to allow them to attend the Russian classes.

Another problem was recruiting. Carrie informed all the other instructors of these students of the opportunity to study at the special school, hoping for enrollment. This is when rivalry evolved. Some principals did not encourage her to speak and recruit their students.

However, another phase of studies opened up after Carrie went to the assistant superintendent with her idea of offering Russian studies to upper elementary students. She was able to implement classes in several elementary schools and a junior high school. Most principals were happy to have a unique offering right at their school. It was fun for the students to learn Russian songs, some conversation, and master the alphabet. It was from one of these elementary settings that a fifth grader decided to continue on, even after the special school was closed. His mother phoned Carrie to request tutoring for him because he planned to continue Russian in college. His family even ordered computer lessons to strengthen his background. Eventually, he was to become an Eastern Orthodox priest.

Were all her efforts worth the struggle? Sometimes even fellow staff members were hostile. One discouraged a very bright student from continuing by calling her a *commie*. He felt that her enrollment in his drama class would suffer. After nine years, the special school discontinued, and Carrie's career as a teacher took a different path.

She had been informed by letter that the school was to discontinue the Russian program. After her many years of experience in teaching language, Carrie expected to be placed in an English-teaching assignment, hoping that her new future principal would advocate offering a course in Russian. Previously, a high school principal had advised her to transfer to his school, and he would offer the course in-house. He greatly disapproved of having his students bused out to the centralized special school. The year that followed the discontinuance of the Russian program brought about five different assignments for Carrie. The first was one for which she had very good qualifications, not only because of her strong personal interest in Literature and writing since high school days, but her college had also prepared her with unique instructors who loved Literature as Carrie did.

Carrie knew she would miss teaching Russian, but told herself she would be happy to teach English Lit again. She recalled the five years she had spent in the suburban high school and her experiences during those years. She particularly enjoyed the Sophomore Honors class. Her principal encouraged Carrie, after examining her planned curriculum. His motto was to make Honors English something special.

"Students can get an easy A in regular English, but in Honors, they have to do something special to earn it."

Carrie had pondered for a time before writing up the curriculum. These students, though only age fifteen, were already adult-level readers, who needed challenges. Recalling her studies in Lit and Philosophy, she asked herself, *Why do they have to wait until college to learn about the ancient thinkers, medieval contributors, as well as those who opened the Renaissance and modern thought.* So she designed courses to cover classical writers in this order: the first three months studies would be on ancient thinkers, including the Ancient Greeks and sections from the Bible. The following three months would cover medieval writers. After that, the students could select writers in the Renaissance period, closing the school year with selections from more modern writers. The course was rewarding for most of the students. A few rebelled.

"Why should we study Plato or Aristotle? What have they got to do with today's world?"

Smiling, Carrie replied positively, "That's exactly what we want to find out."

Another student asked, after reading up on St. Augustine, "You know, I'm a liberal, so I might not agree with his teachings, but his early life was sure interesting!"

Carrie assured her that being a liberal as she claimed, made her reaction and presentation that much more valuable.

When all the papers and presentations came in after the study of Ancient Thinkers during the first three months, Carrie felt a great measure of success. Another student, giving an account of *The History of the Peloponnesian War* by Thucydides, concluded that it had brought to a close the leadership of Ancient Greece. Still another gave an account of the biblical Abraham and brought laughter when pronouncing the word heir like *hair.* Another found research into the influence of the Egyptians upon Ancient Greece in ideas and culture.

By the time they entered the study of Renaissance and medieval thinkers, Carrie was particularly impressed by the paper on Dante, written by one rebellious student. She had dissected all of the *Divine Comedy* and wrote of Beatrice as if she had become an intimate friend. One student came to tell her privately that Thomas Aquinas was "cool."

Sometimes a measure of time, perhaps a decade, helps a student to recall his or her experience in high school, and realize the value of what he has learned.

One student, married to another in that Honors Class, had joined the church to which Carrie and Matt belonged. It was about ten years later, that they met while leaving their church service, and he approached Carrie with the words, "I received a revelation today while teaching my eighth graders in Sunday School. They were arguing with me, declaring they were *entitled to their opinion.* I found myself retorting with the same words you used with us back there in Honors Class, *How can you state an opinion before you have examined all of the facts?* Back there, we thought you were putting us down, but now I realize you were trying to help us THINK."

Such are the intangible rewards of teaching!

Carrie was to struggle through nine years with the special school, but her total assignment never met more than 90% of the school day. She had classes in the middle schools, as well as the high school, and after the fourth year, two elementary principals requested she teach their fifth graders. It was from one of these that she had the student who was to continue studying Russian with her until he graduated from high school. He continued Russian studies in college and then enrolled in a seminary that led him to become an Eastern Orthodox priest.

His parents expressed their appreciation for the efforts Carrie had made to help him continue his Russian studies. They invited Carrie and Matt to his ordination at his church and to the reception held for this celebration of his priesthood. There, Carrie was to meet his wife. If priests were to marry, they must marry before they become ordained. His young wife graciously asked Carrie, "Please pray for us." A number of years later, an incident in Carrie's life, while traveling in Alaska, proved to be rewarding. *

It was the summer of 2001. Carrie and Matt, together with Wren's two daughters, Johanna and Julianna, were visiting in Alaska at their cousin Elizabeth's home at Elmendorf Air Force Base, where Elizabeth's husband, Eric, was stationed. Alaska had many Russian historical and cultural features—churches, schools, and graveyards, and Elizabeth was eager to share these with her Oma Carrie. She identified Eklutna Park, just north of Anchorage. They drove there to tour. A little souvenir shop at the entrance sold tickets to tourists. Here, Carrie encountered an Orthodox priest from California, accompanied by several of his parishioners. He introduced himself as Father Josiah and told of their interest in the Russian contribution to Alaskan culture, particularly the missionaries who had come to serve the natives. During their conversation, Carrie told of her experience as a Russian teacher and mentioned the name of her former student, who had been ordained into the Eastern Orthodox priesthood. He responded eagerly:

"Father Tom, you know Father Tom? Well, you must've done a good job. Do you know every time the archbishop goes to Moscow, he takes Father Tom with him to interpret." Carrie protested that she was only his *beginning* Russian teacher, for the student had continued his Russian studies on through college to become proficient. Nevertheless, the tie revealed here manifested the far-reaching results of Carrie's teaching efforts. She and Father Josiah, though thousands of miles away from home, had a common friend.

And again, Carrie experienced one of those priceless rewards of teaching.

Durinda, dressed in native Slovak costume, is hanging an ornament on the Czechoslovakian Christmas tree at the local art gallery.

Chapter VII

From Whence We Were Derived

The most important part of their twenty-fifth anniversary celebration was their trip to Europe where they hoped to visit family in Holland and Czechoslovakia. Their plane was a KLM jet that flew them from Chicago to Amsterdam.

Upon their arrival in Amsterdam, they were met at the airport by Matt's cousin, Reta. Warm and hospitable, she assured them, "Your bed is ready for you," acknowledging their jet lag and need for rest. Matt drove their rental car, following his cousin. Carrie's eyes guarded Matt, as he drove on the narrow highway situated between two rather deep ditches. Reta's home was a *boathouse*, about the size of a small American ranch house, set on the hulk of a boat, moored on the shore of a lake. The view from the living room window overlooked the water and the picturesque shore across the lake. The bedrooms were on the lower floor, and Reta led them down to comfort and sleep for several hours. Carrie was softly lulled to sleep by the waves splashing gently on the sides of the boathouse.

In the evening, they were hosted to a delicious home-cooked meal, and later visited by other cousins, Reta's sister, Caterina and husband, Harry, and their brother, Darius, whose appearance strongly reminded Carrie of Matt's late father. This was Matt's family, all right. The Dutch cousins recalled that the last American cousin to visit them was a mutual cousin of Matt's, who had served on President Truman's Berlin Airlift as a pilot. When he had leave, he traveled to Holland to meet his Dutch family. Now these cousins expressed a strong interest in their American cousins and their plans to visit Czechoslovakia. Maps were brought out, and the road recommended through Germany was pointed out. Summer meant many other travelers would be on the roads, and guesthouses and restaurants would be open late into the night. Being advised of this situation, Matt decided he would like to begin their travel on the next day. They decided to leave in the late afternoon and travel the six hundred miles during the night.

Bidding the Dutch cousins a warm farewell, they crossed into the German border, and stopped in a restaurant in Koblenz. There, they struck up a conversation with a native couple who invited them to come to their home. Although they declined, Matt and Carrie were impressed by their graciousness. They gave much attention to Wren and gifted her with several German coins. She had begun to collect coins in Holland. It was hard to believe these people were enemies of Americans just a few decades before. The food was tasty. By the time they left the eating place—actually a pub—it was already twilight. But Matt decided to drive throughout the night, hoping to reach Nuremberg by daylight. Driving through rural areas, villages and small towns, Carrie was impressed by the architecture. When they arrived in Nuremberg, Wren awoke. She was fascinated by the "double streetcars," and insisted they take some photos. Finally exhausted, Matt parked on a side street, and napped behind the wheel. They awaited the opening of an eating place nearby where they hoped to buy breakfast. The snacks they had from Holland were almost gone.

Arriving at the restaurant, and consuming a hearty breakfast, they were then faced with a new situation. The waitress would not accept their travelers' check. She held up German paper money to indicate that this was what she expected. So, leaving Carrie and Wren at the restaurant, Matt proceeded to the bank on the same street, to cash a travelers' check for German cash to pay for their breakfast. After that, they stopped at a deli, where they purchased luncheon meat and bread, pastries, and cartons of juice and milk to take with them on the road to Cheb, Czechoslovakia.

The day was pleasant. The travelers encountered many mountain climbers en route, using wooden carved canes. Before their arrival at Cheb, they stopped and had a picnic lunch with their purchased food and drinks. On occasion, they stopped for a "comfort stop," and noticed how different these were designed from most in the States. One had merely an opening in the floor, and Carrie found herself explaining to Wren that perhaps the local taxes did not provide enough revenue to pay for the facilities she was used to having at home. When they arrived near the entrance to Cheb, the full impact of what the other world was like was felt by all of them. The fence surrounding the entrance was at least fifteen or maybe twenty feet high. Close to the entrance were several cars on the road ahead of them. And there they waited. And waited. Finally, Carrie, needing a comfort stop, left the car long enough to walk up to the guard at the gate. Learning of her need, the man pointed to the field, and told her that was available. Noticing the area—the fence, the watchdogs, and the armed guards at their posts, Carrie reluctantly decided to wait, hoping it would not be too long. Altogether, it was about an hour when their car was finally allowed inside the gate, where a very polite woman directed her to a ladies' facility.

Then there was the necessary paperwork. For each of the three family members to enter, they were required to exchange a certain amount of dollars for Czechoslovak currency for each day they planned to stay in the country. Matt and Carrie had previously budgeted a time span of eleven days. Having completed these requirements, they drove on toward *Karlovy Vary*—Carlsbad. This town in former times was known for its spas, enjoyed by many of the crowned heads and aristocracy of Europe.

En route, Matt encountered a hairpin turn which their car navigated successfully. However, after another turn, they were flagged down by a highway patrolman, who stopped long enough to collect a fine of about five American dollars. Indignant, Carrie retorted in her best effort at the native language, "Is this the way you treat visitors to your country? My husband drove very carefully within your speed limit around a curve that was not even marked in advance, to allow the driver to know it would be a sharp one."

The only response Carrie received from the patrolman was the repeated hunching of his shoulders. It was difficult to determine from his body language what his true intent was, other than collecting the five dollars which he pocketed, without even offering a receipt. When they arrived in the outskirts of Carlsbad, they sighted a gas station with a line-up. Matt, cautiously concerned that they would keep their little car adequately filled, decided to take his place in the line-up, counting about five or six cars ahead of him. As they neared the pump, a man just sort of hanging around the gas station, approached them. He seemed to know they were Americans, and opened his heart to Matt and Carrie.

"I was in England during World War II. I wish I could have stayed there. Here, since the commies have taken over, times are hard. Now I drink every day."

They understood his attempts at English but did not know what to say to encourage him. They were later to observe a dichotomy of reactions to the present form of government in Czechoslovakia. Carrie kept recalling the ideas of Masaryk and his hopes for the country when it was founded after World War I. Could all of this have been lost, or was it a temporary situation? What she was not prepared for, as yet, were the attitudes others had, and she was soon to learn when she met the family members.

Having fed their vehicle, Matt drove on to a motel that was recommended to them by the travel agency, where they had inquired for information about food and lodging. Arriving at the motel, the clerk refused to register them when Carrie indicated that Wren had her own sleeping bag.

"Oh, no," she insisted, "she must have a separate bed. She is *a vooman*." It was true that Wren was tall for her age, but Carrie countered by giving her age—nine years old. So Carrie decided to try another accommodation. This one was a hotel, and their rooms were on the second floor. Bathrooms were down the hall, but there was a sink in their suite, and here, Wren had a bed in a separate adjoining room from that of her parents. The bathroom looked scary. The windows overlooked a courtyard, and Carrie, now having a taste of this present culture, recalled the defenestration of the late Jan Masaryk, who was reported to have been pushed out of just such a window by his political opposers. She was also uncomfortable about having to leave their passports at the desk. She wondered, *Would my prayers for safety here, help us?* They settled in their room, and then went down to the restaurant. On the elevator going down toward the restaurant, they met a couple from Boston. "I know you must be Americans," the wife pointed to Matt's feet, "because you're wearing white shoes. We're from Boston. We've been here for three days, hoping to find some of my husband's family, but without success."

When Carrie told her they were to meet her family in Prague on the following day, the lady indicated how fortunate they were, and assured them they would find this trip here well worth their efforts.

Shortly after they were seated in the dining room, a young woman came and sat down in the empty chair at their table. She did not talk very much, but expressed a strong interest in remaining there with them. The waiter who took their order for food did not offer to serve her. In fact, he rather ignored her, as if she did not really belong with this party. The food was delicious—Prague ham, *knedliky,* roasted potatoes, and beets. Desserts were homemade torte and coffee was black, Turkish-style. Wren took such a liking to the Prague ham that she was to order it again a number of times throughout their stay in the country.

Leaving their visitor behind, they returned to their quarters and settled down for the night. The beds were comfortable, and breakfast was served before they packed to leave. Alas, Matt could not find the key to the car. He had gone down to the parking lot adjacent to the hotel with Wren and some of their luggage already, only to realize he did not have the key. After scouting through his suitcase, which was still in their room, Carrie located the only car key in the pocket of his trousers, which had already been packed. Handing the key to Wren, who had been sent up to Carrie for help, she advised her very strongly, "Hold this tightly in your hand and don't let it get dropped or lost and go straight to Dad with it."

After finishing their packing, and retrieving their passports at the hotel desk, they entered their car, ready to travel towards Prague. Before they left the parking lot, an elderly man approached them with a map. "Going to Prague?" he asked, and when Matt nodded, he held the map up and indicated with his pen the road to be taken. Matt gave him several Czech coins. By the time they were at the outskirts of Prague, Matt indicated he needed to nap a bit. While Carrie and Wren waited, Wren asked to go see the flowers in the field around them. She was so enchanted by the poppies; she took many photos of them, using up much of the Kodak film in the camera, which later proved to be very difficult to buy.

Arriving in Prague, they looked for the International Hotel. Unsure of their direction, Matt stopped to ask a man in uniform, who turned out to be a Russian officer. He asked for their passports, and satisfied, he gave the directions, which proved to be accurate. Matt offered him an American fountain pen, one of a number Carrie had packed before their trip because she had been advised this was a wanted item. The officer refused to accept it, pulling out his own pen, to indicate he did not need one from Matt.

Old Town Prague.

The International Hotel, where Carrie and Matt were to meet her Aunt Eva, was a wedding cake-style building, much like one built during the Stalin era in Moscow. Once inside the building, not sure exactly where they were to meet their hosts, they proceeded to knock on a door where a meeting was being held. It appeared to be a party meeting and surprise was expressed in the face of the woman who answered. She obviously expressed disapproval. Although she did not welcome these intruders, as she indicated they were, her tone softened when Carrie explained they had come here to meet her aunt, her mother's sister. Even under the existing regime, family seemed to be respected. So she directed them to a lounge by the hotel lobby, where she believed they would meet their hosts. And so, they did.

Aunt Eva was holding a photo of Carrie's mother and father that had been sent to her many years before to identify herself. Accompanying her was her son-in-law, Vaclav (Wenceslaus), and there was immediate joy expressed by all at this meeting. Wren, who was practically the same height as her great aunt, immediately bonded with "Tetka Eva." Their itinerary was prepared, the result of Carrie's letters to Aunt Anna in Slovakia, prior to their trip. Long before. Carrie had collected photo books of Prague; now they toured many of the highlights—Prague Castle, St. Vitas Cathedral, the National Art Museum, the *Divadlo*, the National Theatre for which the Czechs are most famous, and many other enchanting places, including *Karlovy Most,* the Charles Bridge, built during the time of Charles IV, in the fourteenth century. In spite of the current Communist Regime, the statues of the saints and historical Christian figures were being preserved.

They were to see all of these and more. Over several days' time, it seemed there was no end to the wonders and beauties of Prague. Carrie asked to see the statue of Jan Hus, the morning star of the Reformation, located in the square. Jan Hus, who opposed certain tactics of the Roman Church practiced at that time, had been martyred. In spite of being promised safe sanction, he was burned at the stake. Yet he predicted that even if they destroyed the *hus*—the goose— they could expect the coming of a swan, and within a century, Europe was to welcome Martin Luther. Around the corner from the statue of Hus was the astronomical clock, and close by, the sidewalk revealed the markings of the sixteenth century defenestration of Prague. There was the *Zlata Ulicka*, the Golden Lane—the target of alchemists, and what especially fascinated Matt was the home of Tyco Brahe. When one believed he had seen the ultimate, there would be another surprise, sometimes just around the corner.

Overnight, they were hosted by Carrie's cousin, Emily, and husband, Joseph, whose home was in the suburb of Prague. Aunt Eva's son-in-law was their tour guide and Matt was to follow his car for guidance to all the sights. What astounded Carrie and Matt was the graciousness of their hospitality. The family gave their most comfortable beds to their guests, some bunking on sleeping bags on the floor.

Aunt Eva insisted on paying for all their meals at various restaurants, until Matt decided it was his turn to treat at a Russian restaurant whose manager had served with the Czech army in England. He spoke English quite fluently. Carrie asked for borscht. Alas, they did not have any left, though it appeared on the menu. Seeing Carrie's disappointment, he asked if they were in a hurry. If not, he would ask the cook to prepare a pot. Beet soup was as great a favor here as it was in Russia. Finally, after the soup and other gourmet foods, Matt took the check. When Auntie began to protest, he smilingly threatened her with one of his few vocabulary words, "I will spank you on your *dupa!*" Surprised at his use of this common native word, Aunt Eva joined his smile.

Earlier, the travelers had been advised in their travelers' brochures that they were to report to the police station in Prague. Auntie had to ask for directions, and after completing a rather long stroll, when they entered the building, they were met by a uniformed host. Aunt Eva explained this was her niece, with husband and daughter, visiting from America. The look on his face softened with a smile, and both hands were waved forward with the words, *"Tieraz ne musite!"* It was no longer necessary to report to the police. This was still only 1974, but could it have been a prophecy of the coup to take place fifteen years later? Communism had taken its toll since the close of World War II, when the country had come under its yoke, but now, it was a generation and a half later.

Aunt Eva explained to Carrie that she wanted them to see as much history as possible, so one of their major excursions would be *Karlstejn*, the castle built by Charles IV. How can one explain the history of this great edifice? One must climb a hilly path to reach it. Trumpet blowers in Renaissance costumes were playing a classic German tune that Carrie recognized was also the music of a Christmas carol.

Karlstejn Castle.

How can one explain the magnificence of this castle, built in the thirteenth century? Ever the geographer, Matt expressed his imagination—one can look down from the castle and visualize peasants working the fields below. For indeed, their gardens were lovely. The people lived close to the land, their *mother*, their *nurturer*, that kept them fed.

Inside the castle, they toured the various sections allowed. Most beautiful was the chapel lit with gold. Even more interesting was the tiny chapel, hidden in a very plain, nondescript concrete hallway. What a contrast! Inside the tiny chaplet, the walls were covered with precious stones, some of which are described in the book of

Isaiah, Chapter 54:11–12, wherein the Lord promises: "I will build you with stones of turquoise, your foundations with sapphires, ... and all your walls with precious stones."

Returning to Prague, they were taken on a tour that spoke of another tragic event in World War II. It was at the church where the assassinators of Sebald Heyden sought sanctuary. It was told they were captured by drowning. World War II left many scars in the memories of Czech and Slovak people. It was as if the war had just ended yesterday.

On the following day, after bidding their hosts farewell, the two cars drove to Brno, the capital of the Czech portion of the country. They did not tour much of the town, for their destination was the home of Vaclav, where they would be hosted by him and Carrie's cousin, Svetlana. Svetlushka, her Czech-translated name, proved to be an excellent cook. She served them stuffed peppers with freshly baked rye bread. Matt, who particularly enjoyed a second serving, was surprised to learn that Carrie had often eaten these in her childhood homes. She also admitted she knew how to prepare stuffed peppers.

"Wow!" was Matt's response. "I had to come far from home to find this out!" Carrie promised Matt to cook some for him when they returned home.

Vaclav and Svetlana had three young sons. They were fascinated by their American cousin, Wren. One son was to leave home early the following morning to fulfill his obligation of clearing fruit trees of pears and apples, to be brought to a special market for distribution to low-income families. Every child eight years or older was signed up to a task as part of his training in civic duty. Also the visitors learned that every young man, at age twenty, was required to sign up for military training. They were to be responsible for the protection of their country.

Matt and Wren were invited for a stroll, so the boys could acquaint them with Brno, leaving Tetka Eva and Carrie behind to have tea with Svetlana. The women were happy for this chance to visit. It was during their conversation that Svetlana informed Carrie that she was an atheist: "I do not believe in God."

Viewing the surprised look on her niece's face, Tetka Eva tried to explain to Carrie, "See, this is what the war did to us."

Carrie pondered. How could she respond? She certainly did not want to compromise her faith. From somewhere, the words came from her sub-conscious. Nodding in agreement with her aunt's words, she stated, "I know there were many evils done during the war, but that should not force one away from belief in God."

A moment or two passed. Then Tetka Eva asked Carrie if she still remembered the hymn, "Hrad prepevny est Pan Buh nas"? A mighty fortress is our God. When Carrie nodded, Tetka Eva asked if they could sing it together. And *all three sang it together.* After that, there was no further discussion about religion. Just warm conversation between members of the family, long absent from one another.

After hosting them overnight, they were again to travel and visit Eva and husband, Zdenek, in Hodonin, a town very close to the Slovak border. Svetlana did not join them. She explained that there would not be room enough for all of them to stay.

Young Eva, who was the sister of Svetlana, proved to be a very gracious hostess to her cousin, Carrie. She took her on a bus ride to the center of Hodonin. There, they entered a bookstore, where Eva gifted her with a special book telling about their country. Eva also proved to be a very good cook. Their meals, all made at home, were delicious. What proved to be most interesting about their visit was the strong interest expressed about Carrie and Matt's life and livelihood in the United States. They wanted to know all about *Amerika.* Thinking about their conversation later, and explaining it to Matt, Carrie referred to it as the *Hodonin Dialogue.*

Carrie had read much about the first president of Czechoslovakia, Thomas Masaryk. She admired his philosophy and beliefs. Not far from the young Eva's home was located a park, at which stood a statue of the first president, who had been dearly loved by his country. Although Eva's mother did not appear to share Carrie's admiration, declaring Masaryk to be a *bourgeois,* undoubtedly influenced by the current communist regime. Carrie defended him, reminding her European family of his many heroic acts that stemmed from his love for his country and a strong sense of justice.

After Matt, Wren, and Tetka Eva had retired, Carrie found herself alone with young Eva, her husband, Zdenek, and Vaclav, with whom they had been traveling and touring during the days following their first meeting in Prague. Before the young Eva began her questions about America, Carrie responded to the information she received when they first arrived. Eva explained why she was at home caring for their baby son, Thomas, who was still less than two years old. She was given leave of absence from her teaching position until Thomas was two and toilet trained, at which time he could be enrolled in a government-operated preschool. Her job as teacher would be held for her at full salary. However, now she was being paid 80% of her normal wage, while at home with her infant child. Carrie stated this was a hope that they in the U. S. would be able to pass a similar law to arrange for their mothers and babies.

"Ano" (Yes), nodded Eva. And she began to enumerate other benefits this communist government had provided. Everyone had a job. Many of them had gardens that provided a large percentage of their food. Children were trained at an early age to participate in the distribution of fruits and vegetables to accommodate all citizens. One year of military service was required of twenty-year-old men to be trained to protect their country. Their memories of World War II and invasion of the Germans was still fresh in their minds. The Russians were considered their liberators from their Nazi invaders. Now as their leaders, the Russians had provided farming equipment. It was also true that a huge percentage of crops yielded were sent to Russia. There were bonuses of travel. Factory workers, such as Zdenek, who met their work quotas, were rewarded with trips to other countries behind the Iron Curtain. But travel to western countries was strictly limited. Limited also were the churches. Although they still existed and the clergy were paid wages by the government, they were not allowed to teach religion to the young.

Both Eva and her sister, Svetlana, were baptized and confirmed in the Christian faith. Their churches' ties were with the Lutheran Church in America, but they called their denomination The Church of the Augsburg Confessions. Carrie recalled the conversation at Svetlana's home in Brno. She wondered, was this a defensive statement about atheism to protect her family? Now, in her conversation, Carrie defended both her American freedom of religion and freedom of speech. She found herself quoting from Masaryk's words about Christian socialism, a socialism that was democratic. Many of the benefits Eva and their family now enjoyed would undoubtedly have been carried out, had Masaryk more time. Two decades between two wars was not enough time. Yet after Carrie offered the comparison in their lives, Eva responded positively: "I believe Karolina believes the same way we do. We agree on so many things."

Carrie, steeped in the writings accounting for the prison camps documented by Solzhenitsyn, withheld agreement. She also recalled the many written accounts by *Samizdat* writers, asking why there were so many underground writers opposing the communist hierarchy?

Eva's response was that there were many mistakes made under the Stalin administration.

"But how then can you call the death of twenty million lives *mistakes*?

"Yes, but many things have improved, especially if one joins the Communist party, and I am glad that Vaclav here introduced us, so we could join."

"Vaclav?" Carrie stared at him in disbelief. She and many others in the U.S. had been led to believe that all communists were bad, like hardened criminals. Senator McCarthy's propaganda against Russian communists had persuaded Americans how evil they were. Yet, Vaclav? This gentle, thoughtful man who had guided them on their journey so conscientiously, so hospitably, a *real communist?* Never. Impossible. Carrie looked his way with wonder in her eyes. He nodded. Yes, after the horrors of the war and the help from the Russians, he saw their aid and their partnership as the way to go, to protect his country.

All were silent for several minutes that seemed like hours. She believed Vaclav to be a man of good character, genuine, wholesome. There was nothing artificial about this person. Carrie's response now came from her heart.

"Ja nedbam ze ty si Komjunist. Ja teba lublyu!" *I don't care if you're a communist, I love you!* And she walked over to his chair and hugged him. End of *Hodonin Dialogue*.

If they felt weary, their exchange assured them that their personal goals and ideas were compatible enough to allow for a continued visit as a family, despite their differing governments. All were looking forward to continuing their journey the following day. They would, at last, visit the family at her mother's village, from which Carrie felt she had been derived.

At the entrance to Klátova Nová Ves, the village from which Carrie's mother came, they received a unique welcome. Matt drove behind Vaclav's car with Tetka Eva. Both vehicles were met by a large flock of geese, forcing both cars to slow down to a crawl to avoid hitting any of the honking fowl. Entering the village street, the geese seemed to form a line straddling each car, escorting them to the gates of Tetka Anna's cottage.

Later, Carrie asked her aunt, "Those were your geese, Tetka?"

"Ano" (Yes). The fowl seemed to know that Carrie and Matt, together with Wren, would be her visitors. Their loud honking announced their arrival. Neighbors and other villagers were in the habit of allowing their geese to run free throughout the village during the day, yet each gaggle seemed to know where it belonged when it was time to return home at evening. After they returned, the gates at the entrance to each home were closed for the night. Carrie wondered at this measure of security, was it really needed? For the village appeared quiet and peaceful.

Young Eva accompanied her mother and brother-in-law to Tetka Anna's home. Eva wanted to visit her Slovak cousins, which did not happen very often, it seemed. Close to her age would be her cousin, Anička, who with her husband, Milan, and son, lived in the neighboring town of Topoľčany. Milan was a professor of animal husbandry and agriculture at the Institute in Topoľčany.

Living next door to the elderly Tetka Anna were her son, Štefan, and wife, Teresa, and their daughter Janka, (pronounced Yanka). Both Teresa and Anička were expecting—for each it would be the second child, to arrive in the fall. Their children, Janka and Milan, were close to the same age, and while visiting their grandmother, played together a great deal.

It was Milan, Anička's husband, who suggested that they tour the Tatra Mountains.

"How far away are they?" Carrie asked.

"About six hours, one way."

Calculating time and hopes for touring, Carrie replied, "I would rather see things that are close to here, where my mother lived. That is most important to me. I would like to visit the church where she attended with her family and see the home where she lived."

The group agreed. Carrie was their visitor and they were eager to accommodate her. The compromise was a visit to *Bojnice*, the large castle/museum close by. Here, everyone was required to place cloth slippers over their shoes in order to preserve the beautiful wood floors of the castle. As they toured, Carrie noted the lovely furniture that had been preserved since the days when the *Hungarian* lord of the manor resided there. Now the castle belonged to the people, that is, the state. For a very modest sum, tickets of admission could be purchased. The cousins would not allow Matt or Carrie to pay for a thing. All was taken care of by the hosts, eager to treat their guests with utmost hospitality.

In addition, when Carrie mentioned her strong interest in the late President Masaryk and his ideas, Štefan decided they should visit the summer home of the president in Topoľčianky. Here, Carrie was surprised as they toured the library, to see on display a third-century copy of the Bible, handprinted by a monk in the local monastery, many centuries before. The whole family accompanied them— Pavel, the older brother of Štefan, and his wife, Martha, as well as their two children, daughter Evočka and son Stanislav.

They entered the castle, and as on their previous tour, were given cloth coverings to cover their shoes so as to preserve the floors and carpets on which they would be walking. The historic furnishings gave everyone an aura of things long past, now being shared with a generation and culture that was indeed separated by time and style.

When they returned, Tetka Anna had a dinner prepared that seemed like a feast. Carrie saw her reimburse her son for the costs of the tickets and items purchased on the trip. She also presented Carrie with a beautiful doll dressed in native Slovak costume.

Tetka Anna with two grandchildren—first cousins
visiting and playing at their grandmother's.

It was Saturday evening, and the plan was that Carrie and her family would attend the church in Nitrianska Streda, on Sunday. Carrie affirmed the plan with her aunt. "Zajtra bude naš deň." *Tomorrow will be our day.* Her aunt nodded, smiling.

What an event that Sunday turned out to be. Tetka Anna was dressed in her native Slovak costume. Her daughter, the younger Anna, and husband, Milan, together with Štefan, attended the service. Carrie tried to count the number of persons attending, mostly elderly ladies with heads covered with kerchiefs. There were forty in addition to Carrie's family. The sparse attendance left the church more than half empty. When praying, the minister thanked the Lord for the visitors and especially for those who had returned after a long absence. Carrie was reminded that her cousins were subjected to the laws of the communist regime. Young people, educated and controlled by the regime, were forbidden to attend worship services. Their jobs, their community status, their very safety as individuals

Tetka Anna's son Štefan—first cousin to Carrie. Štefan is a philatelist and is seen here with part of his stamp collection.

were at stake. There was no compromise. It was a miracle that her cousins even dared to accompany Carrie, Matt, and Wren, along with Tetka Anna.

Studying her surroundings, she noticed the fancy lettering of the words high above the altar. They contained the Edict of Toleration issued by Joseph II in 1781. This improved the situation for Protestants, freeing them from the restrictions of a half century earlier, when the Resolution Carolina of 1731 upheld the restrictions imposed by Leopold I that limited worship, allowed only Lutheran grammar schools, forbade conversions, and required the swearing of a Catholic oath upon entry into the public service. No wonder Masaryk strongly endorsed the separation of church and state!

The church itself was more than two hundred years old, probably built close to the year of 1771. Its interior was lit by three beautiful chandeliers, not matched, but unique in design. The altar was flanked by two statues, and two angels hovered over the table used

Carrie with Tetka Anna and Tetka Eva, Carrie's mother's sisters.

for the communion vessels. The tempo of the hymns was much slower than those sung in the American English services back home. But those who sang did so from their hearts. Maybe only a remnant attended, yet still it would be. This remnant persisted, in spite of the Russian-led Communist yoke.

Carrie was reminded of the words spoken by the Russian Christian philosopher, Nikolai Berdyaev, who responded to the Americans' confrontation, inquiring about the Soviets' opposition to Christianity. Berdyaev declared that Russians had become Christians a millennium ago, they have remained Christian in spite of the regime. Currently, their government is temporarily in Babylonian captivity. World War I ended with the Bolshevik takeover of Russia in 1917. Was this a prophecy by Berdyaev, for Carrie and all the world to see, some seventy years after the Bolshevik takeover? For while Gorbachev was president, changes took place, freeing the entire Soviet Union and its satellite nations from this Communist captivity? (Consider this comparison with the Israelites' Babylonian captivity of seventy years.)

After the service, the family was invited to visit with the pastor and his family for refreshments. Tetka Anna presented the pastor with her tithe to the church, expressing thankfulness for the life of Carrie's mother and for the visit of her niece and family for the first time in Slovakia. Matt presented the pastor with a small white Bible and a copy of the new Lutheran hymnal. The pastor's teenaged son eagerly opened it, and placing it on the stand of the piano, began playing the liturgy, *This is the feast of victory for our God."* This tune was like a bit of home for the visitors. The pastor and his wife welcomed everyone warmly, and his wife urged Anička to come again.

Taking leave of the parsonage, all drove to stop at the cousins' as they had promised. What they did not expect was the banquet prepared for them that noon. Tetka Anna lamented, for she had prepared her force-fed goose for a dinner, along with many of her homegrown vegetables and potatoes. However, everyone politely sat at the table prepared for them and ate of the gourmet village delicacies—homemade sausage, potato salad, tomatoes with lettuce from their garden, beets, cabbage slaw, and coffee served Turkish style. Here, it is important to reckon the influence the Turks had on these people during their century and a half dominance. Foods often had a Mediterranean flavor, with spices and herbs introduced by their Turkish captors. Carrie could not consume the inky black coffee served and only sipped a bit to be polite, but it was readily accepted by the natives; it was quite unlike the western coffee they had been served in Holland.

But this was not all. Later in the day, as they planned for a walk in the village, Tetka Anna declared, "We must go to see my friend Karolina. If I don't bring our visitors there, she will not speak to me for the rest of our lives." There proved to be two Karolinas— mother and daughter. Again, Slovak hospitality prevailed, with large selections of food, homemade sausage, salads, vegetables, and liquor. Carrie chuckled as the daughter and she exchanged greetings.

"I have never before been in a home where there were three Karolinas," she declared. And poised on top of the archaic radio was a wedding photo of Carrie's mother and father. "I have never seen this photo," Carrie told her hosts. Young Karolina promised to make a copy for her someday. The elder Karolina remembered Carrie's mother well. She reminded Štefan to take Carrie to the former home of Maria I, which he did on the following day.

The lodging was one of a connected series of four apartments. As they walked around the building, Štefan struck up a conversation with one of the neighboring inhabitants. She remembered Carrie's mother. In fact, it was she who reminded Štefan that after Maria died, her widowed husband (Anton) had written Maria's mother, requesting her to send another of her daughters to be his wife and help him care for his three little daughters who had been half-orphaned by Maria's death. To this the mourning mother replied, "I have already sacrificed one daughter to America. I do not intend to sacrifice another." This tale had become part of the village legend. Štefan explained to Carrie that her father's request was not an uncommon one. Often when a young mother died, her sister might become the wife of the widower and substitute mother to the half-orphaned children.

During their first ten-day stay, the cousins took them to many spots in the area. They spent one day in Piešťany, where the spas had formerly hosted many crowned heads of Europe. One unique eating place served sheep's cheese, which neither Carrie nor Matt had tasted before. One cannot exclude seeing the mountains in Slovakia that are inhabited by the native bagpipers. They did not wear plaid skirts like the Scottish musicians, but their music was pleasant to the ear. The cousins took care of all expenses, buying tickets and paying for lunches in restaurants where family members were usually divided, seated at separate tables. Often the tables were small and round and could not accommodate all hosts and visitors together. Noticing all this, Carrie was to arrange for a change in their seating arrangement before they left, in Bratislava.

On their eleventh day in the country, it was time to leave. Their visa only allowed for the days already paid for in advance. The cousins accompanied their visitors to the border at Bratislava. But first it was Matt's idea that they invite all for dinner at the hotel. However, the *classless society* in which they lived proved to be otherwise. For when they entered the dining room, Štefan and the other family members were not allowed to be seated. Carrie, who momentarily was in the ladies' room, was hastily approached when she joined them with the request that she speak to the headwaiter, affirming that she, with her husband and daughter were visitors, and wanted to have her Slovak family members join them for dinner. Only her statement allowed all of them to be seated together. They were served by several different waiters. One poured water. Another made certain all had menus. A third took orders for drinks, wine, *Becherovka*, beer or plum brandy, called *Slivovice*. This dinner was delicious. Carrie noticed that other guests in this dining hall were admitted. Štefan explained they were allowed to dine there because they were select party members. Later, when it was time for Matt to pay the bill, he presented his credit card. This was another unusual event for the maître d'. It took quite some time for the card to be authorized and payment to be completed. At last, they were leaving the hotel.

Recalling this event after they were homeward bound, Carrie believed that this was a special opportunity for the cousins to raise their self-esteem. Their closed society had many limitations. But they would not accept the hospitality of their guests without doing something in return. Going to the gift shops close by the hotel, they entered with Carrie and Matt, insisting that they choose gifts to take home with them. Cut glassware and china plates, products of their country's artisans, were selected and wrapped carefully. These were added to the many gifts already given by Tetka Eva and her daughters, the books and perfume bottles, as well as the gift items they had brought back from Russia.

That was another event they shared. Each worker who faithfully completed his or her given quota over a period of time would be given as a bonus a tour, expenses paid, to the Soviet Union, usually to Moscow or Leningrad. Several of the family members were employed in the shoe factory close by. Products manufactured were shipped to outfit people in the Soviet Union. Once, while touring with the cousins, they watched tractors working in the fields. Štefan's wife pointed to the huge vehicles and remarked, "These were given us by the Russians. We had none after the war, and they helped us with our farms by sending their equipment." Teresa expressed respect for the Russian dominion with tenderheartedness.

She was now looking forward to the trip with Štefan to Leningrad. They had already traveled several countries within the *Iron Curtain* and Štefan had shared his experiences going to Hungary, Yugoslavia, Romania, and East Germany. In contrast to former decades, especially under Austria–Hungary, those who chose to follow the rules exacted by the communist party fared well. There were certain restrictions. Cousin Anna pointed them out during her conversation with Carrie on one of their walks in the village. Although she and husband, Milan, and Štefan all attended church with Tetka Anna, accompanying Carrie and Matt, she explained that in order to have employment and other benefits, one could not be a *Lutheran*. She and Milan were both teachers. She taught home economics and Milan was a professor of agriculture. He proudly arranged a tour of his office and the building where cows were milked on a circular platform, machinery purchased from Sweden.

Their experiences were the source of much conversation when they reentered the western world.

Chapter VIII

Visits in Free Europe

It was hard to describe their feelings of relief after crossing the border from Bratislava and driving toward Vienna. The entire atmosphere was different, and Carrie, who usually had no difficulty describing situations, found herself pausing before trying to explain the feelings she was now experiencing. Was this like the sun shining after a heavy rain? Now their destination was to drive into Germany and find a store in Munich that carried parts needed for Vaclav's razor that he was unable to get in his own country. She had written these parts on her note pad so she could explain what was needed to the store clerks. Although Tetka Eva kept assuring them that "we have everything," this did not prove true. One item they had looked for and were not successful in finding was film for their camera. It was possible to find Kodak film, but not the size needed for their camera.

Matt found driving to be somewhat challenging, for traffic proved to be quite heavy. On one road he had unwittingly cut off a driver who was not German, but Dutch. At one stop sign this driver and his wife decided to stop Matt's leased auto by driving around and blocking his path with their car to give Matt a lecture on safe driving. The man's English was heavily accented, and he scolded Matt about his driving method. Matt tried to explain, apologetically, but his efforts were not appreciated and the Dutch driver accused Matt of driving without a license.

After their scolding, the adversaries remained parked in Matt's way for several minutes before finally driving on. By the time they arrived in the motel in Lenz, all three were hungry and happy to find a restaurant close by. The food was homemade and tasty. Noodles with beef, and what had become a favorite, white asparagus.

Returning to the motel where they had reserved a room for the night, they found themselves ready for the shut-eye, under the comfortable quilts awaiting them. But all they had for funds were the travelers' checks they had brought from the Credit Union in the U. S. One kind Austrian came to the rescue. He appeared to be a close friend or relative of the motel owner. Speaking English with an accent, he explained, "If we go right now, I can take you to the bank. They'll cash a check for you, but they close in twenty minutes." Leaving his wife and daughter to wait for their return, Matt accompanied the kind native. They returned in less than half an hour. Having paid the owner, the travelers were ready to settle down for the night.

Morning included a typical European breakfast, to which they had already been introduced—warm cereal, eggs, and sausage with home-baked rolls and coffee. Packing suitcases and double checking to make certain nothing was left behind, they parted with the host in the office. Before traveling on to Switzerland, they were determined to keep their promise to Vaclav.

What surprised them at the border to Germany was the reaction of one of the border guards when he examined the windshield of their car. He spoke in German, which neither Matt nor Carrie understood. He pointed to their windshield and shook his head. Matt gestured with open hands, trying to indicate he did not understand. Moments later, the guard was accompanied by his colleague, who fortunately seemed to know some English. Having heard the complaint of his fellow worker, he nodded and leaned at the driver's window to inform Matt of the problem. The windshield lacked the letter of the country from which they were traveling. Then Carrie and Matt both recalled what had been missing already in Czechoslovakia, the letter *C*, which some citizen, eager to acquire a souvenir from this visiting American's car, had removed from their windshield. What to do?

"Buy one here, only this would be one of ours." The cost was less than about 25 cents in American money, and both guards watched as Matt cooperatively pasted the German letter on the windshield. Off they went.

"Whew, I was afraid they might want to search our luggage. I wonder if we would have been charged a fee for all those gift items the family gave us back in Czechoslovakia. It's good that Wren slept on the *perina* Tetka Anna gave us to avoid any charges."

"It seems like a lot of fuss for such a minor matter," Matt commented, laughing.

They finally arrived in Munich. Traffic was heavy, as it might be in the U. S. at late afternoon. It was certainly unfamiliar territory, yet they did locate a hardware store where they were fortunate to find the part for Vaclav's razor. Carrie referred now to her notes, listing parts needed for the razor. The clerk was helpful, for he did speak English. When Carrie explained they wanted to mail the razor part to a cousin in Czechoslovakia, he found a small padded envelope in which it could be sent. Carrie addressed it, and after purchasing the correct stamps, the clerk directed them to a postal box. (Weeks later, after they returned home to the U. S., they received a letter confirming the arrival of the package. Vaclav did not inform them whether he had to pay any extra postage or a tax for receiving a package from a foreign country.)

Completing their mission in Germany, they drove on toward Switzerland. Next to the Swiss border, they stopped and drove through the tiny country of Liechtenstein. En route, they stopped for dinner. While they waited for the meal to be served, Carrie approached the telephone booth. Depositing the coins left over from their purchase, she dialed the number of her former professor's home in Switzerland. Happy to receive her call, he advised of the roads Matt would be driving. "And you have been in Munich?" His voice expressed empathy, for he was aware of the crowded streets they had braved at that time of day.

They were warmly welcomed at the Tchirky's. Their home was large and comfortable. The children enjoyed entertaining Wren. She was given a bunk bed in the room of the youngest daughter, who was close to her age. Matt and Carrie referred to her as the

Tchirky's *honorary American*, for she had been conceived before they left the U.S. eight years ago, while the professor was teaching Carrie's Russian class at the new fledgling college.

"Yes, who would have predicted eight years ago that you would come to accept our invitation to visit us?"

The visitors were given a comfortable bed in the guest room. Wren slept in the bunk bed with the youngest little girl. Adelle treated them to meals of Swiss cuisine. The days took them to various spots in their village, including the three-centuries-old cathedral.

Carrie brought out several of the souvenirs they had purchased in Czechoslovakia, asking her hosts to choose one of them as a gift for their home. The choice was a framed photo of a doll dressed in the native village costume. Both the host and his wife showed a fond appreciation for the art of this country that they had not yet visited. However, the professor had chaperoned students to Russia at least five times. He was quite experienced and familiar with the culture in an Iron Curtain country.

By the time they prepared to leave on the third day, it was evident that their hostess was worn out. So, the older children, now in their teens, prepared breakfast for their visitors prior to their leaving. At the professor's recommendation, they planned to visit Zurich and Basel before leaving the country.

Zurich was enchanting. Its history reminded Carrie of the home of Melanchthon, Martin Luther's close associate and friend. They visited the church where he had preached. Ever eager to bring home souvenirs, they bought Swiss-made watches on pendants. Years later they were to become gifts to two of their great-granddaughters.

It was in Basel that a personal statement by a Swiss native touched Carrie's heart. While she was cashing a cashier's check for Swiss currency, the bank teller, surmising the check was from the U.S., addressed Carrie: "You are an American?" Responding to Carrie's nod, he expressed with sincere sympathy, "Oh, I am so sorry for what is happening in your country." European newspapers had informed him of Nixon's plight and resignation and the presidential office now being held by Gerald Ford.

This news had already been presented by the Czech cousins. Vaclav's wife spoke of it, and showing their local paper's description of the event, she then gave the copy to Carrie to keep. Carrie thanked the teller for his kind words and returned to Matt and Wren, awaiting her. They were now going to return to Holland to their waiting family, before boarding their plane for home.

Before they got to Holland, they drove through Luxembourg, where Carrie was totally enchanted by the beauty of the gardens. In France, they drove past a church with a stork's nest on its roof. Carrie so wanted a photo, but Matt didn't want to stop, telling Carrie, "Oh, we'll see a lot more of them, let's go on." They saw no more.

In Belgium where they were low on gas, they had difficulty at two gas stations where they refused to take their American travelers' checks, so at the third stop, Matt parked by the gas tank and filled up before paying. He had coins and some paper money in his hands from three countries—Austria, Germany, and Switzerland—and held them open in front of the owner. The man studied the money, and then picked out what he wanted. Smiling, he handed a piece of paper serving as a receipt to Matt and waved him on. He appeared to have relieved them of the Austrian coins, whose value was the lowest of all. As they drove away, Carrie asked Matt, "Don't you think this guy shortchanged himself?"

"I wouldn't know. Even if he took more, I wouldn't argue. I can't speak his language, but my gas tank is full, that's the main thing!"

It was late afternoon on Saturday when they arrived to the cousins at the boathouse. They were accompanied by other cousins, one from Utrecht; he and his wife both wanted to meet their American cousin and his family. They enjoyed supper and then were informed there would be church to attend on the following morning. Gifts from Czechoslovakia were given—carvings, pottery from Modra, and cornhusk dolls. There were bottles of *Slivovice,* the native plum brandy, of which all were fond. Their hostess happily served it with their meals.

The family atmosphere was somehow more advanced by the friendliness and openness of Reta's six-year-old son. He showed

Carrie his children's-sized buggy filled with stuffed animals that he called his *friends*. He also told them that he wanted to be married while he was young because his mother and father were able to sleep together and he had to sleep alone.

Matt and Carrie found themselves discussing what they had learned about the inhabitants' lives in Czechoslovakia. In comparing certain benefits with what the Dutch cousins already enjoyed in Holland, it was evident there was much social progress for the Czechs and Slovaks, yet it was at the cost of losing their freedom of religion. It was as Anička had told Carrie, "One cannot be a Christian and enjoy the approval and benefits of the present government."

Their last Sunday in Holland gave Matt and Carrie an opportunity to attend the church with Reta and Ger. The service was entirely in Dutch which made Carrie wonder about Matt. Did he understand very much? Did the language bring back thoughts about his father? He had on this trip met only one of his father's brothers, his Uncle Brat. Reta and Ger took them to visit him. He had not seen Matt's father for many years, for his brother had never returned for a visit after making his home in America.

The following morning, the visitors boarded their plane for home. The jet lag took its toll. When they arrived at Betka's in Chicago, all three fell asleep in their basement rec room. Betka had a surprise to show them. The postcard mailed from Basel had already arrived, an unusually short travel time. Carrie tried to recall, was it four or five days? Carrie had the newspaper given her by Svetlana, describing the decision to impeach Nixon which forced his resignation.

When Matt was representing the city's teachers in the Republican party, he had opportunity to confer with Jerry Ford, who represented Michigan in Congress. Now Matt and Carrie were returning to their country that would be led by him, as their new president.

Chapter IX

The Marriage Encounter

Ah, Love! could thou and I with Fate conspire

To grasp this sorry Scheme of things entire

Would not we shatter it to bits—and then

Remold it nearer to the Heart's desire!

—Omar Khayyam

The struggles continued. Here it was, the twenty-eighth year of their marriage, and something was going wrong. What was it? They were hardly speaking. Why? *What happened to us*, Carrie wondered. We have been through so much together. We weathered Matt's business problems and losses. We both finished school, repaid our loans, and our jobs seem stable enough now. Timmy's learning problems and challenges do keep us on our toes. Durinda appears content with her marriage to Chad, after an unhappy first with Clark. Yet the vicissitudes in our current life have changed us, from lovebirds to almost strangers. *What has happened to us*, Carrie wondered again. Neither wanted to part. Neither had even mentioned the word *divorce*, but living together now had somehow become strained. What to do?

It was while Carrie was rummaging through old files and papers that she came across them. Why had she saved these? From a previous era in their lives, this was *old stuff*. Should these have been discarded years ago? But curiosity overwhelmed her and she began to read.

"Dear Lover-buttons ..." We were so close, so romantic, she recalled. When he wrote, proposing to her, she recalled his father's words, that she did not have to forget Matt or he forget her, but "you are so young, you must take your time ..." and "My wife was twenty-eight and I was thirty when we married."

Her response was to tell Matt that he must first write his parents to inform them of his intentions before she would answer him. The answer actually came from Matt's mother, telling Carrie that Matt writes "You folks are planning to marry," and an invitation, "You might as well come here and live with us until he arrives home." And Carrie did.

They were married the following July. Just kids. Matt turned twenty-one in April and Carrie was eighteen. How young we were! How naïve! How could anyone foresee life as it had evolved? So much has happened. Their coupleness grew into the parenthood of two daughters, then three children with the arrival of their son, and behold, a fourth when the others were already partially grown. Anna was fifteen, Durinda thirteen, and Timmy nine, when Wren was to join them. Carrie recalled the excitement and the tragedies of that summer when Wren was born.

But they were resilient—Anna with her severed finger; Timmy with his broken leg and many changes of school before the age of nine; Durinda with her change of schools for Timmy's sake. Carrie leaned on Matt's strength, which always seemed to be there.

Matt's father died when Wren was six. Was this when Matt began to change somewhat? Carrie pondered on Matt's reaction. He who seldom drank since their marriage had begun to come home after school each day and drink a couple of Bloody Marys before settling in with the family. It seemed he was trying to run away from something. Hints were given when Carrie attempted conversation. He felt there was much unfinished business with his dad. He recalled his dad's promise, that someday he had things to tell him. There had never been any intimacy between father and son. Why? It was hard to tell.

Tony, as Matt's father was called, had come from the Netherlands as a young man. He met his future wife at the Psychiatric Hospital where both worked as nurses' aides. He spoke English with a brogue, somewhat uncommon in the second-born generation community where he resided. He fell in love with this beautiful young woman and proposed to her. Before they would wed, he built their home. They were frugal people who made maximum use of their resources. Their first child, a daughter, was born three years before Matt. The health of his mother was poor, and she remained hospitalized for a long period of time, so the infant Matt was kept in the nursery at the hospital until both were discharged.

Something happened to Matt's father during the years of Matt's childhood. All the facts were never discussed in the family, but Carrie received two hints. One was from Matt's mother and the other was from Matt's sister, Beth, during her visit from the state of Washington. There was a change of employment for Tony. Why? As Carrie became familiar with the household routine, she realized that Matt's mom ran the household around her husband's work schedule—six weeks of seven nights' work for twelve hours and a seventh week of complete freedom. It was his task to run the laundry at the hospital. All had to be done during the night to provide linens, ready for the following day. After breakfast he slept all day and was wakened for an early supper prepared by his wife in time for him to eat before he left for work. Carrie was puzzled, because she recalled Matt telling her his father had been a nurse's assistant.

Finally, his wife shared her confidence with Carrie. "Yes, Papa had a better job, but something happened and certain employees had told lies about Papa, and so they demoted him." Later, after his father's retirement, Matt expressed his resentment to Carrie. "Yeah, my dad ran the whole laundry himself, but now they hired four people to replace him doing the same work!" Perhaps the elder man's time was so taken up making a living that little time was shared with his son during the boy's growing years. Once Matt, now in adulthood, recalled attending a men's breakfast at his father's church, a rare occasion for the father and son. En route to the event, Tony confided, "I wish I had spent more time with you when you were a little boy." Much of the training and discipline was left to his wife. *Could this have had its consequences on their marriage,* Carrie wondered. His later words were to relate his childhood memories of his mother.

On another occasion during the time when Matt's sister, Beth, was home visiting from Washington, in the course of conversation with her brother, she raised the question, "Something happened in the hospital to change Dad's position. I wonder what it was—did a patient die, what went wrong, for him to be changed?" Yet very little was known about the incident, for neither parent shared the facts with their children.

Carrie and Matt both grew up in homes where skeletons lingered. Were they victims of circumstances that were beyond their control? If they were, they were soon to learn how to deal with them. Yet it would be an adventure that was not without pain.

Wren was to visit with Carrie's Maria IV—their close family friend who was *Aunt Marie* to Wren and was often referred to as her *fairy godmother.* The two had become acquainted after many church dinners together and both were delighted about the forthcoming visit. For Wren, she was a substitute for a grandmother figure; and for Marie, a welcome fulfillment of a gap in her life, for she had neither a child nor a grandchild of her own.

Leaving Wren with weekend clothes and her pet cockapoo at Marie's, Carrie and Matt drove on to the building to be occupied by the married couples meeting for the weekend in the Marriage Encounter. This building was part of a complex destined to be used for a retirement community, which was not yet occupied. The rooms were comfortable and meals were to be provided. *What a welcome change from their busy lives,* Carrie thought, as she unpacked their suitcases.

The call for supper was early and the first gathering was social. Another couple from their own church was among the group attending. Directing the group was a priest from a parish north of the city whose ministry was to come to the aid of married couples. Unlike many clergy that Carrie had encountered, this man wore neither collar nor priestly garments, but was dressed in casual shirt and jeans. He went around from table to table, introducing himself

Carrie and Matt at the Governor's Mansion on Mackinac Island,
where they were guests of Governor and Mrs. Milliken. Matt
represented the public schoolteachers for the Republican party.

as Father Donovan, noting their nametags, and extending warm welcomes to each couple, twenty-nine in all. He said very little after their supper except to advise each couple to focus completely on each other this weekend, with the promise that their real work would begin tomorrow, on Saturday.

When they gathered after an early breakfast Saturday morning, their meeting did begin with a prayer. Then the priest introduced the participants to the program. Primarily, he repeated they must each focus on their marriage partner. Before announcing their first assignment, he offered some background information. Carrie noted that Matt was taking careful notes of the priest's presentation.

Each husband and wife was given their own notebook to be used for separate writing assignments. There would be a series of questions for reflection. While writing, it would be best to separate for deep personal concentration. Silence was required. No need for small talk. Concentration was to be given to each other. They were to write honestly. Later, joined in their room, they would read each other's notes.

"Hand each other your writing *tenderly*." The priest advised them to read their spouse's notes several times and try to think what was behind the words. Remove time pieces. Read with your head, then again, with your heart. Dialogue with care.

The first assignment: *Why did I come here this weekend? What do I hope to gain?*

Both Matt and Carrie expressed desires for improving their marriage. Matt's words revealed more than his desire for *a more perfect marriage.* He confided, "I wanted to take time to be alone with you, my wife, away from the cares of our daily routine. I really like being alone with you, but so often there are other concerns/pressures that interfere with a precious moment spent together, worries that tear down a positive relationship between us. I often feel like lashing out, but try to stop and think how you must be thinking and why; so silence is better until I have an opportunity to think and allow time to give me objectivity that I may not have at the moment."

Carrie was happy to read of Matt's desires to spend time together, alone. This was a hint of the former Matt, the one who always arranged for time alone up to the time before Timmy, their third child, was born. Her letter recalled times of their history together. Carrie expressed agreement in wanting to come to their Marriage Encounter and much more.

"For a long time, I have felt like my attempts to share feelings with you or to tell you certain things were a failure. I wondered what was wrong. Because in reflecting on the history we have created together, we had a very real and strong attraction for each other. I remember the closeness we shared during our engagement (word study 'my mouth is *sanguinary*'); the hopes and dreams we shared (You pointed to a blond curly-headed youngster in church and told me *Our kids are going to have blond curly hair like that);* and the warmth and tenderness during our first year of marriage; the cute way you hovered over me when I was pregnant for Anna. Do you remember the morning rituals with *Mother's Friend?* The pride and happiness when our children were born, the affection and care you lavished upon them. But somehow, the last few years, you and I seemed to be in conflict with each other. And so many times the things I have wanted to say right, with intent to communicate *clearly*, either came out wrong or were misunderstood. The BHS has helped, counseling was a big step back to what we were, yet not really back far enough."

While Carrie delved into their marriage history, Matt focused on expressing *What do I hope to gain?* Carrie found agreement in their dialogue. Matt had enumerated his hopes—*to gain a better marriage, a closer relationship; a more trusting relationship; to respect each other's needs and wants.* Matt opened up to his own weaknesses.

"Each time I leave home, I try to think of a positive way I could have handled a situation which caused stress between us. I hope that through better understanding I can listen to you, but also have you listen to my needs. I don't feel we do that nearly enough. I hope to be able to do things without being questioned at *length*." *The English teacher in Carrie penciled in the last word which was misspelled and wrote, "ok Tim sr."*

Upon reading their first letters, both felt the barriers between them for so long had been removed. But this removal proved to be only temporary. Much more effort would be needed before they could resume the closeness they had shared earlier in their marriage. Now it was time to meet with the priest. There were to be special presentations by couples who had previously attended Marriage Encounters. The openness of the presenters astounded Carrie more than Matt. One couple discussed finances, how handling them had been difficult and conflict resulted. They resolved it by each writing out a plan to meet needs and expectations. The other couple shared a personal physical problem narrated mostly by the wife. She shed tears as she explained her lament—that her breasts were too small, and she could not offer more to her husband. His reaction was that he loved her *whole* person, her personality, her soul, not just her physical shape. He was not looking for a *Marilyn Monroe*.

Their next writing assignment was to be announced. The priest prefaced it with discussing the four phases to be covered—*The I phase; the We phase; We and God; We, God, and the World.* "Write only your own feelings," the priest advised. "Feelings are not a morality. Feelings are not right or wrong. It is *how* we use a feeling that determines morality. Identify your feeling; substitute the words *I am* for *I feel*."

The writing assignment was to cover answers to four questions: (1) What do I like best about you? How does this make me feel? (2) What do I like best about myself? How does this make me feel? (3) What do I like best about us? How does this make me feel? (4) Openness to God's plan for our lives.

Matt began with his self-description: "I am a forty-eight-year-old grandfather. Often, I look for good things in myself and others. BHS has made me more aware of forgiveness, and so I try to be more forgiving and understanding to myself and others. I used to speak out quickly, but now I wait until I have something substantive to say or do (uniqueness). I remind myself God does not make junk! I belong to God. He made me. He loves me. I like myself. I like my knowledge, strength, insight, lovingness, sincerity, patience, helpfulness, carefulness. This makes me feel wanted, needed, appreciated and cared about, important. I dislike myself when I am false, don't speak out for Jesus or witness positively; when I do not act supportive to family members; don't think things out. These make me feel like a jerk, unwanted, unneeded, a failure, hopeless, inadequate. My masks—Mr. Cool, hardnose, efficient, knowledgeable, sharp, witty, power-backer, politician, strong. Almost always, these masks make me feel less of a person than I really want to be. Each evening, I confess my sins/shortcomings to God, and I know through Jesus Christ, He forgives them all. I feel worthwhile because Jesus is my Savior and Lord.

I feel uneasy with strangers, so I don't go out of my way to talk to them. Carrie can start a conversation with almost anyone, but that often makes me embarrassed/inadequate. I need *unconditional love—Carrie's and God's love, family and friends*."

These insights Matt revealed about himself brought out the *real Matt,* the one that Carrie fell in love with, many years ago, after their first meeting in Chicago. His letter to her also recalled his preface to his early love letters,

Dearest Lover-buttons,

I feel you are the most wonderful person in the whole earthly world. I like you because you make me feel worthwhile. I love you because you are so warm and loving towards family and friends. I feel that our marriage is the best marriage in the whole world. I feel that no matter what obstacles are between us, I will always love you, care for you, and take care of you. I feel that there is nothing we can't do/say to each other that we can't handle. I am trying to overlook/understand / forget/forgive all the symptoms of disillusionment, because I checked most of them. Praise God!

> With all my love forever,
>
> Matthew martyr

Carrie was happy for Matt's candid writing, for she herself felt release from all masks and pretenses when writing to Matt. What did she like best about Matt? "Your strength, though sometimes it seems almost brutal—it's there, and I feel secure when you exercise it confidently and gently."

When writing about her likes of herself, she felt a release she had never before been able to put into words. "I like my ability to *imagine*—it takes boundaries and barriers away. I feel like Jonathan Livingston Seagull and I want to soar the heavens—cross timelines—I feel like Time and Eternity are all one continuous ONE. If Man, if we are really *immortal*, then we are already living in Eternity now. Life is one continuous series of phases—birth; life; death; new life and the mystery of the Beyond; and a closer relationship with God. I feel joy when I can just let go and believe and love and be unbound by manmade barriers, and I want to set about to fulfill my dreams of expression and to share this great feeling of joy. And I feel at peace with myself when I can be my true self. As for US, we're something really special. If we can strip away the garbage that piles up, resulting from daily care and concerns and artificial facades, and just really be ourselves, like when we were first going together, if we could really put each other first … (I'm at a stopping point, because I can't seem to think beyond this for the moment, anyway.)"

For a few moments, Carrie stopped writing. Then she retreated to her memories, reminiscing … that first night, when she and Matt met, "You need a cup of coffee," and his words to her, "You have the most beautiful eyes." When they were engaged, he wanted to replace her frayed watch band, "Here's money for a new watchband," and "You really do want that silverware, don't you?" The surprises, such as the lovely necklace and earring set from the same jewelers where they got their rings. "Thanks for that cup of water."

She continued her writing: "If we could put away, discard all pretenses, and just be *us* to each other, not what someone else might have wished us to be, nothing else would matter."

"Something else," Carrie added, "I really wasn't mad this afternoon. I was only pretending, beating you to the draw, because I was afraid you'd holler at me for dawdling and I really wasn't—and you're right about the *blocks* set up by the ENEMY. But we didn't get waylaid, did we? And I was relieved that you rested, because you were out so late last night."

Then Carrie revealed her innermost feelings about herself. "I feel scared inside. Nothing I accomplish ever seems good enough. Unwanted. Deserted, perhaps by death? Deprived; I envied girls with their own mothers, especially when I had my own children. The need to fight, to feel forced to use unusual means to carry out proper ends. I could not identify with my stepmother; with her I felt rejected, unloved. My high school teacher, Durinda Hansen, was my role model, and in some ways, Aunt Mary. I give to compensate for what I would like to have been given to me. Right now, I find myself super-compensating for our daughter, Anna, for my deceased mother, as well as for myself."

Two hours had passed. It was time for the married couples to again meet with the priest. This time, while coffee was sipped with morning refreshments, the priest played an audio portion from *Don Quixote,* in which *Aldondza* expresses feelings of no self-worth. Later, he urged the writers to consider compliments they might receive from others who react to their personal interaction, their capabilities, appearance, and personal qualities. List your virtues and your weak points.

For Carrie this was not too hard. She believed her virtues included thoughtfulness of others' needs. Imagination led her to the use of creativeness, putting together unrelated things. Her weak points? She admitted to dishonesty or masking of irritations until they "pile up," and confessed, "Then I blow up!" Added was a possible solution, "It might be better to handle each problem right away, as it arises, and settle it promptly, than to let it add up and fester." Carrie's self-knowledge was revealed in her self-description.

"I am a person who dislikes limitations. I want to soar high and explore, often going beyond and above structural boundaries, and bending over backwards to be flexible, and unite or seek to unite two totally different segments (like Milton and Mills or Plato and Wordsworth in synthesizing). I have great independence of mind. No one has anything on me. If I'm wrong, I have a right to make mistakes. However, I do want to analyze why the error was made, mostly for the sake of learning. As was stated at our meeting, God does not make junk! And He opens a window when a door is closed. I feel special because He has cared for me, even when others that I should have been able to turn to have deserted me."

Now they were to return to their room and spend the entire time in silence and writing on three assigned topics: What do I like about myself? How does that make me feel? What do I dislike about myself? How does that make me feel? What are the masks I wear? Briefly describe them. Then when both have finished writing, hand your letter to your spouse. After you have both finished reading, take time to dialogue.

Carrie scanned her most innermost thoughts. "What a question! I'm not sure I even like myself. It seemed when I was a child few people ever showed they liked me, so why should I be likeable? Grownups preached at me, grudgingly directed me and gave me the necessities of life, but one very important thing was lacking— making me feel like someone worth anything. The only one that ever did this was Grandma Fisher, and her daughters, who followed her example. She did this naturally, out of love, the love of God, and her faith just radiated around her. Unfortunately, I only remained with her for a few months out of each year, from the time of my mother's death until my father's remarriage. After that it was only for certain weekends. My stepmother didn't seem to want me. I was just a dredge on her plans to have a family of her own. Looking back, I see she was incapable of directing me in a positive way. And I could not seem to talk over my feelings with my father. He worked nights, so he was gone from home when I returned from school. I was completely subjected to our stepmother's moods, whims, nagging, and beatings. The pressures were too much to cope with, and at the age of thirteen, I *ran away* and went to live with my Aunt Mary. Two positive mentors during my teen years were my pastor and my high school teacher, who was also my homeroom teacher. Today, I understand the weaknesses of those who abused me from an intellectual standpoint. But I still bear the emotional scars. I have said I forgive them and I want to; but periodically, things occur, which open up a whole new bag and recall the hurts of the past. I want to learn to forgive as Jesus did when He was dying on the cross: *Forgive them for they know not what they are doing.*"

"Do I wear a mask? Probably; at times it is that of an intellectual. And yet, I do take the idea of timelessness and God so seriously that I feel a real oneness with people like Thomas Aquinas, Augustine, Sts. Cyril and Methodius, Comenius, Solzhenitsyn, Sakharov, and lots of others (also Barbara Walters). I love to think, to introspect, and to learn new things; so maybe it's not really a mask, but what I want to become. And I love people. Do I really wear a mask? I'm not sure that I wear one. Is this wrong? I'm simply most happy when I can be myself; thoughtful, yet immensely critical of blatant general judgments or divisive ones to mankind. For I seem to seek always to create a synthesis, to build bridges. This seems to come naturally. I see no drama as interesting to me as that of my own life. And as my relationship with God grows with my own maturity, I find I can look back and reflect upon His constant care for me, in every crisis and predicament. I want to make every moment, hour, and day count for something positive resulting. I don't want to wait with my actions till I'm closer to the *hereafter*. I want to act (perform?), be in practice for the Eternity with God, of which I feel I am a part. I feel a real fellowship, a companionship with God as a loving Father who cares for me and arranges things for me in such a way that when I reflect on my imperfect relationship with others, the memories of the hurts and scorn fade away, in comparison to God's love. I feel the warmth of the Holy Spirit in day-to-day activities, which take on special meanings as I go about them. But if I talked about this to just anyone, they might laugh or call me a *kook*. Yet Solzhenitsyn touches on spiritual matters in *One day in the Life of Ivan Denisovitch*, when he compares Alyosha, the believer, to Ivan, the skeptic. Summarizing, I have to learn to cope with (1) carrying out my ideals and becoming the person I wish to be, to fulfill God's laws and to carry out God's will; (2) deal with hurts from the past which arise and haunt me from time to time. I should pray for people that I want to stay away from because they have hurt me, and thank the Lord for those who have made me feel good."

Matt's letter, as most, began with a term of endearment, no matter what type of content:

Dearest,

I feel you do not understand time/time relationships. I feel like if you did, you would start sooner to get ready/ leave sooner/arrive earlier. I feel so much less tension since I leave by myself with Wren in the morning. I feel like the day is brighter when I can go home when I'm ready at night. I am frustrated when you start getting your makeup on/going to the bathroom/checking the doors/asking unnecessary questions/checking Wren's hairstyle and clothes. I am angry with you for waiting until the last minute, when I feel you could have done it well in advance of the leaving time in an unhurried way, avoiding much of the resentment, confusion, helplessness, self-concept-destroying behavior patterns. I feel like you are putting all or most of the responsibility for the success of our marriage on my shoulders. I am resentful when you seem to expect me to make your coffee, know what coat you are going to wear and get it ready for you, wait patiently while you come on the scene to replay all the things/preparations over again, or wait patiently out in the car.

Your loving husband, lover, father, breadwinner,
Grandfather M.

Carrie had to admit Matt had a point, and wrote, admitting, "I am a horrible procrastinator at times and I wonder why? Is it a symptom of a hidden problem? I will try to plan better."

When Matt read Carrie's response, he walked over to where she stood and put his arms around her. It was a peak experience of special closeness. Carrie wondered, *Is this a step back to where we were, or a better step forward for what we can both become, together?* What a contrast to Matt's letter after their former dialogue!

Dear Carrie,

In our last dialogue, I didn't feel in control. I wanted to be open, but I felt that the dialogue wasn't accomplishing that. I was hurt, angry, frustrated. I wanted to leave the M. E. and tell you off. I REALIZED THAT THE DEVIL WOULD HAVE LOVED THAT. {Then a transition in the very same letter.} I feel like we may be able to communicate after all. I feel that we can if we are completely open with each other about everything in our lives, even if it means hurting each other's feelings temporarily. If we are gentle and loving in our dialogue; if we are following God's plan, then we are going to meet success.

Love,

Dad

Carrie noted Matt's use of his parental name, which they sometimes substituted when speaking to each other, especially in front of the children. She recalled their notes from the priest's teaching earlier and wondered, was Matt experiencing feelings of vulnerability by being *too* open to me, his spouse? We become more aware of God's love through loving another person. The basic love relationship in the world is the love of a man and woman, a relationship ordained by God. God's plan is to find happiness in and through each other. A closer relationship with God and being open to God means one will be open with one's spouse. Couples were urged not to give up with dialogue, for we can only gain through more visible love for each other.

Marriage involves three stages. It begins with romance. After a time, there is the cycle of disillusionment, but ultimately, can become joy. In resolving disillusionment, there is fighting. But fighting is a form of communication. The priest offered eight guidelines; most important, "Hold hands and look into each other's eyes as you fight; listen to each other; stick to the subject; be fair, do not hit *below the belt;* do not repeat past history over forty-eight hours old; no silent treatment or name calling; *throw only marshmallows;* do not go to bed mad!"

The next assignment given to the couples was to write describing three specific instances when each felt close to their spouse, telling this closeness in loving detail. For Matt, this was not difficult. He was to recall the time they were transporting a car from Chicago. Those miles always included the area with many crowded roads from south Chicago, through Gary, and the remainder of northern Indiana. Carrie noted his endearing address at the beginning of his letter.

Dearest Carrie,

The first instance I am describing was when we were coming back from Chicago, driving the white Cadillac. I was beset with fears of having done something wrong/ stupid. I had had the car given some repairs in Chicago and was already having doubts as to the wisdom of my purchase. We were driving on the I-94 and we stopped because the lights were growing dimmer while it got darker and darker. I couldn't see the road very well either. Anyway, we stopped and I was almost defeated. You said, 'We can make it.' Then I felt like there wasn't anything I couldn't do, and we did make it safely.

The second instance deals with recently, when we were driving to school in the morning and we were talking, communicating harmoniously, when I felt like everything was sunshine and roses, just a beautiful feeling.

The third instance was a recent Sunday morning. We were all ready early, not the usual last-minute interruptions or anything, and we had plenty of time to talk with each other, do different personal things; well, I just felt so good, like I was on a mountain top.

Love,

Matt

P. S. I'm sure there are many other similar instances, but at the moment I feel like there aren't nearly enough in our lives, like most of the time there is oppression and no communication."

Carrie recalled instances from their history together and wrote from her heart.

Dear, dear Matt:

Probably there are more times that I felt super-close to you than I can remember. However, right off, these are the ones I think of now. I still remember you kissing me—it was a *long* kiss—on our wedding day, right after Pastor Samuelson had declared us husband and wife. You told me how you had arranged to borrow a car so we could go on a wedding trip to Saugatuck (your kiss was actually more than a prolonged kiss, as it appeared to our friends and family around us; it was the way for you to take the opportunity to tell me that you had provided for our honeymoon in such a sweet, concerned, and affectionate way—that I will always remember it).

Another time was when you told me how you prayed for me and Anna when I had gone into labor, before her birth.

And when it was over, how you thanked God that Anna and I were both fine and how thrilled you were to have this little daughter. Your warmth and love for her as well as me, and your open expression of faith in God made me feel confident and warm and secure with you.

We have shared many joys together and also some sorrows. Our children were both a responsibility and a warm tie for us. Often the feelings you have manifested towards them made me feel close to you. Or the concern, such as when I had a threatened miscarriage when I was carrying Timmy. I'll never forget the grave look on your face. You wanted this child—a son—and you wanted all to be well with me. How loved I felt! And I was not afraid. Or the day we brought Wren home from the hospital. You talked about understanding God's love more because you loved Wren—your love had broadened to include her—yet you did not lessen your love for our other children. Then, when she woke us up that first night home, you were patient and affectionate, even though you were tired after a hard day at the playground, and still you willingly helped me with her. I wonder if the security I felt in your love and affection didn't appear as if I was taking it for granted?

Then there was Thelma's wedding and the free manner in which you willingly went to El Paso—without counting the cost—to give her away, was still another occasion when I felt close to you. Love is contagious. The closeness you have for those around you is one of the most loveable qualities I cherish.

My warmest devotion,

Carrie

Carrie recalled how easy it was, after receiving Thelma's letter describing her bridal shower and thanking Carrie and Matt for their gift, to make the flight reservation for Matt by phone. He would be the only family member present for this important day in his younger sister's life. When he arrived home from school, Carrie approached him, handing him the letter, and informed him, "I have a reservation for you. Your bag is packed. We can pay for the round trip with the money no longer withheld by Social Security from our paychecks this fall. Do you want to go and be there for Thelma?"

"Of course, but I want you to go with me."

"We can only afford one getaway this time. Maybe we can visit together next spring."

Carrie had already called ahead and spoken with Thelma's roommate, who assured her they would meet Matt at the airport and also provide accommodations at their apartment for him. So, off they went to the airport. Later, Matt told Carrie, "This was the work of the Holy Spirit, guiding you so I could be with Thelma and Larry at their wedding."

They read each other's letters, but there was almost no dialogue. Instead, Matt beckoned to his wife, "Come here!" She was in his arms, and for the first in a long time, longer than either one could remember, they made love as the lovers they had been from the very beginning. *The two became one.*

When the group met, Father Donovan again offered more inspiring talk. It was late Saturday afternoon. There were bottles of soft drinks and water, as well as light snacks and chips offered to mend appetites. The next letter assigned would be their last before dinner. This time the topic for careful consideration would be *feelings and love.*

The priest explained: "Love is a *Decision,* not a *Feeling.* Love is a decision to love each other. One can say he loves someone, even if he doesn't *feel* it at the moment. To love is to give; to share; to look for the good in the other. Do not quarrel with your spouse's feeling or your own; this makes a judgment. Rather, share the feeling; reach for your spouse's feeling, to understand. Feelings are not either good or bad; they just *are.* Go beyond quarreling or questioning spouse's feeling in order to respond. Write an answer like a love letter, tender and personal, letting your love come through. Check for symptoms present in your marriage. Pick one which hits you the strongest.

You don't have to include all. Focus on feelings which come from symptoms. Focus on the person to whom you are writing."

The priest's words stimulated Carrie's thinking and memories were recalled, memories that made her somewhat conscience stricken. She found herself addressing her letter three-fold:

Dear Dutch,

Matthew,

Sir;

There are times when I have become so wrapped up in my career that I have not been available emotionally to consider and share your daily frustrations. Or when I listened to you relate a problem such as you had with the administration at your present school during your first year there; it was not with respect to your personal viewpoint and reasonable cognizance of the other person's own weakness and contribution to the situation. It was only that of a person 'hearing out' the problem of *a kid who is in trouble again.* Part of this stems from an old-fashioned ignorant view that 'Matt can't get along,' which I inherited from former parental influences on our marriage. Please forgive me. It is past, and I find myself wanting to share more of your life, your hopes and dreams, and the things you want to do.

I love the way you have shown how you care for me and our children. Your strength. Please be more patient with me when I don't seem as strong or when I need to cry. Yesterday when I was packing and getting ready, I realized how many things you do for us, which I take for granted.

I don't care anymore about the past. We each did our best (or worst?) in a given framework I just want us to love each other *now*, like this is the first day together for the rest of our lives. We are each other's gift to each other from God. Did I say that right?

How do you like that? I'm not really satisfied with this, so I'm starting all over again …

Dear Matt,

Once upon a time I called you *Dutch* or *Dutchie*. However, in view of the man you have become, and in view of my more mature regard for you, I would like to call you Matt. Matt comes from Matthew and it is a very nice name. I once heard your mother explain that she named you after the disciple Matthew, the writer of the first book of the New Testament, and William, after William of Orange. Our son, Tim, is very proud of his middle name and that it is the same as his father's. I decided a long time ago to love you. If I have let you down or reneged, please forgive me and forget it. OK?

Carrie

Matt noted from the priest's talk that the love relationship is a growing experience, an awareness of each other. He made a small diagram, illustrating the gift of daily dialogue as one of giving and receiving. On this same page, he developed a chart listing the procedure and contents of what spouses write, exchange, then dialogue with each other. The priest recommended a 90-day trial period of continuing this procedure following the weekend of the Marriage Encounter.

In his letter to Carrie, Matt chose to answer, "What feelings did I have today that I wanted to share with you, that I either could not or did not share?"

Dearest Carrie,

I don't really want to write this letter. I feel like at the close of a school day, before I've had a chance to unwind. I don't feel very objective right now. Since I'm sitting here, I might as well write a couple of feelings, but not necessarily meeting the above criteria. I felt perfectly comfortable when you wanted to share in this last session; while earlier today, a couple of times, I didn't feel as free about your comments 'i.e.,' at breakfast this morning and one other time today. Maybe that's a good sign. Well, anyway, I don't have any big pressing concerns at the moment. I did feel especially receptive to Father's comments about getting ideas/thoughts/ material/ from Christ's love letter to us. I feel like I've been doing that for some time now, so if that's the kind of results that will be coming from our dialogue, I think that will be super.

Love,

Dad

Again, ending with his parental name reminded Carrie of Matt's role as *father*, as well as that of *husband*. Sometimes, they did address each other as *Mom* and *Dad*, especially around the children. Anna and Durinda were married now and living in their own homes. Tim and Wren were still at home with them. At twenty-one, Tim was uncertain what his goal for the future would be. Wren would be a teen next year. She was still attending the private academy, with excellent study habits and grades. She did not choose to become a teacher like her parents. Instead, she planned to enter the business world and become wealthy. It was Anna who had become a teacher, with a major in Art and elementary education. She was assigned to several schools. Her husband, a Vietnam vet, was having his struggles. Enrolled in the local junior college, he was uncertain of what his future would be. Carrie found herself worrying about their future. She also felt concern about Durinda, whose life had taken a weird evolution from that which Carrie had desired for her. Basically, she felt unloved. She felt her parents loved Tim more than they loved her. Carrie shared some of this concern with other mothers in the association designed to help the parents with children who experienced learning disabilities. The group named the Michigan Association for Children with Learning Disabilities— MACLD—had goals to both serve as support group and provider of information. At that time, the education structure was not set up to help children with dyslexia. Children like Timmy were often excluded from school. Timmy had been in five school situations by the time he was nine years old.

She recalled one mother of five children who shared her concern for a son who had run away because he had, like Durinda, felt unloved. He believed his younger brother, who was dyslexic, was loved more than he. Carrie saw his absence from home take its toll on the mother. Her appearance was gaunt. She admitted to many sleepless nights and loss of appetite. The parents had no knowledge of where he was or how to find him. Finally, after a year's time, he called home, asking for funds for air fare home. The parents arranged for his air fare directly with the airline that was to bring him home, to ensure his arrival and rejoining with his family.

Carrie recalled the similar situation with Durinda and her response to the attention given to Timmy, attention that she would not have wanted in the same way, for she did not experience the learning difficulties her brother had. Some of her activities were bizarre. Joining the hippies. Carrie and Matt traveled to their compound and brought her home bodily, over their daughter's protests that she was not happy at home anymore. Three days later, she ran away. When she called again, it was to announce she was ill. Timmy began to cry. His words revealed what may have been the problem—"Drugs!" That was not all. There had been a son born out of wedlock. At this time, Durinda opted for adoption. Every child should have both a father as well as a mother, she decided. Her marriage to a Vietnam vet proved to be a disaster. Her divorce was barely completed when she accepted Chad's marriage proposal.

Carrie recalled trying to explain her older sister's situation to six-year-old Wren. The younger sister had become somewhat fond of her brother-in-law. The separation saddened her, especially in the light of the religious teachings she was receiving at the private Catholic Academy she attended. She had already been informed about the infidelity and abuse toward Durinda. Well informed, she called his action *adultery.*

Wren responded with a maturity somewhat precocious for a child her age. "But I know something more important than adultery," she replied. "It's forgiveness."

"But he doesn't want to ask for forgiveness," Carrie tried to explain.

Wren again whispered to Carrie while they were seated at the church, just before the ceremony to unite Durinda and Chad was about to begin. "Why didn't he want to ask for forgiveness?" Shrugging her shoulders in response, Carrie quietly pointed to the altar where the pastor was ready to begin the marriage ceremony. Accompanying Chad and his intended bride were Anna and her husband, serving as witnesses. Chad's parents and sister joined Durinda's family. They had met Durinda and appeared happy that their son was getting married. Because of the hastiness, the ceremony did not have the fanfare of Durinda's first marriage. She wore the gown Chad requested, the Gwahili Indian gown Anna had brought her from Venezuela, where Anna had completed her practice teaching in a program sponsored by her university.

The marriage—living together—got underway smoothly at first. Yet Durinda tried to explain reasons for the mistakes she had made in her teen years. After that, Chad took a protective stance that resulted in hostility toward Timmy. He blamed Tim for Durinda's mistakes. Family get-togethers were not attended and Timmy was not welcomed to visit.

Carrie's concern for Timmy and these related family difficulties led her to accept Father Donovan's offer for a private one-to-one meeting. She found herself relating the family matters openly. The priest listened intently. Then he asked Carrie, "Are you letting these behaviors affect your relationship to Matt?" "How is Matt responding to this situation?" Food for thought, Carrie realized.

"Your first obligation is to each other," and "You undoubtedly are both doing your best to help your son. As for your daughter and her husband, allow them to make their choices and do not comment. Show your concern for each other. These family things have a way of working things out, so don't let their problems or challenges create a barrier between you."

On Sunday morning, mass took place. The priest, now garbed in official collar and robe, spoke of the covenant of marriage as holy before God. Strengthening the relationships of couples would strengthen our society, our communities, our nation, and our world. He prayed particularly for Christ's message of love to be poured into the hearts of every couple present. All members of the Marriage Encounter were invited to participate in Holy Communion, non-Catholic included. He stated, "The body and blood of Christ was shed for you. You are all welcome." Although both were raised as Protestant believers, Carrie and Matt accepted. Carrie's thoughts recalled Martin Luther's catechism and wondered at this respect for Christ's *Invisible Church*, no barriers.

After a brunch was served, it was announced that the couples would continue with their letters and dialogues until dismissal time, late in the afternoon. Topics now would be centered on family relationships. First would be a brief analysis and sharing of the relationships of one's parents. *How do you feel about your mother? Your father?* Later, relationships with siblings. *How do you relate to your sister(s)? Your brother(s)? How do you relate to the siblings of your spouse?* Revelations abounded. To Carrie, Matt's letters raised questions in her mind—Is Matt equating our relationship to that he had observed of his parents? Is some of the resentment expressed toward me a latent feeling he has had toward his mother?

There were incidents that occurred throughout their married life, when problems arose, resulting from actions taken by the parents toward Matt and Carrie. Part of this was caused by Matt's resentment toward them, particularly toward his mother. Yet, from the first that Carrie met her, she seemed motherly and kind. It was later that certain demands were imposed. Now, in greater maturity, Matt was able to clarify his feelings more acutely.

How do I feel about my mother? As Carrie read Matt's response, she noted he began with words of gratitude for this day, itself. He also addressed her lovingly.

Dear, dear Carrie,

What a super nice day we had, P. T. L. I feel like a child of the King. P. T. L. for all our blessings. What a blessing it was to have sunshine and warmth today. What a blessing it was to be able to do so many things today, both of us. I feel very little warmth toward my mother. When I was growing, she was always cleaning/working/washing/canning/darning. I don't remember one time that she showed emotion, like my dad sometimes did. I don't feel strongly toward her, other than I know it's my responsibility to be available if she needs me. I suppose she tried to be close, but didn't really know how. I remember when she attended R. B. I. and got a 'B' grade in English. She was so proud. I feel that she had/has a terrible inferiority complex. I don't feel that I reject her or neglect her either. I respect her as my mother, but I don't feel I have much in common with her in a lot of other ways.

Love,

Matt

Carrie was able to coordinate certain memories and bits of information from Matt's mother that revealed the shaping of her personality. His maternal grandfather had held certain antiquated ideas about his children. Of his six living daughters, Matt's mother ranked third. An émigré from the northern part of Holland, called Friesland, he had been deprived of an education as a youngster and reportedly did not learn to read until he was twenty-one. He farmed the land in the northern part of Michigan and niggardly saved his earnings. His children were all taught to work hard, but their chores varied. The oldest sister was assigned to work inside their home, assisting their mother in cooking, baking, canning, and laundering clothes. It was Matt's mother who was assigned the outside chores—milking, gardening, and at least one time, was involved in the harvesting. She once told Carrie when one of the horses used in the field became ill and was unable to work, her father harnessed her and commanded her to work beside the other horse. Is it any wonder the young girl felt inferior, to be equated with a working farm animal? Now all members of her household were geared for hard work. She often emulated her father's didactic manner. As they grew into adulthood, all but the youngest left home for faraway places. Beth, who had become a nurse, went to California. Matt joined the Marines. Jean married and moved with her husband to the northern part of Michigan. When Thelma graduated from high school, she immediately signed up for mission work in New Mexico. Only the youngest remained at home, and she eventually served as her mother's caretaker and confidante.

How do I feel about my father? Carrie found an interesting repetition of a pattern. Again, Matt began his letter with current experience, prior to reaching a response to the main subject.

Dear, dear Carrie:

P. T. L., yes, I did feel like taking over and picking up Tim, even though it was a humbling experience; I mean by that I wanted to see Tim, but I wanted him to come to me on my terms, not be flexible. I feel that my father wanted me to communicate with him and I didn't know how. I went to everybody else—I never tried to talk to him after my teen years—just busted my butt getting his approval, when I could have talked with him—instead of talking, trying to impress him with new cars/jobs/titles, etc. I guess, too, I was trying to find the success formula that I grew up to pursue: the idea that everybody can become rich/prosperous/successful in the USA if they work hard (25 hours) daily/think big/etc., etc. I feel that my father was a lost soul in mainstream USA, but really had it all together in the spiritual realm. He had found a peace/joy that was really his richness; he was a humble man, not a braggart/big shot/a *real child of God.* What a rich spiritual legacy he left me. P. T. L.

Love,

Matt

Carrie had to agree with Matt about his father's spiritual depth, which led Matt into his own deep belief. His dad was always thoughtful of Carrie. He planted lilies of the valley in her yard. When their bungalow needed painting, he got the color pink she wanted and painted it. He was well aware of his wife's temperament and dominating spirit. One time when he was visiting, she phoned, and when Carrie answered, she demanded to know "why Papa was still there," for he had chores to finish at home.

"Oh, but I just made him a hamburg!" Carrie declared, after setting it before her father-in-law. Gently taking the phone from Carrie, he assured his wife he would be leaving quite soon. After hanging up, he rapidly ate the sandwich, but in between bites, he told Carrie that one must understand *Mama,* and that he was used to her, but he did not expect her and Matt to live the same. Matt's father and Carrie had some things in common. Although she was born in the U.S., in Chicago, no less, Carrie had been raised by European-born family members and had learned to speak the Slovak language quite fluently. Her father-in-law's Dutch accent did not seem strange to her. One time when he was driving her to the lake where their cottage was located, in the process of their conversation, he suggested they both sing the hymn, "A Mighty Fortress is our God," each in their native language. "I will sing it in Dutch and you may sing it in Slovak." Carrie loved her father-in-law as much as she had loved her own father.

How do I feel toward my brothers/sisters? Carrie felt sorry for Matt. This had been somewhat of a deprivation in his young life. Again, he began this letter in an endearing way.

Dear, dear Carrie,

Well, my sisters are really not part of any significant part of my life, 'i.e.,' when I was very young, Beth was working at home and I was usually outside. When I came back from the service, I wasn't home much with Thelma or Polly. I really didn't start to develop any relationship with any of them until much later. Of course, we all have our own immediate families now, so we can't really develop any separate relationships apart from them. I guess I feel that, somehow, I'll never have/or have missed out on any childhood relationships. I feel close to my brother-in-laws, but again, in kind of an extended fashion.

Love,

Matt, the sweetie

How do I feel about your brothers/sisters? This letter was short, but it was again prefaced with Matt's loving address. Matt expressed his response honestly, but not unkindly. He had not had much opportunity to get to know the other sisters because visits had been sparse. The two younger brothers were very little boys when Carrie and Matt married, so there was scarce opportunity for them to interact and develop relationships.

Dear, dear Carrie,

   I really like Betka, she's the one we've had the most interaction with. I can't really feel much of anything towards your brothers and sisters, except for Betka.

Love,

Matt

A few years later, Matt did get to correspond with Milka, the younger sister, after both had computers. That is when a relationship actually developed between them. Both revealed a strong sense of humor. They enjoyed sharing jokes and funny stories, as well as newsy items.

Now it was Carrie's turn to write Matt about her feelings toward her family and his. Actually, what she was about to write was what she had told Matt already, long before, but after reading his letters, she found new meaning in her own life history. It was the realization of how her life had been shaped, just as she learned of his. In comparing their childhood situations, she saw that, although he did have his own mother, there was definitely a lack, just as there was in her young life, a void that now reached into their life together.

How do I feel about my mother? For some reason that Carrie could not explain, she did not begin her letter by addressing it to Matt. Her thoughts took over her writing: "My own mother, my real mother is dead. I cannot relate to my stepmother as a *mother*, perhaps because she never related to me as her *daughter*, as I have tried to relate to my own daughters. Going to Europe and meeting my own mother's family had a very healing effect on me. I realized that my mother was loved, that I was loved, and after observing the closeness of the family in Czechoslovakia, I felt that both my mother and I had had an identity and family ties that I could relate to.

This type of relationship was entirely alien and foreign to my stepmother, who always 'put down' my mother to me. Also, she always said and did things to me to make me feel like a *non-person*. In complete contrast, she waited on her own children hand and foot, built them up, became almost a servant to them. Sammy, of course, was favored most. I once forgave her for the beatings, psychological and emotional wounds, and all she did to me as a child. But she played her antics over and over again, and now I realize she was really, in many ways, a sick, depraved person, and if she was incapable of loving me, it is because there was something really lacking inside of her. She manipulated and used my father against me because I would not be manipulated. I realized at thirteen that I would have to fend for myself—and if I'm too independent at times with you (or seem that way), you'll have to understand *why*. I never had adults around me that I could turn to and trust, as a child or adolescent. By the time I came to live with Aunt Maria and Uncle Jan, a lot of the distrust was permanently instilled. Seven years of continuous abuse was too much to combat. It was not until I married you, and had Anna, that I began to really feel a sense of wholeness. But there was another conflict. Because of the void in my life, I tried very hard to identify with your mother. As you know, that was not only impossible, but also proved to create many conflicts between us.

But God did not fail to provide a model for me. He did put Mrs. Hansen in my life through four crucial years (ages 13–17), and then I was able to relate to someone who had many common interests with me. (That's why I've always loved books and learning.) Today, I don't feel *alone* so much, since we've had your B of HS and our ME in our lives. It is only when I feel you've deserted me that I regress and feel depressed. I need your strength and emotional support— especially when our children rebel against me. Love, Carrie."

Matt, somehow, knew how to work around one instance when an antic was played, while he and Carrie were visiting in Chicago. Somehow an argument had fermented between Carrie and the stepmother. They left with bad feelings on both sides. Most of the weekend was spent with Aunt Maria and Uncle Jan. However, as they were about to leave the city homeward, Matt headed for the home of Carrie's parents. When Carrie questioned him, he merely responded that he wanted to stop and say goodbye to her parents. Responding to Matt's knock on their door, both parents were surprised to see them.

As they beckoned them to enter, Matt greeted his father-in-law cheerfully, "We just wanted to stop a minute before we left for home."

"Sit down a minute. Would you want some coffee?" Maria usually was hospitable to Matt.

"We really shouldn't linger, it's at least three and a half hours of driving, but thanks, just the same."

After chatting a few minutes, the grandparents focused on the two granddaughters. Each was given a dollar in spending money. As they were leaving, Maria III approached Carrie and uttered what came closest to an apology she would ever give, "You know me ..." and she reached out her hand in a semi-embrace.

Later, Matt explained his decision for stopping there. "We had to do it, Car, or we wouldn't be able to go back again." Ever the peacemaker, Matt was.

How do I feel about my father?

Dear Matt,

My father is the only real parent I remember. He took care of me evenings and weekends from the time my mother died when I was just two, until he remarried, when I was five and a half years old. For some weeks and months, I was cared for in Congress Park at the home of my great-aunt and uncle, whom I called Grandma and Grandpa. There, just as with my father, I was exposed to the Slovak language, which has remained with me all of my life. Most of all I remember the stories my father told and the songs he sang to me, all in Slovak, just before we fell asleep. I used to snuggle and sleep next to him in the big double bed. Later, after I was six years old and attended church school on Saturday mornings, he gave me formal instruction in Slovak. I still remember the repetition of the vowel sounds he had me do as he instructed me.

There are other things I remember about my relationship with my dad—(1) when my tonsils came out; (2) going with him to the Slovak shoemaker's on Saturday mornings and singing songs for the friends gathered there; (3) watching the trains at the railroad crossing just five blocks from home; (4) the putty incident, for which he gave me his only spanking when I was about three; (5) tight shoes and blistered heels; (6) going to church and not being allowed to go to the bathroom, result: an accident; (7) his promising me a *new mother* to replace the mother I will see again *na sudny den*; (8) waking up early on Sunday mornings to find him already dressed, ready for church with his watch pocket chain hanging from his vest pocket, and reading from the Slovak *Tranosius* or his Bible. I'll have to tell you about these. They take too long to write about.

But as I reflect on my father's life, I realize his own history—as a child caught in Europe without parents during World War I; coming to America and going to work; losing my mother; the old-fashioned views of his parents, which formed and shaped his life. In a sense, it stunted his growth for American social integration; and their closed-society immigrant church added to his limited development. I feel he was secondary in decision making. He earned the money, but accepted matriarchal decision-making as to how it would be spent, both by his mother and later, by his wife. This undoubtedly helped to develop my concept of a man being the breadwinner, but having very little voice in the economic decisions of the household, or in the rearing of the children. During my childhood, the woman was in charge.

And when he remarried, the companionship I had with

him in the interim years between my mother's death and his remarriage was expired. He was meek. He accepted his lot without questioning it—even the dictates of his wife. He was never a person in whom I could confide or lean on for strength. This factor, plus the reality of not being able to relate to or identify with my stepmother, forced me to go on my own—to do things independently. It also forced me to grow up too fast, in one way; but it did not allow for any of the carefree, frivolous times all children should experience before they shoulder the responsibilities of adulthood. In addition, I am sure I felt a measure of resentment to persons in authority, because of the fact that I had parents whose own development had been arrested by certain causes beyond their control (?)

It was probably because I learned early in my life that I could neither rely upon, nor receive the emotional support I needed from my father (or my stepmother), that I sought elsewhere for direction. I got it here and there; and it added up to quite a rich storehouse of resources, I realize now, as I reflect. There were Pastor B., Durinda Hansen, and some pretty fine bosses I had at part-time jobs, while I was in high school and later. I made mistakes. But someone was always there to help. Since then, people like Len A., who helped encourage us through college, and many others. Proof that God does not desert us; He fills in the gaps, one way or another. Now I feel I don't want to be so independent, so self-sufficient anymore. I want to lean on you and have you take the helm—not to shirk my responsibility, but to share feelings and thoughts with you in such a way that they are not burdensome; that as I relate to you, I gain a more objective perspective on myself as a person. Like tonight when I told you about the Easter eggs. I also am going to let our children do more for me and do less for them, to give them a chance to see me as a person, not just as a *ruling force.* Will you help me?

Love,

Carrie

Matt responded with a hug. "This letter's a long one. But you know what, I'm taking over the budget. That should relieve you somewhat, because you have lesson plans and all the work at home to take care of. But now, it's time for us to go." It was snack and meeting time. Carrie would finish later.

How do I feel about my sisters and brothers?

When I think of my sisters and brothers, I have to think in several dimensions. At one time I worshipped Ria as a "special little sister," in much the same way as Durinda does Wren. In recent years, I feel she has become a rather bitter person. It must be difficult for her to see my sisters and I married, with families, and to realize she is still home, forty, without any prospect of being married and having a home of her own. I feel the forced purchase of the folks' latest home, and the lack of understanding about the black situation, was merely a cover-up for Ria's real feelings about the lacks in her own personal life. I feel uncomfortable about Samuel's relationship with us. As for Don, he has broken away. I was happy my friends, returning to their home in the East, were able to stop and visit him in June, and bring the gifts I sent along for their home. When we attended our nephew's wedding, he expressed warm feelings, and held out an invitation to visit whenever we were traveling out East. We may do just that sometime. I love my sisters, Milka and Betka, very much. We had the same mother, and there really is something special about our relationship. Both of them experienced the same family challenges I had. Each handled them differently. Milka tells me she has buried them. Betka wants very much to have the approval and acceptance of authority persons, but cannot have it; and is in constant conflict, trying to be her real self. Our stepmother's relationship with us has not been really motherly. I have spent the greater part of my adult life working myself away from this sad situation. And I have determined not to have this type of relationship with my own children. Those things which I felt were lacking in my own childhood I sincerely tried to provide. I admit it was easier with Anna than it was with Durinda. But I know I did all I could with Durinda. As for Wren, there are newer ways and means—different from either Anna or Durinda—which I am seeking to discover. But I need your support. One most important thing and way for us is daily communication, via dialogue.

Affectionately (and less angrily now)

Carrie

Carrie did do some real thinking about her stepmother. What had shaped her personality, her character? We are taught as Christians to forgive. Pastor B. knew this best of all. That was undoubtedly why he selected her confirmation verse from Ephesians 4:32. Now in greater maturity than her childhood and teen years could offer, Carrie could begin to empathize. Maria II (as Carrie called her to herself) had a difficult life. Early in her childhood, she lost both her parents. She and her younger sister were cared for by their grandmother, who did not spare the rod. In fact, Carrie recalled Maria II saying, "It was good for me." They had struggled through World War I. When they were still in their late teens, the two girls traveled from their European home to America. Naïve and inexperienced, in strange surroundings, they were relieved of their earthly possessions by thieves shortly after their arrival. Their sponsor was an aunt, who together with her husband, ran a small grocery store. The girls were hired as maids and nannies for upper middle-class families. The money they earned was banked by their guardian aunt. The 1929 crash consumed their savings. It was not until many years later that some of it was recovered. Carrie recalled that a check arrived from the bank to compensate for the loss one fall, just in time to buy new winter coats for her and her sisters. If one were to target blame, it should be the regime under which the Slavic people endured when it was Austria–Hungary. Too often, the cruelties were emulated towards the children.

How do I feel towards your brothers and sisters?

Dear Matt,

I guess I could feel warm toward your sister Beth, and I am especially fond of her husband, Lisle—and as you do, I feel very warm toward Thelma. I hope we can get to Germany and visit her and Larry. Polly is something else. I try, but it can be trying at times. But in the last year or so, it has seemed better and more possible to get along. Again, we either have geographical barriers or psychological ones—and very little background that would foster mature social relationships. Part of it stems from feeling guilt whenever we participate in recreational activities. Another is that both our families come from environments where inheritance—or rather the threat of withheld inheritance—was used as a manipulating device (I'm talking about your Grandpa and my Grandma). Religion was a didactic tool or agent rather than a loving activity. It is a hard thing to overcome and it affects succeeding generations.

Now I am beginning to wonder—is dialogue a *real help* to our relationship? I don't feel warm toward you this evening. When you finish your put-downs, *nagging, complaining*, or other derogatory adjectives, I don't feel close; and worse than that, I feel like I couldn't care less whether we will become close again. Why should I have to guard every word; why can't I just be myself, without constantly being on my guard for fear of reprisal for something not even meant with anything but good intent? That's ridiculous. One way that would really help is a greater effort on your part to sincerely be open; to communicate; be receptive to my communication; and set aside your ego. I wonder if that is really, actually possible. Or do you have too many ghosts haunting you from the past?

Your wife,

Carrie

Why did I write so frankly; was I too hard on Matt? Carrie wondered. For a short period on this Marriage Encounter, they experienced the *Mountain Top,* but soon they would be returning home, the family environment where conflicts can quickly arise. Carrie's thoughts were interrupted by the priest's announcement.

Their last assignment given was yet to be completed: *How do I feel about our sex life?* Prompting the couples in his fold, the priest spoke openly, admitting that sex is difficult to talk about. Sex is part of the ground rules for marriage. It is not merely for release. (A woman is a person with feelings, not just an instrument to be used.) It is a *total* sharing of *total* people in a *total* way, or a means of fulfillment, an important non-verbal communication, a *sharing of each other.* Lovemaking is a celebration of our closeness with each other. There is more than merely writing a letter. Be honest. Paint pictures in words. Get feelings out. Write with feelings of strongest impact. Reach out and share yourself. Then read your spouse's letter with deepest feeling. Armed with the Father's advice, Carrie and Matt proceeded to write:

Dear, dear Matt,

Probably more than anything else in our marriage relationship I have valued is our sexual relationship. It is a special closeness that we have had always, right from the beginning. This may come as a surprise to you, because there have been times when I have not felt in the mood for sex. And when I said *no* to you or rebuffed you, it was rarely without a sense of guilt. I realize now that possibly it was because I needed badly to communicate with you in other ways. More than that, I needed your assurance that you loved me for *me,* and wanted to share other parts of me, such as my thoughts and my feelings, and allow me to share *your* thoughts and feelings. Maybe we misunderstood each other.

During our life together, we have had many anxieties. It is so helpful to share a problem or a trouble with you. When I know that you know about it and/or have taken care of it, I am reassured of your love for me, and I feel confident with your strength and courage. Spontaneous, thoughtful reassurance of your affection means so much to me. Like the cup of coffee you make for me in the a.m., or the rose you bring me from your garden, placed in a bud vase at my bedside table.

XXXXX

Carrie

It was interesting to Carrie that, when listening to a marriage counselor on TV, he spoke of the difference between men and women. "Men want sex. Women want to talk." Carrie wondered, *Am I so untypical, then?* Matt's letter, however, came to her as a great surprise.

Dear, dear Carrie,

How do I feel about our sex life?

As the new freshness after a storm, that's how I think about our sex life.

After the calm, cool, refreshing breeze off from the lake has swept the hot muggy air away, that's what I think about our sex life.

When a flower like a rose blooms, that's what I think about our sex life.

As spring bursts forth after the cold of winter, that's what I think about our sex life.

As the autumn hues give forth their glorious colors, that's what I think about our sex life.

I feel that our sex life is lousy/beautiful; used as a weapon/used to express our deepest love for each other; something God gave us/something the devil can never take from us. Our children are our living remembrance of our sex life together.

Love,

Matt

Romantic, poetic! Sex is *a total giving of oneself to your spouse*, the priest had declared. But Matt had always been romantic, even when they were first courting. Looking back, Carrie recalled the letters he had written when he was courting. Of course, they were boyish, youngish, but sincere in declaring his love, and as young as he was, he declared his faith. Sometimes while still in the Naval Reserves, he did ask for a special package to be sent. Cigars, peanuts, oranges, whatever! Usually, Carrie complied.

Later, Carrie recalled, there was another set of letters she had saved. Matt wrote her daily while she was in San Francisco. She was busy studying and did not often join in the social activities that occupied the leisure time of her teacher colleagues. But she did miss her family—specially little Wren. She wondered, did this little two-year-old daughter miss her mom? Will she remember me? Of course! The child proved to be highly intelligent with a good memory. After all, Carrie told herself, I was just her age when my mother died, and I have never forgotten her. Once while eating in the college's cafeteria, she spotted a child in a high chair next to her mother. Tearfully, Carrie approached her, asking if she could hold her baby, who seemed to be the same age as Wren. Smiling, the mother nodded, almost knowingly, as Carrie consumed her baby fix.

Matt detailed each child's activity. Timmy was doing well in summer school. Durinda, now fifteen, took careful care of Wren, as well as pitched in with household chores to assist Anna, who had now gotten a summer job. At seventeen, she expressly affirmed her independence and asked to use her earnings to travel west for a week or two, and visit her young aunt in New Mexico. Both girls adored their infant sister and doted on her, but not more than did Wren's father, who had declared that this, his youngest child "had wrapped herself around my heart!"

Beyond the Marriage Encounter

Somehow, we have to pick up the pieces and put things back together, Carrie thought. The priest advised the couples to continue letter writing and dialogues as they had on the ME: "Continue for at least three months." Would they succeed and hold their marriage together, and hopefully experience the enrichment for which the priest had prayed? It was Carrie who expressed her thoughts the next day.

Dear, dear Matt,

I feel a real letdown this morning. For a weekend we had nothing to do but focus on each other—and now all of a sudden, I am thrust back into my routine—where I feel the pressures and find it difficult to cope. What a high! And what a low! But I'm thinking of you. I was pleasantly surprised and happy about Durinda's singing last night—this is one of the things I have always wanted for her. And now it has come to pass. Wasn't she beautiful? I want her to be happy.

We need to make a schedule—determine what is really a priority activity for us and stick to it as closely as possible.

The question we were going to discuss has begun to occupy my mind—why do I feel self-conscious when you are talking? Maybe we already hit on the reason—I have a greater tendency to be verbal, and maybe when you want to say something, it takes a few more seconds to get it out and say it the way you want. I find that often I attribute to others the same quick verbal keenness which I believe I possess, but don't have the patience to see the need for others to think a second or two; e.g., I need more patience and less need to be concerned about what others think— just like you can perceive things with care faster and more accurately than I can. Now I'm going to make my list for the day's activities. It seems that when I do that, the whole list of my responsibilities seems somewhat reduced, and I chip away in order of importance and get all the chores done. I love you—*the real you.*

Carrie

P. S. I set up those books for us to write more easily—for now. Okay?"

Home again. It was as if they had climbed down from the mountain top. Now they had to face the valley of everyday life again. But at least they were armed. For indeed, there were communications that had been promised them. Supportive letters arrived from the Community. The first community letter, written by a couple who had formerly attended their marriage encounter, revealed their *ups and downs.*

"We're not alone. Other couples have had struggles, too," Carrie noted, handing the volume to Matt. "Just look at this! They haven't forgotten us!"

It's hard to believe we're the same couple we were a year ago, before our Marriage Encounter. We have experienced many ups and downs in our dialogue, as well as in our relationship, as we go through each stage of romance, disillusionment, and joy. Our dialogues have helped us grow together in our love and knowledge of each other and Christ. Now we can see more clearly His love for us and for everyone. We enjoy being zone coordinators and your willingness to continue dialoguing and continuing the communications begun at the Marriage Encounter give us the love of Christ present in you. We love you all.

"Let's follow through now," and grabbing pen and paper, Matt handed a sheet to Carrie, with one of the many pens in the souvenir cup on his desk. He proposed writing about something weighing on his mind for a while—Carrie's job. Did her career, with its responsibilities, create a chasm between them?

Dear Lover,

New feelings today/tired feelings/looking forward to vacation, I feel that at one time I really depended on you for your job; that is, I felt you were obligated to work/help bring in some of the money. Now I don't feel that way anymore. I still realize that in our capitalistic society your ability to earn can provide things for us, i.e., trip to Europe, two cars, etc., for our children/grandchildren. I feel that each day God provides our every need, if we but ask and trust Him. He will even give us the faith and trust. In other words, no matter what we do, we need God's strength for our lives, to get us through. I used to feel caught because you were working and we depended on every penny; but now I can see that (by) your working, we were provided for by God. It's kind of like Drs. M. and P. Her family didn't want her to throw away her efforts. I feel that you have always contributed a great deal to society because God had a purpose, just like He has a purpose for everyone's life.

Love,

Dad

Carrie gave thought about her job, her teaching career. Matt had always supported her desire to finish college, to major in both English and Russian. She recalled the letter from Durinda Hansen, her former high school teacher and mentor, in reply to Carrie's letter informing her of her college studies. She wrote, "You must be married to a *superior* man." She always remembered that special look he gave at her college graduation ceremony. It was one of both pride and compassion.

Carrie's Slavic language background gave ready access to Russian studies. The NDEA Studies in Russian that took place in San Francisco, with forty-four other Russian instructors from all over the U. S., had required her to be away from the family for eight weeks that summer. Matt's daily letters encouraged and assured her of his deep care for her, as well as their family. Two summers later, another absence from home took place, when she enrolled at the Russian School in the East. When she wrote that she was crying every day, Matt boarded the plane and rented a car to bring him there for a weekend with her. Matt shared her goal to teach Russian, as her contribution to acquaint American children with Russian culture, and do her part in promoting understanding and hopefully, peace. The Cold War was raging. Carrie thought, my mother's family, my first cousins live inside the *Iron Curtain.* Must my children shoot them or be shot by them? Then there was the question, how much will this exposure benefit? Yet, there had been serious students. Several became teachers. As mentioned earlier, one continued his studies in Russian throughout college and entered the Eastern Orthodox priesthood. Another student completed a master's program with a scholarship and became a social worker for the Slavic Gospel Association, assisting many émigrés from the Soviet Union, when 10,000 were released and came to Chicago. Was this worth her efforts? Dear Matt had stood by her, supporting her all the way.

Dear, dear Matt,

How do I feel about my job? Sometimes I love it. Sometimes I feel it is frustrating, and sometimes I feel it comes between us.

I'm writing this letter in between all my a.m. chores. I haven't fully focused in on the question we discussed, about my job. There have been times when I really felt discouraged about the whole Russian program and my involvement with it. Also, at times I envy women who are at home and *can* do things more thoroughly and efficiently at home, than we working wives.

But when I experience the nice things with my job, I'm glad I'm involved and forced to pull myself together, and be alert and aware. Otherwise, I'd stagnate. However, I still hope to do more writing, perhaps after my M. A. T. is completed. Remind me to tell you about the two courses—timewise, etc., I can do this summer (enclosed).

I do want to share my day with you.

P. S. We still have to decide about Easter. So, my day can be filled with numerous activities, without my ever working. But my mind needs fulfillment with challenging and active accomplishments. Teaching, learning, and writing fulfill these.

Hey, it was great sharing *The Family* with you last night. Also, the news. Only—can you wait until 11:20 next time, so I don't doze off and wake up at 1:30, as I did—I'd really appreciate it.

Love,

Carrie

For the first week after their ME, there were letters and some dialogue almost every day. Later, they became sporadic. The newness remained with them for a while. Then when an incident arose that had them grasping for resolution, they had to remind themselves of their need for communication. Yet at the beginning, Matt seriously took the initiative in sharing. Only a few days after their return home, he was to write something he considered important for their marriage.

Dear, dear Carrie,

I was reading the ME calendar last night—listen to this—April 1970, great discoveries about feelings are made! (1) Feelings just are. (2) I feel that is not a feeling, it's a judgment. (3) Feelings are neither right nor wrong. Summer 1973, Our most common feelings such as inadequate, guilty, and rejected are found not to be feelings, but judgments. From my ME notes: focus on feelings/give to each other/not complain to each other; look beyond surface feelings, use descriptive words; if I were to take a picture of my feelings, how would I describe it? Further information: *Mark 11:25 And whenever you stand praying, forgive if you have anything against anyone; so that your Father also who is in heaven may forgive you your trespasses.* I feel my feelings are all cloudy/hazy/misty about the question we dialogued on last night. Also, I feel that we are really on the threshold of some real terrific dialogue. At first last night, I began to get frustrated, but later, I felt really good about the whole thing. P.T.L.

Love,

Matt

They talked. Carrie noted the serious effort Matt was making, as well as his relating his faith with respect to feelings, and how important it was for both to consider them when attempting to understand each other. She tried to express this in her next letter to Matt.

Dear, dear Matt,

This morning after having had an opportunity to express my feelings, I became aware that I no longer felt the same level of frustration and resentment I did prior to your acknowledging that I had a right to my feelings. I felt supported. Now I can reexamine the situation more objectively. I still feel the same way as I did before—only I am able to view it with more compassion. Still, I feel the need of your support. I need you to be tender. Because I am a responsible adult, I resent authoritarianism in any shape, manner, or form. The command to pour the wine, without sensitivity, produced my reaction which you called *snapping*—but actually it was an outward sign of my compounded frustration. Please try to be more sensitive to my situation. And please have the dignity to give our coupleness first consideration when you want to put me down. Exercise greater self-control. I try to do this in front of guests, friends, and others, because I want their respect. Can we both try to do this?

Love,

Carrie

They talked about the dinner with the family after the baptism of their granddaughter. Matt, when confronted about his action with the wine-pouring, asked Carrie's forgiveness—a milestone in their relationship. Carrie felt compelled to respond with a short note.

Dear Matthew,

Of course, I forgive you. But it's like a new beginning. In order to avoid what happened last night, we should dialogue and get to know each other better, and understand each other—while happenings are fresh in our minds.

Love,

Carrie

Many days passed. Ups and downs. Yet, communication strengthened. Trials were met with renewed effort to resolve each with new resilience. Support was given in the monthly newsletters sent to them by the Marriage Encounter Association, assuring them they were not alone in their struggles. Though their letters were sporadic, they continued. Often, it was Matt who took the lead in attempts at communication and resolution. The tasks were not easy. Debates and arguments were pursued in written form. It was as if piled-up resentments and sins inherited from their fathers and forefathers were being swept away to leave a cleaner slate on which to rewrite their new, more stable relationship. There were mornings when Matt, the early riser, knelt beside Carrie's side of the bed with special petitions to the Lord for success in this, their new budding phase of their marriage relationship. Often, he held his hand over his sleepy wife's heart.

After two years had passed, with a strengthened marriage, they celebrated their thirtieth wedding anniversary with a second trip to Europe. This time, unlike their first trip, when they had landed in Amsterdam, they arrived in Frankfurt, where Larry and Thelma met them at the airport. It was Larry's first tour in Europe; he was stationed in Heidelberg. Their stay in Europe was twice as long, six weeks instead of three, allowing them a longer visit in Czechoslovakia. And they did not neglect visiting the Dutch cousins, with an opportunity to visit many they had not seen on their previous visit.

Interestingly, they were to be met with a new challenge in the following year, which greatly altered Carrie's professional career. Their experience with Marriage Encounter had prepared them to wade through this stream of changes which we shall explore, after joining them on their second adventure in Europe.

Chapter X

Return to Europe

Five years had gone by since their twenty-fifth anniversary trip. Now their approach to Europe differed. Unlike their first landing in Amsterdam, this time it was in Frankfurt. There they were met by Thelma and Larry, who had driven from Heidelberg, where Larry was stationed. Much had occurred in their lives since their former trip abroad.

The major event had been the Marriage Encounter in '77. Matt, who proved to be eager to preserve their marriage and strengthen their relationship, assumed a leading role by following the advice and communications offered by the other experienced married couples. By the time their thirtieth anniversary approached, both Matt and Carrie were totally convinced they belonged to each other. This togetherness proved to last firmly. Both credited the leadership of the priest who had directed the Marriage Encounter. Disagreements, now fewer and farther apart, actually evolved into mild debates. Both enjoyed the openness they continued to experience. Now they both were armed with a new, stronger level of confidence, not only as a couple, but also each one, as an individual.

This second trip abroad was planned to be twice as long, six weeks instead of the former three. The plan allowed for three of those weeks to take place in Czechoslovakia. Thelma, Matt's younger sister, had plans to take them on tour to a number of the German towns she and her husband had already toured and chosen. There was also to be a special visit with Matt 's family in Holland.

Carrie, who had researched more of the history of the Moravian Brethren, hoped they could visit Naarden, which they did.

Matt's sister had made friends with a close German neighbor who had offered the lower section of her home for Matt and Carrie. Wren would remain in the apartment with her aunt and uncle. Their German hosts shared their war and post-war experiences. They had been sent to Hungary to work during the war. After peace was declared, their Hungarian hosts required that all the Germans sent to their country leave. They were very glad, for now they were free to be in their own country, and escape living under the Iron Curtain. They were fortunate to be able to buy their home, with separate floors to accommodate themselves with one of their mothers, and an upper floor for their married daughter and her family. Spacious, the home was able to accommodate four generations under one roof. The lower level they offered to Carrie and Matt included bedroom, bath, and sitting room, with stove and small refrigerator; private and safe, these quarters were comfortable for visiting guests.

After taking a day or so to settle in and accommodate their jet-lagged bodies, they began their first step in touring the surrounding area. Thelma and Larry lived in the suburban town of Leimen. Larry first drove them to the U. S. Army base to inquire about information on travel to Vienna—then a stop at the bank to exchange their travellers' checks for German cash, before browsing through a few stores on the base. Most items were very expensive. For example, a new wallet was priced at about four times the cost of a purchase in the U.S. Other prices might prove lower, but still were expensive. Postcards were bought, ready for quick greetings by mail to Carrie's already prepared address labels to friends and family members in the States. Later, after dinner in the early evening, Larry again drove them toward Heidelberg, to show Matt the exact direction to drive; the tour departure point leading to a number of the town's highlights, to orient them for the following day's excursion.

The next morning from 10 a.m. to noon, found Carrie and Matt on a bus tour of Heidelberg. In the Old Town was a castle. Its ruins were brought about by the French. Yet these ruins were not hindered further during either World War I or World War II. The largest wine casket is located in this castle. However, the *largest* was disputed later, during Matt and Carrie's travels in Bohemia. Matt loved the apothecary shop that captured his interest. Another interest to both Carrie and Matt was St. Michael's Basilica, dating back to the 11th century, that they hoped to return to and tour.

Heidelberg was not damaged. The tour guide explained that while the rest of Germany was being bombarded, Heidelberg was only bombarded by leaflets, informing its citizens that Americans did not want to destroy their city, because they planned to have their military live there after the war. With Larry being stationed here with his family, this decision made by the Americans gave personal meaning to the visitors. Among the tour group was a young German student with whom Carrie and Matt became acquainted. After chatting with her, they exchanged addresses. She was hoping to travel to the States, and they welcomed her to visit them. Dinner in Heidelberg was *okay*, but not extraordinary. Thelma had prepared them to expect restaurant guests to be accompanied by their dogs, who, crouched under the table by their master's feet, waited patiently for dinner to be consumed. Finishing the main course, they drove on to Leimen, where they stopped in a small café for coffee. Carrie replaced dessert for the rye bread served with butter. She decided this was probably the best place to eat in Germany. The destination on the following day was Frankfurt, where the rented French car awaited them.

After picking up their car, the decision was to take a short tour of Frankfurt. They visited the home of Goethe. Inside the Town Hall in Frankfurt, they viewed a hall containing full-length pictures of the emperors of the German states, including that of Charles IV, who was a Luxembourger. His mother was a *Přemyslid,* descended from early Bohemian royalty. Another group of paintings included the Old Testament kings; beyond a gap they are followed by Charlemagne, and after another gap, the German rulers of later centuries. One very beautiful painting revealed the wisdom of Solomon, who was prepared to have his soldier cut in half the infant, when two women were attempting to claim the child as theirs. Both Matt and Carrie agreed that one of the main attractions for them in Europe was the great appreciation shown for history, recorded in art.

More history would be recalled when they toured St. Peter's

Cathedral in the city of Worms. It was Thelma who suggested they tour Worms, reminding them of its importance to Luther's history. As Carrie and Matt toured this cathedral, they found its appointments almost breathtaking. Sometimes referred to as the Emperor's Cathedral, it is a unique example of German-style Romanesque architecture. It was constructed and dedicated in the 11th century. Added was the Nikolaus Chapel with its beautiful vaulted Gothic-style ceiling in the 14th century. In the 15th century, the elaborate baptismal font was added. A prince left enough money to have a high altar built of gilt wood and multi-colored marble.

Politics and changes in religion affected the structure ominously in the 16th century. During the Thirty Years' War, while Swedish troops held the city of Worms for three years, the cathedral was used for Protestant services. During the 9 Years' War, Worms was one of four cities devastated at the command of Louis XIV. The cathedral was heavily damaged by fire. A bishop had the cathedral restored in 1698. The renovation was nullified by French Revolutionary troops. In 1792, Worms was one of four cities sacked by revolutionary troops. The cathedral served as a stable and a tavern. Full renovation did not begin until 1886. Much more detail can be appreciated by visitors to the cathedral—the replacement of church bells; the graves and burials located inside the church; the cathedral's current function as a parish church. However, its ties to Luther's history and reaction to political and church leaders must draw our attention.

In April of 1521, Martin Luther was called by the Holy Roman Emperor (Charles V) to appear before the assembly of prince-bishops of the imperial states to be held in the cathedral. He was to answer to the Pope Leo X papal bull that denounced the 95 Theses of Protestant Reforms Luther had nailed to the church doors at Wittenberg. Luther refused to recant his views. He escaped arrest ordered in the Edict of Worms, and hid in the Castle Wartburg in Eisenach. There he began his translation of the Bible, which was to transform Christianity. Later in this chapter we will relate the further influence of the Protestant Reformation under the leadership of the pastor of the Moravian Brethren, Jan Amos Comenius.

On the following day, all three visitors left Thelma and Larry, and headed for Zurich. Their rented car had to have an oil change, which they planned to have done in Zurich. However, unlike American responses to quick oil changes, the Renault service dealer told them he could not do the change until the following morning. This would require them to stay in Zurich overnight. He was able to refer them to the Olympia Hotel, less than a block away, where they registered for a room. The dealer did promise them he would have their car ready by noon. While the car was being serviced, they took a bus tour of Zurich. Stopping to phone Carrie's former Swiss professor, they learned from his daughter that the professor and his wife were vacationing in the French portion of Switzerland, in Crans–Montana. She told them they could see her parents there, but time was limited, with other plans.

They had memories of their tour of Zurich during their first trip five years before, so it was not altogether strange to them. One of the stops was at the church where Luther's buddy, Melanchthon, preached. Carrie noted the Estée Lauder factory. All remembered the beautiful blue waters of the lake. Carrie wanted to stop at the jewelry store where she had purchased Swiss fob watches. However, they learned that the cost had more than doubled the price she had paid five years before, so she decided to pass.

After lunch, they got their car and checked out of the Olympia. One room plus three meals cost $82. Then Matt tried to call Sabina in St. Gallen. When there was no answer to his call, he decided to drive there. After some difficulty, they found Rorschach and the Tschirky home, thanks to the direction of the gas station owner, who knew the family well and could lead them there. Sabina hosted them to a coffee while they visited for a short time.

Then they went on to the principality of Liechtenstein. Nestled between Switzerland and Austria, this beautiful, tiny country, occupying 62 square miles, has somehow maintained its independence. Its official language is German. The country had suffered devastation during World War I that brought about a monetary union with Switzerland. It chose to remain neutral in World War II and sought advice from Switzerland. Ruled by a prince, whose net worth of six billion dollars ranks him the sixth richest monarch in Europe, its population of less than 40,000 enjoys a high standard of living. The very low tax rate attracts companies to settle there. The mountainous region attracts tourists who enjoy winter sports. The visitors stopped for postcards, a few souvenirs, and a bite to eat, before going on to Austria.

Now they were indeed in the Alps. They decided to spend the night in a guesthouse in Bludenz. Matt, ever the geographer, loved this mountainous region. None of the three objected to the cold heights, for snuggly featherbeds protected their warmth. All enjoyed the view of the Alps, as they ate their hearty breakfast at the *Gest Haus,* where they had spent the night before continuing their journey. On Matt drove them through the Tirol country, stopping only for some food at Landeck. The native women wore their traditional hand-embroidered costumes. Carrie splurged on an extravagant souvenir, a delicate handmade and painted little box, decorated with flowers, in a manner typical of Tirolean art—a gift designated for her oldest daughter, who herself was an artist. On they went all day, driving through the Alps. They stopped briefly in Innsbruck before continuing to Salzburg, where they planned to spend the night. They wanted to tour Salzburg before journeying to Vienna, which was now only 200 miles away by *autobahn.* On this trip they experienced their long drive through the *Arlberg Straßentunnel,* nearly 14 kilometers long, and reported to be the largest tunnel in the world.

Matt, Carrie, and Wren were happy to take a walking tour of Salzburg after sitting so long in the car. This city is very old, very clean, and very expensive. Some of its architecture and art is truly beautiful: old spires and old churches unseen in the U.S. Streets were washed daily. Instead of a restaurant, they stopped for sausage and fruit for a picnic lunch at a park-like setting, before going on to Vienna. Carrie was scared as Matt drove through the very narrow curved roads in the Vienna Woods. Wren, who had mostly been silent, joined her dad in teasing her mom, as Carrie, concerned about the numerous, winding hairpin curves and turns, expressed squealy concerns. They had stopped at a *travel informat* to reserve a room at the Hotel Anker in Klosterneuburg, near Vienna. All proved to be quite luxurious in Klosterneuburg. They came to the dining hall with hungry stomachs. After being satisfied with a delicious meal of Austrian *schnitzel,* they were escorted to an adjoining room where a table about ten feet long was adorned with luscious pastries and desserts.

"Wow, how does one choose from all this delicious-looking stuff?"

Their appetites appeased, it was time to enter their room and rest, to prepare for a super busy day. They hoped to tour Vienna for half the following day before crossing the border into Slovakia at Bratislava.

Unlike their first European trip when their time in Vienna was too limited, they were now able to go through selected palaces that once served as homes to Austrian monarchy. Between the two chosen palaces, they met a Japanese couple. Although they did not have a command of English, they approached Matt and Carrie, hoping to get directions to the palace of their choice. Producing their map, the man pointed to the destination they sought. Matt was able to help them by finger pointing the correct direction. The man's wife expressed her appreciation with a formal bow. Unlike most of their fellow tourists, Carrie noted this Japanese couple was attired in more formal wear—he, with white shirt and tie; and she, head covered by a classical bonnet with a partially-attached veil. It was as if they wished to show special respect towards the country they were visiting.

They toured the magnificent Schönbrunn Palace and the Belvedere Palace with its lovely gardens. They ate the food stored in their car. It was getting toward late afternoon. Looking at his watch, Matt announced it was time for them to head for the border for Czechoslovakia.

"We do not want to miss our cousins."

It was already late afternoon when they headed for the border. Carrie wondered what the guards would be looking for, as they lined up their car for inspection. Carrie greeted the man looking through her suitcase in Slovak. His question was whether they would be visiting their family. "*Rodina?*" She felt a bit embarrassed as his hands rummaged through the soiled laundry. When his coworker (*Could this be his boss?* Carrie wondered) approached, with a question about his approval, the inspector affirmed that all was fine. "*Dobre, dobre*" he repeated the word, and nodding his head, he closed her suitcase and shut the baggage door. Then he gestured for Matt to drive on. Matt did, then stopped, as the only car ahead of theirs was answering the questioning guard and showing a paper, which undoubtedly was his passport. This was a reminder for Carrie to prepare for this next check, and she removed their passports from her handbag.

After this brief encounter, the drive was very short, and they were met with warm greetings and smiles from cousins Anička and husband, Milan, who were accompanied by Štefan and wife, Terka. They mentioned that they had been waiting for a few hours, and had watched as a number of cars entered their country, hoping each one would be Carrie's and Matt's. They did not want to leave, fearful they would miss their entry, but decided to wait for one more car, and it, fortunately, was theirs. All got out of their cars for hugs, before beginning their rather lengthy drive to the village, Klátova Nová Ves.

Carrie's cousins and their spouses (left to right): Milan, husband of Anička; Terka, wife to Carrie's cousin, Štefan.

*Carrie's cousin, Anička, and her husband, Milan,
with sons Peter and Milan, Jr.*

Terka (Teresa) and Štefan with daughters Janka and Mirka.

Matt followed their car, and their drive, which began during twilight, ended in darkness. Their arrival to the home of Tetka Anna and Strychko brought about many happy greetings. Paul, the older brother of Anička and Štefan, was there with his wife, Martuska (Martha), and their little daughter, Gabrielka. The excitement kept all of them wide awake. There was much to tell. Carrie found herself translating for both Matt and daughter, Wren, who knew only a few words in Slovak, but were eager to join in conversations. Cold cuts of meat, cheese, Slovak rye bread, and kolach were served, along with Becherovka and *Slivovice* (home brewed plum brandy), and tea for those who preferred something warm to drink. Carrie dug into her travel bag to give Štefan a special meaningful gift from America. A philatelist for most of his life, Štefan collected postage stamps from all over the world. Now his American cousin brought him a rarity. Since their visit five years before, the United States had celebrated its Bicentennial year as a nation, and the U.S. post office printed commemorative stamps. Štefan was delighted to receive these. After 1:00 a.m., all were ready to turn in for the night. Their hosts announced there would be surprise visitors joining them on the following day.

The following day was spent close to the home of Carrie's aunt. Matt was relieved, for he had driven many miles since their arrival in Europe. The three accompanied their hosts for a very long walk around the village, as well as the neighboring village. At the start of their walk, they met an acquaintance of Carrie's aunt, who, after learning of the guests from America, told them about her two daughters who had left the country for America in 1968. What was unique about their location in the United States was that both daughters, now married to American husbands, lived in homes less than thirty miles away from Matt and Carrie. She persuaded Matt and Carrie to visit with her while they were in the village. They promised they would try, not yet having devised a schedule of tours and other visits with their host family.

They stopped to eat *halushky*—a Slovak recipe for a delicacy like homemade noodles served in a silash. Being teachers and book lovers, they were happy to learn that the eleventh-century castle they remembered seeing on their previous trip was being restored and would become a library.

When they returned to the home of her aunt, Carrie was introduced and greeted by Emanuel, the oldest of Tetka Anna's children, and his wife, Helen. They had traveled by train from Bohemia. Their conversation revealed that the length of their journey from their home to the village took as much time as it had for Carrie, Matt, and Wren to fly across the Atlantic from the U.S. to Europe. Eman, as everyone called him, and his wife were to accompany them on some of their tours during their visit. They particularly looked forward to visiting the Tatras.

The following day was Sunday, and the visitors went to the church in Nitrianska Streda they had all attended on their former trip. They also visited the pastor and his wife after the service. What had happened with churches during these past five years? Surprise. Since their previous visit, a new church had been built in the town of Krncha and their host pastor served that church, as well. He invited Matt and Carrie to attend the worship service there on the following Sunday and gave directions to Matt on how to drive there. He also reminded them that services were two hours earlier than the church at Nitra so he could serve both churches.

Visits were fun. All returned to Tetka Anna's. Then they all went on to the home of Pavel and Marta. Their daughter Evočka was playing badminton with Wren. Evočka had been studying English and could practice speaking with Wren. Close to the same ages, the girls had fun together. Before all left for home, Anička suggested they stop to visit the neighbor whose daughters were now living in America.

Carrie was happy that allowing more time in Czechoslovakia on this second trip took them to more places. On Monday, Štefan drove them to *Jankov Vrhsok,* a memorial built especially for soldiers who had lost their lives during World War II. Later, Štefan showed them the bunkers used by the partisans and where they were killed by the Nazis. The surrounding woods were quiet and peaceful. Then they drove to the village of Závada, where Anton, Carrie's father, was born. There, they saw the home built with stones, where he had lived as a young boy. People came out to greet them. They met Anton's cousin Adam and his wife, as well as the wife of Anton's godfather, with whom Anton still corresponded. Veering back toward the Topoľčany area, they stopped to see Milan at the Agricultural Institute where he taught as a professor of agriculture. On their tour, Milan proudly showed them the new experimental circular machine that was designed to milk ten cows at once. This machine had been purchased from Sweden.

Hosts and visitors all left the village at 6 a.m. Their destination, the Tatra Mountains, would require a six-hour drive. Milan drove Matt's leased Renault. Carrie felt that Matt was grateful that Milan had offered to relieve him, after all of the driving throughout their European travels thus far. Wren rode in Paul and Martha's car, to accompany her cousin Eva, as did Anička, and Emanuel, with his wife, Helen. Their caravan stopped in Martin, the town known for its museum and other special buildings containing much Czechoslovak historical information. Martin was formerly named St. Martin of Tours, but was shortened to Martin by the Communist regime to avoid recognition of Christian saints. Carrie was delighted to visit a bookstore where she was able to purchase a Russian/Slovak Dictionary, as well as a newly-published Slovak/English Dictionary.

Their entry to the Tatras found them almost gasping at the beauty surrounding them. After a walking tour in one section, they found a cave that had been discovered in the thirteenth century. Carrie was happy she had worn her raincoat as they strolled through the chilly dampness. The group drove into the town for lunch. Returning, they went on to an area called *Rysy*, where they took turns riding on a cable car taking them over a valley and crossing to another section of the mountain. Now it had become misty—*maraseet*—just as the Russian instructor had described the mountains in Vermont. But the view was breathtakingly beautiful. Carrie found the ride on the cable seat to be scarier when returning back to the first side than the first ride. Thankful for a safe return, she was happy when their departure for home was announced. The plan for the following day was to tour Bratislava, the capitol of Slovakia.

Bratislava, sometimes known as Presburg, its German name, is a very old city. It was much favored by the former Austrian–Hungarian rulers. When they stopped to visit St. Martin's Cathedral,

Štefan's wife, Terka, sitting beside Carrie, reminded her that this was where the coronation of Maria Theresa took place. The interior was beautiful with its art work. Some renovation was now being done. Other visits in the town included the *Bratislava Museum* and the *Bratislava Castle*. Dinner took place at the Hotel Devin. Europeans eat their main meal at midday. The whole group, except for Pavel (Paul), who seemingly disappeared, walked a great deal from place to place. Tired, both Carrie and Terka agreed it was time to stop. The group assembled at a Franciscan wine cellar for rest and wine. Here they were joined by Paul, who sheepishly confessed he had found a corner in one of the museums and had napped in a comfortable upholstered chair. It seemed that the long journey of the previous day had taken its toll on him. Worn out, he took an opportunity to take a nap away from the group. Before they left the city for home, they made a final visit to *Slavin*, the memorial for the Russian, Slovak, and unknown soldiers felled by World War II. There were approximately 6,800 soldiers buried here. Those who could be identified have been. The rest were buried in a common grave.

Home, back in the village, and beds for the travelers were welcomed by all. The hosts announced the plan for the following day—a visit to Piešťany, a popular and internationally-known town for its healing spas that served the needs of many aristocrats of Europe and other countries throughout the world. They would also go to Topoľčhany, the hometown of Milan and Anna, and their two sons, Milanko and Petko.

Piešťany seemed to be a very relaxed town. People from all over the world came here for bathing and healing from ailments such as rheumatism and arthritis and other similar problems. There were many stores and gift shops, including Tuzex. Carrie and Matt, as always, kept an eye open for unique gift items, and here they found two chief gifts for the Kiefers, their hosts in Germany. After going home for a quick lunch, they drove to Topoľčhany.

Knowing that Carrie was teaching Russian in the States, Milan had arranged for her to meet two Russian teachers who were from Saratov, on the Volga. Their government had assigned them to go to Slovakia for one month in order to help Slovak students—

Pioneers and Komsomol members—with Russian oral conversation during summer classes. The goals paralleled those of Carrie. She expressed her reason for teaching Russian—she wanted American students not only to be introduced to the language, but also to learn some Russian history and culture. Hopefully, this was a step toward peace between our two countries, she stated. Both nodded their head in agreement; these instructors had witnessed the devastation and losses their country had suffered during World War II. Already, she continued, there were trade and economic efforts taking place. She recalled the Ford plant built in Russia, as reported at the Slavic annual conference. Carrie eagerly informed them that a number of businessmen had enrolled in her Adult Education Class, so they could at least greet and speak with their Russian counterparts in the business world. There were also teachers, a journalist, and a few hopeful tourists. At the close of their meeting, they parted in friendship. What a unique opportunity this proved to be. Thankful to Milan, Carrie believed it was the Lord's direction that had brought them together.

The following day took them to the town of Trenčín, which dates back to Roman times, during the reign of Marcus Aurelius. Trenčín had been a garrison for the Roman military. The famous castle was being renovated, so they could not go further than a very short walk on the approaching walkway. However, a section of the town called Nové Město, offered some very nice stores where Carrie and Matt could do some gift shopping. Then they visited a cousin of Strychko's, from Eman's side of the family, before returning to the village. This cousin had just returned from a trip to Leningrad and had much to tell. They arrived back at the village in time for dinner. Then they paid a visit to the home of the other two Karolinas.

Everything was the same. Perhaps this sameness was what Matt and Carrie loved about Europe, especially Slovakia. Even Wren commented, "They live so naturally." Already a mid-teen, she fell in love. It was a teenager attraction to Milan, Anichka's husband. As they toured the various places, she wanted to hold his arm. Thank goodness, everyone merely smiled in an understanding way. Milan, as yet, had no daughters, but he, too, understood. He bought Wren a carved walking stick which she cherished always.

Carrie was happy for all the stores in Topoľčhany. She purchased a Russian/Czech and Czech/Russian dictionary. For gifts, she got a number of handmade cornhusk dolls. Štefan bought for her a special gift to honor her thirtieth anniversary of marriage to Matt—*Luchnice,* relating and illustrating in many beautiful photos the famous Czechoslovakian dance team. After shopping a while, they went to Anichka's for coffee before returning to the village. Carrie watched Anička and Terka prepare *shtrudle.* This was another feature Matt and Carrie enjoyed at their European cousins—gourmet food, homemade, from scratch. They packed a portion for Eman and Helen to take with them now, as they left for their home in Bohemia. Carrie was so happy to have met them on this second trip.

That evening, Štefan took them to the cemetery in the village, where they visited the gravesite of Carrie's maternal grandmother. They retired early, as they planned to attend the service at the church in Krncha on Sunday morning at 8 a.m. What interested Carrie and Matt was that, in spite of the present communist regime, it was possible to build a new church. The congregation was much larger and more men were present than at the church in Nitrianska Streda, served by the same pastor. They were able to record the entire service successfully. Carrie was happy to have this service on tape to share with her cousin, John, in Minnesota.

Later that Sunday afternoon, Carrie and Matt went to visit the pastor and his wife to bid them farewell. The pastor presented a lovely gift to Carrie—a Luther rose pendant he had brought from a visit to Germany, one just like the one his wife was wearing. They parted with the hope of meeting again in the future.

Monday morning found them packing again, preparing to travel to Hodonin, the home of cousin Eva and husband, Zdenek, and their two sons. After lunch, there was another visit to the Trenchansky's, the sister of Mike in Cicero, and her family. Her daughter and husband had built their new home since Carrie's visit five years before. As before, they were very hospitable and showed them around their home, a two-story house and very spacious. They expressed a lament that their uncle in Cicero had not come to visit them and wondered why.

When they returned to Tetka Anna's, Carrie visited with her aunt for the last time. They had coffee together. She had gifts for Carrie to take home with her—an oversized pillow to match the one she had given Carrie on their first visit. Also, three handmade lace tablecloths. One was oval, to fit on Carrie's table. The other two were for her daughters, Anna and Durinda. There was something about visiting with her aunt, her mother's sister, that made Carrie feel as if she was visiting with her own mother. She felt an unusual sense of wholeness.

They departed the next morning from Klátova and went to where Terka was working to bid her goodbye. It was sad to say goodbye to everyone. Wren was in tears. En route, they made a last stop in Piešťany and bought several gifts. They wanted to get Nescafe at the Tuzex store, but the line was so long, they decided to skip it. They drove on to Brezová pod Bradlom, and stopped to see the memorial built to honor Štefánik, a patriot, and contemporary of Thomas Masaryk. Carrie wanted to send postcards to her brother-in-law Ed, and John Riban. Milan suggested they have dinner there while they waited for the stores to open. Anichka paid for all the meals. The cost was modest, but the food was good and tasty. After they mailed the postcards, they drove on to Hodonin, where Evochka, Zdenek, Tetka Eva, Strychko, Vaclav, and little Tomashik were all waiting for them.

Here, Milan and Anička, with young Milan and Janka, parted for home in Slovakia. Wren cried when they left.

The date was August 1. Carrie asked herself, *What will this August bring into my life?* She remembered that, as a little girl, maybe only at the age of ten or eleven, when it was the beginning of August, she asked herself, *I wonder what future Augusts will be like? What will I do, where will I go?* And here she was, with her mother's family in Czechoslovakia. It was like a dream come true. Rising from her bed in Evochka's apartment and stretching, she joined the group in the tiny kitchen. It seemed the family members were used to small places and making close space do.

After breakfast she and Evočka took a long walk to Hodonin. There they looked around the town, the Centrum, and Carrie bought picture postcards. When they stopped in a bookstore, Evočka bought her a gift, a book containing written criticism of American and English literature. They rode the bus back to Eva's home and then drove to the town of Breslav, where Tetka Eva was waiting for them, to serve a warm noon meal. Later, Carrie and her cousin took a long walk in Breslav, where they saw not only shops and the Centrum, but a whole new section of the town only recently built. They stopped to speak with a resident whose lawn was beautifully manicured. His home was built of stucco, as were most of the homes, and in a California bi-level style. They discovered a hidden closed Jewish synagogue with a cemetery. Matt took a photo of it. He was also able to photograph another Jewish temple which had been deserted, but was now occupied by some gypsies who now wanted to be called *Romanis*. There were tears in Evočka's eyes as she tried to explain: "But we don't have any more Jews." This brought back for all of them the sad events of World War II.

More history and cultural information was offered when they accompanied Uncle Vaclav and Evočka to Mikulov on the following day. A charming old town, it was close to the border. Here, they visited its *Dietrichstein Castle*, with its interesting scientific and archaeological exhibits and library. Here was located the largest wine cask in Europe, made in 1643, with a capacity of 26,400 gallons. In the surrounding area were many fine Renaissance and Baroque houses. They also saw the *Pavlovský Vrch,* the hill with the stations for penitence offered by the pilgrims as they climbed past, to get to the chapel at the top. On their way back to Hodonin, they left Uncle Vaclav to catch a train to go to work. Then the rest went to *Valtice,* a chateau dating back to the thirteenth century and transformed into Baroque between 1643 and 1730. It was owned by the Lichtenstein family.

Probably the most impressive of all their visits in the Czech portion of the country was *Mikulčice.* Eva was eager to have them see the museum and the opened archaeological findings. These archaeological discoveries revealed that Moravia was already a well-advanced civilization in the sixth century. Artifacts such as earrings, belt buckles, spurs, and many other works of art were on display in the museum. There were crosses that confirm their introduction to Christianity. Graves and churches were excavated. When the discovery took place, there were no government funds available to support a program to start an excavation. A volunteer group of Czech citizens was willingly and proudly formed by the people themselves to conduct an excavation. There is a program with plans to have this entire archaeological discovery on display completed by 1990.

In the evening, Eva and Zdenek hosted Carrie and Matt at an enjoyable wine cellar in Hustopice. There, they met a pair of couples from East Germany. Matt took their photos, and receiving their home addresses, promised to send the pictures, which they did after returning to their home in the U.S.

Strazhnice, the castle visited on the following day, contained a museum and an art gallery. The works of art contained in the museum are peculiar to that area—lace, embroidery, wooden carvings and toys, dolls made from cornhusks, and dolls dressed in native costumes. On display were other Czech/Moravian works of art unique to that region. In the library were musical instruments, including bagpipes and native instruments. In addition, another lovely art gallery contained many paintings by Uprka, who in the 1890s, painted many scenes from Moravian villages, giving great attention to details on the costumes and folk items. This was before the age when photography had become common, so his works have often served as a historical record for studying the national dress.

Carrie and Matt, together with their hosts, experienced much friendliness as they traveled throughout the Czech countryside. They stopped near a home situated at a very large parcel of land, where a man was cutting tall grass with a scythe. Evočka approached him, and pointing to his scythe, asked if she could use it. Nodding, he handed it to her, and she spent a few minutes cutting away at the tall blades.

"It has been a long time since I have done this," she smilingly declared.

"Me, too," responded Matt, and gesturing to the scythe owner, he pantomimed using the instrument. Laughing at this enthusiasm, the owner raised his arm in agreement. Evočka handed him the scythe and all watched for a number of minutes as Matt lowered some of the tall grasses.

They had driven from the home of Evochka's parents in Breslav and stopped in the town of Milotice to see the *All Saints Church* and the *Castle* there. Inside the castle, they viewed displayed a collage that had won a prize at the *Montreal Expo* in 1967; this depicted a symbol of the region of Hodonin. Also displayed were a carved bunch of wine grapes from Mikulov; and the sixth century earrings archaeologists found in Mikulčice. Later, they went to Lanžhot, where Matt photographed a Slovak *chalupa* (cottage) there.

Then they went to Moravská Nová Ves, where they joined *Lidová Slavnost* (a people's celebration). Folks from the village had gathered to socialize, drink wine, and dance. Called *Hodky,* it is an annual celebration commemorating a particular saint. Here, it was St. Ann. Matt took many photos of the villagers wearing their *kroje* (costumes). Leaving there after a couple of hours, they drove on to the village of Hrushk, where they visited Zdenek's parents. Greeting them warmly, they invited the visitors to eat a light supper with them before they drove home.

The next visit was to Brno and Velká Biteš, the home of Vaclav and Svetlana. In Brno, Matt parked their car on the square, *Ploscad Ludy Armady*, and walked to the Centrum. There, they shopped and looked in several stores. They also visited two churches—Saint Thomas and Saint James (Svaty Jakob). They learned that the architect of St. James was a member of the Parlez family. Parlez was the architect of St. Vitas Cathedral in Prague. St. James has very similar high Gothic naves. From there, they went to see Špilberk Castle. They parked by the Hotel International, a very modern building built in the 1960s. In contrast, the castle was an old fortress built in the fifteenth century, in the Gothic style. The only section that was open for the visitors was the dungeon and not very inviting.

However, there were noticeable changes in the domestic lives of some family members. Svetlana had a modern washer and dryer imported from the U.S. She used and displayed household items—sprays and laundry soaps—she had purchased that originated from Amway in Ada, Michigan. She proudly showed these to Carrie.

So, Amway undoubtedly would display the Czechoslovak flags with their international collection displayed in front of their plant in Ada, Michigan.

There were two buildings of much greater interest visited on the following day—*Náměšt' Nad Oslavou and Kralice*. The first, a castle of Gothic style, was built in the fourteenth century; added in the sixteenth century was some Renaissance style. Its main features were the numerous tapestries by Gobelin. These tapestries were gathered from all of the castles located in the surrounding areas in Moravia. This castle had been the presidential weekend residence of the second Czechoslovak president, Edward Benes. Now, the second floor was being used to house visiting foreign guests.

When Carrie related the disappointment she and Matt experienced during their first European trip in not seeing more storks on roof tops, like the ones they saw on a church roof at Alsace–Lorraine in France, Vaclav and Evočka pointed to the two roofs on high buildings in the village. These served as separate homes for the stork parents and the nesting stork offspring. All chuckled at Vaclav's claim that the home of the parent storks was evidently not large enough to accommodate their youngsters.

In Kralice, the visitors toured St. Martin's Church, an old twelfth-century Gothic church, which was originally a Romanesque language-speaking church of the Moravian Brethren. During the flight of the Thirty Years' War, it was left bereft of its members, so it became a Catholic church. The Czechoslovak government recently supplied funds for restoring the church, with its interior, to its original Protestant appearance.

Time to move on. The following day, after bidding Vaclav farewell, all went to Prague, accompanied by Evočka. They planned to visit their mutual cousin, Emilia, who with husband, Joseph and family lived in suburban Hostovice. Her brother Zdenek, whose job as chauffeur for the national teachers' association president helped him to know Prague like the back of his hand, kindly offered to drive all of them around Prague and serve as their tour guide, for which Evočka expressed deep gratitude. They saw much that was missed on their first trip, five years before. They began with the *Memorial of*

National Literature. After their tour of the museum, Zdenek parked the car and they entered the new subway station. They stopped to tour each subway station. Each station was uniquely artistically decorated. Later, they went to Wenceslas Square. On display was the statue of Jan Hus, the fourteenth-century martyr, who had been double-crossed by church officials and was burned at the stake. There were shops for gift buying. Carrie selected a wooden carving of the panorama of Prague. They enjoyed a gourmet dinner at the restaurant *Beryawshka.*

After dinner, they went to Old Town, where Matt snapped the twelve apostles coming out of the Astronomical Clock. Evočka and Carrie wanted to shop some more, so Matt, with Wren and Zdenek, went to tour St. Vitas Cathedral, where Matt took more photos. When the group met back together, they all walked to the museum, where Smetana artifacts are kept on display. The director there spoke very good English and related the life of the composer. She played the *Moldau* while the group watched the river itself. How thrilling it was to hear the music as they viewed the river with its waves bordering the shores.

Later, they walked across the Charles Bridge, which tells its own Christian history. They stopped for coffee with native pastry. Zdenek drove them around some more, taking them to the Jewish cemetery, and several other spots like the Stadium and the Golden Lane. They stopped at the legendary home of *The Good Soldier Schweik.* They also stopped at the Gothic Beer Garden before returning to Emilia and Joseph's at Hostovice.

After bidding goodbye to the cousin in Hostovice, Matt drove to Prague for a little more sightseeing and shopping. Matt took a second series of photos of the twelve apostles, because he feared over-exposure on the first set of photos. Then they walked on toward Charles Bridge and visited the Old Town Hall and toured the entrance, where Matt was able to photograph some very lovely mosaics. They walked to the top of the building, from where they were able to view the entire city. This would prove to be the last time in Prague for many years. They ate a very tasty dinner of beef stroganoff at the restaurant *Moskva*, before boarding the subway to get to their parked car. It was hard to say goodbye to Evočka. Both cousins were in tears. It was imprinted on Carrie's mind how they had waved to each other until they could see one another no longer.

Matt drove to Pilsen, where they stopped for a brief respite before continuing to the border town of Rozvadov. They crossed into the German town of Waldhaus. The only problem they had at the German border was that their USA sticker was considered *verboten*, so they had to get an *F* to grace the windshield of their leased French car. The *F* had been missing since they left Slovakia. It had obviously served as a souvenir for a native. Matt drove on to Nuremberg where he stopped for gas. Then he headed for Leimen, where they arrived at Thelma and Larry's after midnight. Now, they could look forward to adventures, touring in Germany.

Everyone was very exhausted from their long trip back from Prague the previous evening. They visited with Thelma, did the laundry, and Libby did Carrie's hair. When Carrie returned from Libby's hair salon, Frau Kiefer was visiting with Thelma, and eagerly waiting to hear all about their travels in Czechoslovakia. Frau Kiefer expressed a welcome for them to stay at her home again. She also gave a special invitation for a visit when they returned from their final excursion in Holland.

Later at her home, Matt and Carrie gave Frau Kiefer and her husband the gifts they brought from Czechoslovakia. When she unwrapped the first, she beckoned to her husband with a delightful smile and the word, *shpek*—the homemade bacon Europeans love. They also gave her a lovely china canister made in Modra, and tea, as well as a still life (fruit) plaque, carved in Czechoslovakia.

For the next few days, they would see more of Germany with Thelma and Larry. In the Neckar River Valley there is a four-castle corner. These include the *Mittelburg* and the *Vorderburg*, which are privately occupied today; the *Hinterburg*, a small ruin; and the *Schwalbennest*, the highest of the four; and from which one can view the entire town of Neckarsteinach. They also got a view of the *Hirschhorn*, a thirteenth-century castle, located in the town with the same name. The drive with Larry and Thelma was very relaxed and fun, without pressure. Earlier they had stopped at the PX, and upon returning to Leimen, spent time getting packed. Cousin Harry phoned to confirm the invitation to visit them in Vlissingen on the following Monday. We were to meet him at the Grand Hotel Brittania at 4:00 p.m.

The three actually set out twice on their travel toward Holland. About thirty miles away from Leimen, Wren discovered she had forgotten to put her passport in her purse. What to do? Should they just drive on and take a chance she would not be refused entrance into the Netherlands? This might abort their visit with the Dutch cousins. Uncertain, they stopped and asked the German border guards. Fortunately one spoke English. When they related the situation, he merely shook his head. "Best to go back and get her passport. Better to be safe."

Thelma was surprised to see them, but Wren quickly got her passport from her other purse and they set out for the second time. Near Ludwigshafen, Matt stopped to snap a photo of a modern bridge of unusual architecture. At Koblenz, they stopped to buy some postcards, and briefly stopped to see the interior of the *Pfarrkirche Herz Jesu.* In Aachen, they filled up with gas at an Esso station. Then they crossed the border into Holland. This time they had their passports stamped. They regretted not having had them stamped before, in Switzerland, Germany, and Austria. It was five o'clock when they arrived in Vlissingen, an hour later than the time requested by Harry. Yet he and Cathy were there, waiting for them.

Wren asked for Didi, who was swimming. Harry took them for a brief tour. The harbor area was picturesque and meaningful to Harry because his father was born here, and he recalled his own boyhood years here. Then, after getting a large bag of mussels in a fish store, Matt drove, following Harry's car to Rotterdam, to the home of Reta and Gar Nap for dinner. They no longer lived in the boathouse in Zuidland, where they had hosted cousin Matt and family five years before. Now they owned a condominium-type dwelling. Gar gave Wren the assignment as the oldest of the youngsters there to supervise the younger ones while dinner was being prepared. Soon, they were all seated around the large table where mussels, other fish, and vegetables were being served.

Dinner over, all went to Schiedam to visit Ari and Co. Ari was a mutual cousin to Matt, Cathy, and Reta. The plan was for Matt and family to spend the nights in Holland at the apartment of Ari and Co, who proved to be wonderful, warm hosts. Carrie recalled seeing a boyhood photo of Ari in a sailor suit, shown to her by Matt's father, when he was sharing his family pictures some years ago. How happy she was for Matt to meet this cousin and the others in person. She sensed he had acquired a sense of wholeness meeting his father's family in Holland, much as she had, meeting hers in Czechoslovakia. Ari was the family historian, and having a deep interest in sharing family history with Matt, he gave him a printed copy of the family's recorded history dating back to 300 years before. Ari also shared a photo album of the buildings, streets, and areas in Rotterdam, as they were before the Nazi destruction of that city. The Nazis had broken their word to the people of Rotterdam and to Holland. They had promised that if the administration would voluntarily surrender, they would not bomb the city. Although the surrender did take place, the Nazis still proceeded to destroy much of Rotterdam. Some of this destruction also had been photographed. Ari also showed them a number of family pictures and albums.

The next day, Cathy and Harry came to drive the visitors around Rotterdam. One important historical stop was the harbor from which the Pilgrims had departed for America. On the street by this harbor stood the building where they had met to discuss the decision and form a plan to leave. The visitors drove around the old neighborhood and saw the marketplace where Matt's paternal grandfather sold his vegetables. Then they went to visit Tanta Martye, the sister of Matt's father. Her close resemblance to Matt's father was so striking, it brought tears to Carrie's eyes. After doing some more sightseeing, they visited Cathy's mother, Tanta Marie, and Cathy's aunt, Marie's older sister, 100 years old. They lived in rooms next door to each other in a retirement home.

After stopping for lunch and parting from Harry and Cathy, Matt and family, together with Ari and Co, drove to Naarden. Carrie had a strong interest to visit the museum and the place where Jan Amos Comenius was buried. Leading as pastor of the Moravian Brethren, he also became famous as the world's renowned educator. The whole effort to honor and commemorate Comenius has been a cooperative program between the Czechoslovak and the Dutch governments.

Carrie found herself explaining her interest in Comenius to Matt. "Our children share heritage from both countries. What an important legacy they have from each!"

They arrived at the doors of the museum minutes before closing time. However, the director of the museum greeted them warmly and volunteered to stay and guide their tour. He did not mind working overtime.

"I often have Czech businessmen coming to Holland who willingly drive all night to allow themselves time to visit this museum. The Czechs are very proud of this heritage," he explained.

Who was Jan Amos Comenius? Born on March 28, 1592, he died November 15, 1670, in Amsterdam, the city that hosted him during the last fourteen years of his life on earth. Comenius (known also as Komensky) was one of the greatest Czech and European philosophers and pedagogues. He was also known as The Teacher of Nations. His goal as an educator was to interest children in learning. He believed it was important to devote training for parents, from whom children receive and develop their initial steps in learning. Carrie and Matt became acquainted with the life and work of Comenius in the museum, situated next to the mausoleum where he is buried.

The director, who was their guide, told them about Comenius' invitation to visit and teach in a number of nations—among them was Poland. Catholic persecution forced him to emigrate, where for a time, he lived in the town of Leszno; in Sweden; in Hungary, where he tried to establish a pansophic school, which he wrote about in his *Sketch of a Pansophic School.* (*Pansophic* means all things to all people.) And he even lived in France where he was invited by Cardinal Richelieu. Though he was a Catholic, he recognized the pedagogical talent of this great educator. The director also discussed the books Comenius had written: *A Theater of All Things*; A comprehensive dictionary of the Czech language; *The Great Didactic; The Gate of Languages Unlocked; Astronomy; Physics*; and probably the greatest known, *The School of Infancy.* Because he wanted to stimulate learning for children, he wrote books with pictures; in Hungary, he completed the first illustrated textbook: *The World of Sensible Things Pictured.*

During his final years in Amsterdam, Comenius wrote his major work, *General Consultation About the Improvement of Human Affairs*—a plan for reforming human society. Interestingly, only two parts were published in 1662; the remaining five were not found until the 1930s. In summing up his long life, Comenius completed *The Most Important Thing* in 1668.

The towns of Naarden in Holland and Uherský Brod in the Czech Republic enjoy close ties to the memory of Comenius. Every year on March 28, on the anniversary of his birth, the Comenius Foundation honors the memory of Comenius. March 28 is known as *Comenius Day.*

Ari and Co were happy to learn, with cousin Matt and his family, about Comenius and his history in the details that were presented. Thanking the museum director for his kind attention, the group took leave to return to Schiedam. All were too tired to visit Cathy's mother. Instead, they phoned to say goodbye. After enjoying a hearty Dutch breakfast with Ari and Co the next morning, they lovingly bade warm farewells.

It was Matt's plan to drive to Paris that day, where they would return their leased car and have an opportunity to do some sightseeing. Wren had studied French and was able to speak the language quite well. Her two wishes were to visit the *Notre Dame Cathedral* and the *Eiffel Tower.*

But, alas! Travelers sometimes are victims of the errors of well-meaning hosts. Their first stop in Paris was the return of their leased car, which was probably an error. They checked their luggage at the train station and got in line to get their tickets—only to learn that the next and only train going to Heidelberg was leaving within the hour. Carrie had received a train schedule before they left Heidelberg that stated their train would be leaving early in the evening. Matt bought three coach tickets, while Carrie went to the station's store and snack shop, where she bought sandwiches and a French travel book of Paris for Wren. At least, missing the places she had hoped to visit, she would have this travel book.

It was hurry, hurry, to retrieve their luggage, eat their sandwiches, and be prepared to board the train on time. Inside the train, they walked from car to car, looking for the coach. Not finding the coach, they spotted an almost empty compartment, where they joined another passenger who was alone. Wren was spokesperson, asking her if they could join her. She gestured to the leather-covered seat across from her, and all three were able to sit there comfortably. That is, they were comfortable for the first hour or so, until the French-speaking conductor entered the compartment to collect their tickets. He took the ticket from the other passenger without comment, stamped it, and returned it to her. However, when he accepted the three tickets Matt handed him, he shook his head.

"You must pay more," he informed him in French. Wren translated.

When Matt asked why, Wren repeated his question, and hearing the conductor's reply, she explained to her dad: "These are coach tickets and we are sitting in a private compartment, which costs more."

"Then please show us where the coach is," Matt requested.

When Wren asked about the coach, the conductor merely shrugged his shoulders. No one in the ticket booth had told Matt that this train did not have a coach. The clerk there merely sold him the three train tickets. The conductor left them with a rude remark to which Wren used a phrase she had learned from her French teacher. The conductor may not have understood English, but he did understand Wren's French remark, and he told her she was a rude young person.

All three left the compartment and went to look for a coach, which was not available on this train. However, they found another compartment with only one young man in it, and Matt opened the door and asked if they could join him. He spoke English, introduced himself as a military, and more, he was from their home state of Michigan. Expecting to be discharged soon, he was traveling to see as much of Europe as he could manage before returning home to the States. Being a former Marine, Matt and their new acquaintance had much interesting conversation. Wren took time to read and look at the new French travel book, and after a while, it was time to change trains at Mannheim.

On the train at Mannheim, the conductor was unable to speak English, and here Wren's French was also strange to him. So the conductor went to get the inspector who was riding on the train and was fluent in English. He informed the transferring passengers that there was a supplement charge to pay. The fare was an additional nine marks, but none of the three had either German or French money. However, Wren offered her American money; she counted out six dollars, which the inspector accepted. Both Carrie and Matt aired out their grievances. Carrie showed him the schedule they were given before they left Heidelberg. The inspector asked where they had gotten this schedule, and after a quick glance, he informed them that it was obsolete. He proved to be quite sympathetic. When he learned they were headed for Leimen, after departing from Heidelberg, he asked how they expected to get to Leimen. Carrie replied either by streetcar or taxi. The inspector offered to drive them to their destination, the home of Thelma and Larry.

His conversation, as he drove them to Leimen, was rather interesting. He denounced the presence of the American troops, claiming no decent German girl would even think about dating an American soldier, and he believed the sooner American troops were removed, the better. Neither Matt nor Carrie responded, but later, Carrie revealed her thoughts to Matt.

"I wanted to ask him, 'But who started the war?' yet I did appreciate his ride to Thelma and Larry's, and am thankful we got there safely."

It was so good to be back *home* and they all slept soundly. With just a few days left before the flight home to the U.S., Thelma announced she and Larry would like to take them to one more special town before they left Germany. It would be best to go on the next day, because they would need a day to pack and prepare to travel to Frankfurt to board their plane for home.

The town was Ladenburg, the oldest German town on the right bank of the Rhine. When the town charter was issued in the year 98 A.D. by the Roman ruler, Trajan, it was known as Lopodunum. This name came from a Celtic name of a settlement which existed on the same site long before the Romans came. During the Roman period, Ladenburg was the capitol of *Civitas Ulpia Sueborom Nicrensium,* the area of the lower Neckar region. From archaeological finds of this period, it is believed the Romans began to build a basilica in the beginning of the third century that was to be a courthouse and marketplace. The foundation was 73 yards long and this structure would have been the second largest Roman building north of the Alps, second only to the Basilica of Trier. Intended to be the crowning glory of the Forum and rival of all structures in Italy, this plan failed because the structure was never completed, for at this time the Roman Empire had begun to collapse.

Today the St. Galluskirche stands on the original foundation and the floor of the Forum is two to three yards under the present Kirchplatz. The church was probably started about A.D. 1000 and the crypt, shortly after.

In the early Middle Ages, its name was changed to Laudenburg. Today, it is called Ladenburg and is located on the Neckar River, between Mannheim and Heidelberg. Its population is more than 10,500 and the inhabitants are very proud of their heritage. The old part of town is living history. Its old timbered buildings have been restored to their original condition. The old narrow cobblestone streets are lined with relics.

During the Middle Ages, Ladenburg was the seat of the Bishops of Worms who determined the history of the town for 1,000 years. The remains of the Bishops' Palace and the nearby St. Sebastian Church are evidence of once-grand structures. Beside the church in a dug-out area are the remains of a wall dating back to about A.D. 90, as well as a section of a stone wall from the early Middle Ages, probably part of the town fortification. In the Bishops' Palace, a museum contains columns and blocks from a second-century Roman building, as well as archaeological finds from the Ice Ages throughout the Middle Ages, found in the Ladenburg area.

In more modern times, Ladenburg was the home of Carl Benz, the inventor of the first automobile powered by an internal combustion engine. His first garage, considered to be the oldest automobile garage in the world, is still standing there.

The town council of Ladenburg has taken steps to preserve its historical image. An ordinance requires that all repairs, restoration, or roof work be reported to the mayor; and all work, materials, and color retain the historic image of the town.

"Wow, what a climax to all we've seen in Europe this time," Matt's words of reaction expressed the feelings of all. It was as if they'd seen the ultimate before getting ready to pack and fly back home.

Chapter XI

The Grievances

It happened. No matter how hard Carrie had worked to promote the Russian program throughout the school district, it did not meet with the satisfaction of certain members of the administration. It was while she was studying with a number of teachers of Russian from all over the country, including Alaska, that the letter arrived. After nine years, it had been decided to discontinue the class in the Downtown Program. Matt brought the letter with him when he came to Ohio to get Carrie. There had been continuous tension throughout the nine years. Principals resented having their students leave the base high schools to enroll and attend the special courses offered, courses that could not be offered in the base schools, for the numbers attending each of these special classes were too small. Students however, liked attending diverse classes. They did not mind riding buses downtown and they enjoyed meeting students coming from other high schools to the Downtown Program classes. The parents strongly upheld continuing the Russian class each time it had been threatened with discontinuance.

During that nine-year period, Carrie had expanded the program to include elementary and middle school students. Some chose to continue Russian studies on, into high school. Several chose careers in which they benefited from having studied the language and culture. As mentioned earlier, one was destined to become an Eastern Orthodox priest. Another became a social worker for the Slavic Gospel Association. After completing two years in Carrie's classes, she continued studying in a local college and earned a scholarship in graduate school at an eastern university. Upon completion of her master's degree, she was invited to enroll in their doctoral program. However, she felt a calling toward a different course of action.

At that time, a large number of Russian Jews were allowed to leave the Soviet Union. About ten thousand came, as refugees, to Chicago. This was when Carrie's student's skills and understanding of the language were needed to serve them in various ways. Her Christian conscience directed her decision to join the Slavic Gospel Association and help the refugees settle and assimilate in their new country. She arranged for housing, food stamps and monetary assistance, medical help, employment when possible, and the study of the English language, offered in churches and public school evening programs. Working in this assignment led her to meet the man she married. Carrie and Matt proudly attended their wedding ceremony and reception at a church located on the West side of Chicago. Some time later, Carrie was to share her experience when giving a eulogy for Professor Mudry, who had been her first Russian instructor at the fledgling college west of the town.

And when the grown student, who had begun Russian studies in fourth grade, became a priest, Carrie and Matt were invited to his ordination. They observed his first serving of holy communion to his young wife at this service. Later, at the reception being held, he introduced her to his former teacher. "Please pray for us," she asked. (Carrie was to experience another occasion in 2001, when referring to him in a conversation with his colleague while visiting in Alaska.)

These were only a few of the intangible rewards Carrie had experienced when teaching. She did not want to give them up. There were others, particularly in the evening classes. Although the Russian classes were no longer offered in the Downtown Program, they did continue in the Community Education program that met in the evenings. High school students loved the class and were welcomed to attend two evenings a week. They were able to earn high school credit by completing the required assignments and tests. Among them were three students from the same family—a sister with two brothers. For one semester, Wren joined the group. She had studied French previously and learned from her mom how helpful

French was when interpreting Russian literature. Carrie's former roommate at the eastern college told of her successful experience in earning an A in her Russian literature class. Having a fluency in French enabled her to glean content written by French native critics of the novel *War and Peace*, with her instructor, Madame Volkanskaya, an extended family member of its author, Leo Tolstoy.

Carrie remembered asking her roommate, "Were there any corrections on your *doklad?*"

"Only a few corrections on the grammar, here and there, but she complimented me—*Awchen kharawshy doklad.* "A very good essay."

Wren memorized her dialogues perfectly, but she refused to receive credit for any of her recitations or translations. Her reason—"I don't want the other kids to say that you are showing preferential treatment with your grade because I'm your daughter." Carrie honored her request, but she felt it would have been justified to give Wren high school credit and a grade of A.

As popular as was the evening class, the new daytime assignment was not going well for Carrie. It was not until she recalled each situation that Carrie came to realize what was happening. The true motives of the principal and the grave difficulties awaiting Carrie were revealed, not only during Carrie's teaching assignment, but to others who replaced her throughout the school year.

When Carrie attended the orientation program at her newly-assigned high school, she was informed immediately that she would be evaluated this year. Evaluations were never a problem in the past. Often, she was given compliments for methods employed in her classroom and the results experienced by her students. However, now she was surprised at the first evaluation presented. Reading one item after another, she wondered at the contents. How was she to react?

Carrie thought about the experiences she had learned from the Bible history she studied as a child. Maria II felt that Carrie and her sisters must memorize sections of Holy Scripture in the native language. Carrie recalled the story of Joseph. His brothers, jealous of the favoritism shown him by their father, determined to kill him and remove him from their midst. Only the overt objection of their oldest brother, Reuben, prevented this violence. Yet it did not alleviate their young brother's suffering and challenges. Arriving in strange Egypt, he was unjustly accused of attempted rape by the wife of his master, Potiphar. This led to an unjust imprisonment. There, he was given opportunity to use his God-given insight to interpret dreams of his fellow prisoners with accurately predicted results. Joseph was not a stranger to dreams, but his dreams told to his brothers led to compounding their resentment toward him. When the Pharaoh was puzzled by his dream, the released prisoner recalled how Joseph correctly interpreted his, and reported it to his leader. Joseph not only interpreted the forthcoming famine, but when asked, advised the country's leader how to prepare for it. This led to Joseph becoming the Prime Minister of Egypt, second only to Pharaoh himself. He was given a wife selected from Egypt's aristocracy.

I have to state the facts as I see them, Carrie told herself, *and also I must be true to myself.* Examining the first evaluation form given her by the principal, she responded to each item as accurately as she could, choosing her words carefully. Carrie scanned the list of items:

The assistant to the principal wrote her comments on the Classroom Visitation Form, beside the designated criteria for evaluating teachers.

Meets basic needs of students. More than 30 minutes of the class period was devoted to discussion on a test given on a previous class day. Activities should be more varied. Time should be more effectively utilized.

Arranges and manages the physical setting so that it is conducive to learning. Room is difficult to work in for several reasons. The seating is arranged so that bright sunlight is in students' eyes. Wind blew papers around room.

Demonstrates effective planning and preparation. Lesson plan should include a greater variety of activities, better pacing in order to challenge and interest highly-motivated students.

Utilizes instructional materials effectively. Because of temporary inadequate chalkboard space, list of projects written on board could have been more effectively presented to students through use of ditto. List was difficult to see.

Develops and achieves a quality learning experience. Class lacked interest, vitality, due to inappropriate amount of time spent on the one activity.

Utilizes a reasonable variety of techniques and methods for modifications of unacceptable student behavior. More than one student was tardy. I did not observe that the tardy students presented passes to the teacher. The teacher did not request passes.

Carrie noted that only half of the criteria was accompanied by written comments. The assistant principal left the classroom a half hour before the class ended.

Together with the signature of the observer was the assessment written: *Unsatisfactory.*

When Carrie was given the copy of the observation evaluation, she noted each of the items and then wrote her response.

The assistant principal did not consult with me, nor did she follow the Evaluation Procedure as specified in our teachers' contract, pages ten and eleven. I covered the test given to the students previously with the objective of using the review as a learning tool which proved to be needed: (a) as a review and learning experience for all and (b) an opportunity for all to express opinion on an answer and to exchange ideas. My colleagues tell me they do cover tests and results; furthermore, the student adviser, after learning of their test results, ascertained this to be a need. The assistant principal lacked information because she did not follow contractual procedure prior to her visit and become fully informed as to why I was covering the test. Had she remained for the entire hour, she would have observed that students who so desired were given the option of rewriting portions of essay questions missed in the test. Also, projects were discussed, explained, selected, and individual opportunity was given to ask questions about guidelines and to obtain information.

Carrie had changed the students' seating two times. The sun traveled around the south windows to those in the west. She wrote—*The other teacher using this room during the third class hour and I both hope the drapes for these windows will soon be installed, for they will be helpful when the sun becomes bright.* She did not emphasize this was the responsibility of the administration.

She defended her lesson plans, stating—*Lesson plans do include variety of activities, and are planned to meet the needs of all students.*

She also defended her use of the chalkboard, for its position was adequately seen by all students. She wrote—*It will be helpful to have the large chalkboard mounted, for it is awkward having it sitting on the floor beneath student's eye range. However, because the students are able to see the top fifth of the board, it was possible to complete the list of project choices on it. The first half was written on the portable chalkboard standing in the front of the room. Dittos will be provided when students are unable to see the boards.*

Carrie also voiced her disagreement with the assistant principal on the time taken to cover the test. She wrote—*Class seemed vitally interested in their test results and knowing what answers were missed. I disagree with the assistant principal's analysis, for she did not remain the entire hour, nor was she present after class when students crowded around the teacher to ask more questions.*

Carrie explained her reasoning for not sending students to the office for passes when arriving to class a minute late—*My clock varies from the other clocks, so I do allow students one minute without demanding a slip, for often my clock runs a minute fast. Sending a student to the office for one minute's tardiness would add to loss of time, if any is lost initially.*

When asked to sign the evaluation, Carrie refused. She did submit her response, typed up, to the principal. But the problems did not end there. A few days later, the principal herself showed up in her classroom. Carrie felt very well prepared. The students were assigned to study *Main Street* by Sinclair Lewis. Their reactions on various issues and symbols made for lively discussion. Except for a few silent ones, most in the class participated with poignant comments. When the principal left, Carrie believed her administrator should have been well satisfied with her observation. So Carrie did feel a strong level of confidence when she was asked to meet with the principal a day or two later. She was not prepared for the roadblock placed before her at this meeting.

When Carrie entered the principal's office, without being asked to sit, she was met with a host of accusations. The principal declared that a number of concerned parents phoned to complain about Carrie's method of teaching. One parent questioned Carrie's qualifications, stating that students were being treated as elementary students in a patronizing, condescending manner; that the material was not presented in an interesting way; and that students did not understand what was expected of them.

How could you believe this after witnessing the lively participation you observed in my class just a few short days ago? Carrie thought. Before she could respond, the principal added— "I have more complaints from other parents. One was concerned about your rapport with students, claiming her child was already turned off and bored. Another claimed that you had made *racist remarks.* You did not understand why blacks objected to being called Negroes, since that is what they are; that in a poem written in black idiom, you stated that the poem represented the manner in which blacks speak. Recalling this incident, Carrie realized the student did not report what actually had been said—that this was the way that Southerners speak. Another accusation proved to be a distortion of what had actually been discussed. The parent stated that his/her child indicated that the teacher had asked all Catholics to identify themselves and proceeded to say that Catholics should not hate Jews. The discussion had evolved after a study of the historic treatment of Jews in Europe, the prevention of allowing Jews to be employed in the trades by extremists in the Christian community.

An additional complaint was made because Carrie had used a bit of Russian to help a student whose family were émigrés from the Soviet Union. The girl needed help and Carrie was able to translate a sentence to help her understand the context that was puzzling to this student. *The fact that being a trained teacher of Russian made it possible for me to assist this student was looked down upon as something undesirable, rather than realizing this ability was an asset.*

Throughout her relating these parental reports, the voice of the principal became more and more loud and shrill, to the level of shouting. Startled, Carrie asked her, "Why are you shouting?"

"Because my job is so difficult." The reply was accompanied by tears.

Three days later, a memo given to Carrie in which the complaints cited verbally were printed along with directions (1) to treat students in a more adult manner, allowing them to express themselves; (2) give more directions to students, telling them what is expected of them; (3) set up projects so that students feel they are involved in meaningful assignments outside of class; (4) develop lesson plans in a detailed and complete manner. Complete lesson plans are due in my office every Monday morning at 8:00 a.m. (5) Attempt to be less verbal.

When asked to sign the memo, Carrie refused. She asked the principal to recall the lively discussion she had witnessed in her class just a few days before. She further reminded the principal that she had offered to meet with these parents to explain her goals. The reply was that the parents did not want to confront Carrie personally or to be identified, because they feared there would be a reprisal by the teacher—"They're afraid you will take it out on their children who are in your class." A *roadblock, indeed!*

What a contrast this situation was from the one she had experienced during the years she taught English and Literature at the suburban school, and what a difference in administrations. At her former school, books and supplies were ready and available. Classrooms were prepared with adequate seating, window dressing, films and film projectors, and other resources delivered promptly at teachers' requests. Carrie recalled her former principal with a feeling of nostalgia. He related well to her teaching Russian, as well as English, having taught Spanish before becoming an administrator. Now she found herself becoming ill from the stress experienced with her present situation.

Sharing her experiences with Matt, who observed her being

super-tired and unusually stressed, knowing she had always loved and enjoyed teaching, he advised, "Take a sick day and catch up with your rest and restore your energy. Things might get better when you return."

Yet another surprising encounter was to take place on the day Carrie returned from her sick leave. Carrie had used her lunch time to review the afternoon class lesson plans, postponing eating until after her last class, hoping to enjoy the quiet privacy then. Her plan was interrupted. Considering all that had happened since she began teaching at this school, Carrie decided to meet with Rick Johnson, head of Human Services, to discuss her situation. She also requested that Shelly Spooner, her rep from their teachers' organization, be present at the meeting.

Prior to the meeting, Carrie wrote a document describing her teaching situation.

I had been informed at noon that the principal wanted to confer with me at 2:15, after my last class was dismissed. When I arrived at the principal's office, seated there were the assistant principal and three of my eleventh-grade students. Since I had not eaten lunch, I asked to be excused, but the principal asked me to stay for a few minutes and hear these students' concerns. We had an exchange of ideas. I asked the girls why they had not come to see me personally; actually one had, and after our meeting, I considered her problem to be resolved. One girl complained that I had used Russian in class; this matter had been brought up by the principal in Monday's conference, and frankly, I could not understand the principal's failure to explain that I was helping this student as per the principal's earlier request. Kira and another anticipated Russian student had just recently arrived from the Soviet Union. There was a language barrier and both students would need some help. I agreed with the students that I was from a different generation than they, but nevertheless, they might be able to learn from and with me if they tried, and asked them how I could help. One asked about a grading system which I promised to announce soon. Another asked for more specific instructions. I determined that the basic complaint was that I had not made out a ditto'd guideline for the readings in American literature, yet my announced assignments were specific, and when the board was mounted, were written as announced. All three students did agree that the morning's class had been a good one. One matter which I did decide to address was the class behavior of one of the three. Although she was not presenting a major problem in class, she was often unattentive. I asked her to be honest with herself, and ask herself if she had done everything possible to be attentive in class. She blamed me, stating that I had not gained her interest. However, interest in class requires a student to be cooperative and attentive. After the students left, the principal asked me to sign the memo and the two evaluation forms. I refused, for I do not agree with the contents. Much of what is stated is not factual. Nor is it fair to me, in view of the teaching situation I have been attempting to work in. In addition, it does not follow our Contracted Evaluation Procedure. For this reason, I am asking for a meeting with Mr. Rick Johnson of Human Resources, together with Shelley Spooner, our teacher's representative. If a realistic plan to resolve these problems cannot be worked out and met, I would request a transfer to another high school as soon as possible.

Before leaving her office, the principal gave Carrie the copies due her of the Classroom Visitation forms she and her assistant principal had written. She also informed Carrie that she would be given two added hours of preparation time on the following day, because the Art consultant would be taking her first and fourth hour classes. Surprised, Carrie replied that she had lesson plans made. This was more evidence of the breakdowns in communication and organization by this administrator, which affected the teaching planning and results. Then when she arrived the next day, a Friday, she learned that another teacher was also planning on having the Art teacher that first hour. Since neither knew what to expect, both approached the assistant principal. She did not know. Twenty minutes later, she approached Carrie to inform her that the Art consultant would be taking her classes. Carrie took attendance and made a brief statement announcing the following Monday's assignment, repeating it to be certain all were aware and writing it down, before turning the class over to her Art colleague. However, Carrie was happy to learn that the long-awaited texts had arrived. Yet there still was not the Teacher's Guide she had hoped would be available.

Later in the afternoon, the principal informed Carrie there would be a meeting with Rick Johnson on Monday afternoon at 2:30. She stated, "No matter what happens on Monday, I want you to know that I do not hold a grudge." At this point, Carrie informed her that their executive director of the teachers' organization would be present at the meeting. She also expressed disappointment to both the principal and her assistant that they did not offer her the courtesy of a colleague in their handling of students' complaints. The reply was that this was their school's procedure. Nowhere in either the student's handbook or the teacher's handbook was there any statement that their procedure was this high school's policy, to arrange for the students to "evaluate" and "confront" a teacher, without offering the courtesy of informing the teacher of their meeting in advance. Carrie replied, "In the future I do not intend to meet under these types of circumstances without the presence of a Building Council member or an Association representative."

Before Monday's meeting took place, Carrie arrived early to give Rick Johnson copies of her responses to the information written on the proposed Teacher Evaluation forms. Rick took time to read them, expressing surprise at the missing window dressing, the unmounted blackboard, the lack of sufficient texts. When he finished reading all, he handed the papers back to Carrie, stating, "Take this and bury it!"

When the principal and Shelley Spooner arrived, Rick addressed Carrie, requesting her to address her complaints. Carrie spoke of the lack of organization, the attempts at undermining her as a teacher, and the manner in which the principal has conducted their relationship thus far. Carrie tried to speak with compassion, stating, "I am a Christian and I want to be forgiving, but these incidents are repetitive and frustrating. I have never been approached by administrators in this way before at any of the schools where I have taught."

Shelley had been silent, listening to the principal's report of phone calls from parents, repeating much of what she had told Carrie at their conferences. Carrie reminded the principal of her willingness to meet with any of these parents to discuss her goals and plans. Shelley took a different position after hearing both sides.

She addressed the principal by her first name—"Amanda, do you think you and Carrie have a personality conflict?"

This seemed to be an approach at neutrality. It was an easy one for the principal to grasp—"Yes, I think that may be the problem."

When she repeated the same question to Carrie, her answer differed. "I do not believe in personality conflicts. Rather, I would favor honest, open communications between persons working together to avoid conflicts and frustrations."

Facing Rick, Shelley stated, "I believe it would be best for you to consider a different assignment for Carrie. She is an experienced teacher with many favorable credentials, one another principal would be happy to have at his or her school."

Rick nodded, then requested a day to make a decision on a new assignment for Carrie, with the promise to contact her as soon as possible. In the meantime, the principal was advised to assign Carrie's position to a substitute teacher until a replacement would be found. The meeting was concluded and Carrie returned to the classroom which she would be vacating, to gather all her materials and books. It was well past closing time. The rain was pouring hard. Carrie phoned Matt, who willingly came to help her. So did Wren, bewildered by her mother's situation. They each carried a bundle to the waiting car, having placed most of the materials in plastic bags to keep them dry between the school doors and the car.

Rick's secretary phoned the following day, giving Carrie an appointment to meet with Rick the following afternoon. Relieved and excited, she entered his office, expecting to receive favorable news. Previously, she had been invited by the principal at North End High. He never looked favorably upon his students being bused out for special classes, "Get a transfer! Come here and teach. We'll fill up your Russian classes," he promised. Her expectation now was that she would be assigned to teach at his school. However, Carrie was destined to receive a very unusual assignment, not one in a classroom.

"We want you to do some research. You will interview principals and their assistants to learn how they feel about the teaching of

Russian in our school district. Why has it now been discontinued? You will write out reports of your conferences and report to Jack Kendicut each day with your findings. Include the parents of your former students. Include people outside our school system to gather their views. We look for as much information as possible. You can begin by phoning and making appointments with all these people and meet with them. Start tomorrow. My secretary will provide the necessary papers to confirm and also inform the Teachers' Association. I will call Shelley myself."

Astounded, Carrie came home to tell all to Matt. Listening to her review, he nodded and suggested, "Make a list of all the principals for whom you have taught, their ideas and comments. Remember how they all were happy to have your enrichment classes? Put it all in writing. Then we'll see what happens. We may rescue your program yet." *How helpful you are*, Carrie thought, *and encouraging, too.*

One after another, Carrie sought answers and ideas from various individuals. Most felt the program should have been continued. She heard statements like "Our kids need to know more about the Russian people."

"Their generation will have to deal with them."

"Some may want to develop careers, and it will help to know their language and something about their culture and history."

The parents of a former student expressed disappointment that his younger sister was now being deprived of the opportunity her older brother had enjoyed. He even persuaded his parents to approve and finance a trip to the Soviet Union with a university professor and his class several years before. Another parent expressed disappointment because their son had looked forward to continuing Russian studies at the Catholic school where he had studied the previous year. His parents had called Carrie to tell of his feelings. They also commended her teaching. Most spoke about their child's enjoyment of learning another language. Some felt it helped them with their English language studies, as well. The only negative comment she received was from the Downtown School's principal, under whom Carrie had taught and expanded her program for the last six of the nine years she had taught there.

His comment was "We need to change the teacher." Carrie retorted, "Why are you saying this, Ted? You know we had a wonderful program going, elementary, middle school, as well as our high school classes. And the Catholic principal loved it. We had two classes there." Ted had always been moody at times, friendly at other times. His written evaluations of Carrie's teaching had always been marked *Excellent.*

His attitude led her to contact and meet with Dr. V., the assistant superintendent in charge of curriculum. She approached him with questions regarding his assessment of her teaching. He had always been helpful. She remembered his arrangement to have both Matt and Carrie attend a special conference for Geographers in Wisconsin in a previous year. She remembered how hard he worked for kids like Timmy, with dyslexia, to have special small classes at his high school. "Yes, I was happy to see that come about," he concurred with Carrie's gratitude. "Help is needed for the big people with reading problems, not just with the little ones."

Now, when she approached him to explain why Russian classes had been discontinued, his reply differed from that of her former principal. "It was budget cuts. Formerly, we were subsidized by the Feds. Now, laws have changed and Congress has made cuts. That is the only reason. Your experience at the suburban high school was highly praised by your former principal. There's no reason why you cannot teach English and Humanities. Maybe Russian will make a comeback sometime in the future."

By the fifth week, interviews were completed. When she met with Jack Kendicut, he referred her back to Human Resources, as Personnel was now named, and she met again with Rick. "Where do you want to be, Carrie?"

"North End High School. The principal invited me once when I came to recruit students for Russian at Downtown Program."

"Then let's send you there. I think I can make that happen. Report to the principal on Monday morning."

When Carrie reported her new assignment to Matt, he agreed this assignment would be a better one. The principal was Anna's former high school Political Science instructor. At that time he was popular not only with their daughter, but with her classmates, as well. Two years later, he became Durinda's teacher. Carrie's meetings with him as principal when visiting his school to recruit students to enroll in her Russian program were still friendly, in spite of the fact that he did not approve of busing his students out for special classes. Instead, his response was invitational—"Transfer here to our school, and we'll help you fill your Russian classes."

Carrie received another phone call from Mr. Berkley, an administrator assigned to place teachers at middle and high schools, according to their major teaching subjects. "You are to report to North End High School to teach language arts on Monday morning," he advised, "and meet with the principal when you arrive to receive further instructions." What neither he nor Carrie could possibly know in advance was that he would later become the *fall guy* for her situation at a successive school.

Neither Rick nor Carrie, nor even Shelley, could foresee what was to happen in the forthcoming three months at North End High School.

Monday morning started out friendly, but only in the parking lot. Having parked close to the car of the former assistant principal at Downtown High School, she was warmly greeted by him with a peck on her cheek. "Welcome to North End High School, I'm glad you're here!" He, too, had been transferred and seemed to be happy to see a familiar face from their previous assignments.

What a contrast this was inside the principal's office, and what a disappointment for Carrie. "What are you doing here? I don't want you here!"

"But, remember, you did invite me!"

"Now the time is different. They sent you against my will. I am assigning you to be a permanent sub." He introduced her to another instructor who was to show her around the school during the first hour. They stopped at the teachers' lounge. Carrie had already met some of the faculty at previous times, particularly at language arts meetings, as well as foreign language conferences. An hour later, one of the instructors had become ill and as he had to leave for home, Carrie was assigned to sub for his classes the remainder of the day.

Recalling all the principal had told her, she decided to phone Shelley, the teacher's rep who had accompanied her at the meeting with Rick. Shelley was absent, recovering at home with pneumonia. Her colleague, Wes, listened to the encounter reported by Carrie. His response—"Just do your job wherever you're sent. Never mind the principal, leave him to me, I'll take care of him!"

November found Carrie and Matt settling in their new home. Timmy and his wife moved into their former home. The agreement was that the young couple, now married more than a year, would rent with the plan to purchase the house. Carrie found herself content that they would have a comfortable place to live. Yet these circumstances were short-lived. The forthcoming year brought about changes. However, not before other changes took place in Carrie's teaching career.

In spite of the unfriendly beginning with the high school principal, Carrie followed through with each of her assignments. Some changed daily. Teachers absent with colds might require her to sub only a day or two. Twice she was assigned to classes for longer periods of time. There was the French instructor who needed surgery; he was gone for two weeks. Although Carrie, limited to very few words in French, found her years of experience in teaching her foreign language enabled her to apply the same methods with his French classes. First-year students emulated the spoken language offered on tapes played for part of the class period. In the advanced class, two students who demonstrated some mastery in speaking the assigned dialogues willingly led their classmates in practicing speaking the assigned conversations. Written assignments were collected. Carrie used the teacher's manual with answers to check their homework and recorded them in the teacher's record book. There was also a test given. Returning after more than two weeks' absence, their instructor was pleasantly surprised, and pleased that all had been accomplished as he had written in his plans.

As for discipline problems, Carrie was to experience a few of the woes imposed on substitute teachers. Once in the first year

French class, two students entered about twenty minutes after the class had begun. When Carrie followed procedure by asking for a pass, the student very blatantly answered, "Oh, you're a sub. You don't know our customs. My friend and I stopped to visit in another class because we went to sing 'Happy Birthday' to our friend in that room. We don't need a permit for that." The spokesperson for the pair slid by the teacher and went to sit at her assigned desk, assuming her explanation was adequate. Her friend silently followed. Carrie resumed instruction, but also felt she needed more information about this situation.

At the end of the school day, she approached one of the three assistant principals who had charge of disciplinary action. When she finished repeating the student's story, he was shaking his head. "There is no excuse for being twenty minutes late to class without some kind of written permit. I'll take care of this young lady." Carrie later learned she was given an hour after school in the Holdover Room as a disciplinary action.

A few days later, Carrie was called to the principal's office over the intercom. Entering, she found in his presence both Mr. Berkley and Janine Amondson, one of the advisers to the head superintendent. They had come to inform her that because of budget cuts, she would be placed in an involuntary transfer to a middle school. Carrie questioned the reason, as her certification and training was for high school placement. She also discussed the seniority situation. Turning to the North End's principal, she asked, "Aren't you satisfied with my efforts here?"

His reply was negative. "We've had more students in the Discipline Room than ever before, just to support you!" *In two months' time, of the 1,800 students she had taught, there had been a total of 11 disciplinary actions. Carrie had consulted these situations with the assistant principal in charge of discipline in each case, and it was he who determined their being sent to the Discipline Room. The principal himself advised the teachers at their staff meeting to write up students who were involved in behavior problems.*

Turning to the visiting administrators, Carrie asked, "Are you sure you want me at that middle school, after hearing this?"

Both spoke almost simultaneously—"That's between you and this principal. It has nothing to do with your transfer."

Then Carrie, turning to the principal, stated, "I would like to make an appointment with you to discuss activities here at the school regarding my assignments." He agreed that this was *fair.* He asked for a few days' time to arrange it.

A few days later, the principal approached Carrie, handing her the Staff Development and Evaluation Memo, as well as the directive to write up five objectives containing particular emphasis on relationships with students. He made some offensive remarks that someone had not been kind to her for all these years, misleading her into believing she was a good teacher. Carrie did not respond, other than to remind him he had agreed to a meeting when the other administrators were here. He gave her a time, the following Wednesday at 2:30 p.m.

On Wednesday there was a new surprise. Present at his office was the assistant superintendent in charge of secondary education, Sidney Oakton. Seeing him, Carrie hesitated entering, then stated, "I thought I had an appointment with the principal, *alone.*" The principal replied she could still see him alone, but Mr. Oakton was here and he wanted to tell her something.

Mr. Oakton began speaking by referring to an *oral, not written* complaint he had received from Carrie's former high school, which caused him to question her *fitness to teach.* He claimed that whether she was to remain at North End High or be transferred to a middle school, she would be evaluated *fairly and if she were not recommended for rehiring, he, as Director of Secondary Education, would follow through on the matter.*

Carrie thought *Enough!* Then came her response—"a. for the past nine years at Downtown High School, I have received all successful evaluations; b. I was at the other high school only twelve days, had been subjected to unethical procedures and had been transferred by my own request; c. also, I thought the former high school matter was buried, and am surprised that it is even being brought up now!"

Oakton's reply was that just because a teacher had had nine years' good evaluations did not mean the teacher was still fit to teach. He asked, "Who wanted to bury the matter?"

Carrie replied that Rick in Human Resources had asked her to bury it. Then Oakton reminded Carrie he did not have anything in writing. She replied she knew this, and that if it were in writing she would contact her lawyer and sue the parties involved for slandering her professional reputation and attempting to damage her career. Carrie inquired further, why Oakton had felt the need to create a negative climate for her by telling this principal about the tales reported by the former high school principal. Oakton declared he had a right to keep his principals informed.

Carrie reminded him further, thinking of Wren, that she had concerns not only as a teacher, but also as a parent. I, as well as many parents, are concerned about Amanda's behavior as a principal. Oakton declared Carrie had no right to evaluate a principal. A principal can only evaluate a teacher. Carrie pressed him further—"I have had three children come through this system, and now a fourth is in this high school, so as a parent I am concerned about the kind of principal my child has." Oakton told her to bring her concerns to her parents' group. Carrie assured him she would.

Before she left the office, she again asked the principal about their promised meeting, to which he replied, "Will you give me about five minutes?"

Carrie left his office, and went to get the president of the Teachers Association who taught English at North End. When the announcement calling for Carrie came over the intercom, the two headed for the principal's office.

Carrie found it very difficult to talk with the principal, who was on the defensive. He stated that the staff was "turned off" by Carrie, and that the assistant principal who had formerly been assigned at Downtown Program was one. Recalling this man's warm welcome when she first arrived, Carrie asked him to bring the man to his office and tell her this directly. The principal was unwilling to do this. "… Don't you know that middle-class people don't tell you what they think of you to your face?" When he brought up the disciplinary referrals, Carrie replied that of the 1,800 students in 78 to 80 classes, there were only a total of eleven, mostly freshmen. Carrie reminded him that at the November 3 meeting the principal had instructed the teachers to write referrals on any students who were disruptive to the class. So eleven was not an exorbitant number.

Borrowing from her Russian studies background, Carrie remarked that she was always open to constructive criticism when offered in a gentlemanly way, but told the principal that his blustering and offensive manner reminded her of Kruschev, deceased dictator of the USSR.

To Chuck, the Teachers' Association president, the principal revealed perhaps the real reason for his erratic remarks, that he had to cut three people from his staff.

Chuck responded that what Carrie wanted was to be transferred fairly and only because of the contractual matter of seniority, and not have demeaning remarks follow her to the next school. Now the principal seemed to be almost pleading with Chuck, saying he was "not trying to *do a job on Carrie*," and Chuck, you know I never do a job on anybody."

They never got to the evaluation information or objectives. The meeting on the date proposed never did take place.

Looming over Carrie was the reminder that she would be evaluated. She wondered how that would be processed. Knowing the principal's attitude, what kind of judgment would be made? Would it be similar to the procedures attempted at the other high school from which she had departed? Most of the teachers for whom she had subbed expressed appreciation for the manner in which she had handled their classes. Certainly they knew more about her effectiveness than any of the administrators, none of whom had even observed her. She decided to approach five of them.

Carrie kept her request simple. "I'm told I will be evaluated this year. Would you be willing to write a brief letter stating what you told me verbally, regarding your reaction toward my subbing in your classes?"

All five agreed to her proposal and wrote in a descriptive manner, citing from the facts written in their class record books. The first was from the French teacher, who also taught classes in American Life.

Dear Mrs. V.:

I would like to thank you for taking my classes the two weeks that I was in the hospital. It was good to come back and find that the American Life classes had covered an entire chapter, that the test had been given and corrected and recorded; and that the homework had all been checked and recorded, too.

I was glad to see you kept the French classes moving by having them read, write, do exercises, even if you didn't know what they were saying. In French II, especially, I didn't have to spend any more time on the unit on *chateaux*.

Sorry some of my "charmers" caused you trouble, but know that they try my patience almost daily, too. I'm sure they deserved the disciplinary action they got.

Thank you again,

F. V.

Although the manner of writing differed, each of the others wrote of Carrie's actions in their classes positively.

Re: Mrs. V:

Mrs. V subbed for me twice during the first semester of the 1980–81 school year. On both occasions, instructions were carried out as per plan book or my own telephone direction.

I also feel that behavior of the students was well handled, especially when one considers the attitude most students have about substitutes. I believe Mrs. V. did a fine job with my classes and I personally appreciate that.

Mrs. D. W.

Carrie's teaching experience in Russian afforded her opportunity again to carry out methods of teaching a foreign language. Besides, she recalled much of the vocabulary she had learned in her three and a half years of high school Spanish. She had used it occasionally when conversing with people who had a Hispanic background. This particular teacher also knew some Russian, though his family had emigrated from Lithuania, one of the states in the USSR.

To Whom It May Concern:

Mrs. V. substituted for me December 16th and 17th this school year.

I was very impressed by her work. She not only fully implemented my lesson plans, but also kept detailed records of student participation and behavior.

Mrs. V. maintained good discipline and went out of her way to involve all students in learning activities and gave individual help.

Mrs. V. was very dependable, conscientious, thorough, and effective.

V. J.
Teacher of Spanish
North End High School
January 13, 1981

Carrie found herself chuckling at a misspelled word in the Social Studies teacher's letter, yet happy to receive it for its contents.

To Whom it may concern,
Re: Mrs. V.
Substitute Teacher
North End High School

Mrs. V. has substituted for my classes twice. During these times I found that she followed my plans well, and involved herself in their implementation. She expressed a very sincere concern for the development of students. She would always follow up on any problems that may have occurred. Her dedication to the role of substitute teacher on a permanent basis is to me quite impressive. I did not feel that that the time spent in my classes were wasted days.

Thank You,

W. H. H.
Social Studies
North End High School

The fifth communication was brief, handprinted by the Art instructor on school Memorandum paper.

To Whom it may concern
From L. V.
Subject: Art Classes

AVOID VERBAL INSTRUCTION—

Class records and Art Room was left in good order when Mrs. V. substituted for me.

L. V.

The latter did not express Carrie's activity with the students. Yet Shelley, the teacher's rep, called Carrie's attention to this report, that no matter how brief, it was still a positive one, with emphasis on what Art teachers and all teachers would hope for with a sub—the classroom and records were left in *good order.*

Reading each of these reports renewed Carrie's spirit and confidence in the truth being upheld by human nature, by her teaching colleagues.

Carrie was grateful for their Christmas holiday. Away from school, enjoyment with family and close friends did much to restore her morale. Yet January was to contain more challenges, both physical and career-wise. During the second week after the New Year, she found herself catching cold. Trying to avert its becoming worse than a beginning sniffle and soreness in her throat, she phoned her doctor, who willingly saw her at the end of the school day, gave her a shot, and advised her to take a sick day. "Tomorrow's Friday, anyway, and that plus the weekend should help you recover enough to return to school next week."

Carrie had always felt comfortable with Doctor Terry and found herself telling a bit of her experiences at school since the fall semester began. "I think they'd like me to resign!" Her words were almost a lament.

"Don't you do it!" Her doctor had toured Russia with her husband doctor, accompanying a group visit there during the Cold War. Her own daughter had been enrolled in Carrie's Russian class at her elementary school.

Arriving home and announcing her stay at home for the following day, she was warmly greeted by Matt, who brewed them each a cup of tea. Handing her the honey to add, he agreed that a sick day was in order, not only to help her physically, but to alleviate some of the stress. But January weather produced more challenges to Carrie's physical well-being. After a couple of added hours in bed, she awoke, and rising, felt better. Later in the morning, she stepped out on the front porch, reaching for the mailbox. Still in house slippers, she was unaware that what appeared to be a merely wet floor on the cement was actually a coat of ice, and down she went. She lay there, helpless, and then screamed, "Isn't there somebody out there who can help me up?" Her answer was silence. After a bit, cold and shivering, she crawled, and pulling herself up on the stoop by the door, managing to crawl back into the house. Her lower back was in pain. She returned to her bed until Matt came home after school. Describing her pain, pointing to the exact area where it radiated, he expressed concern for a possible broken bone. "Let's get your coat on and get you to Emergency." Helping her to the car, he said, "Schools should have been closed today. It seems we had an ice storm during the night. Driving was slick this morning. I was glad you didn't have to drive and never thought I should have warned you."

The young doctor in the ER introduced himself by his first and last name, just as a friend might. After the X-ray he had ordered was completed and read, he approached Carrie with a thumbs-down sign. Diagnosis: fractured tailbone. "You'll have to take some sick leave. I'll give you something for the pain. When you sit, ease yourself on a donut."

After the next two weeks, Carrie was to spend only one day at North End High School. She was informed by Personnel that she was to report to the middle school to teach in the second semester. Carrie, trained for secondary education with Major subjects, English, Russian, and History was assigned three eighth-grade Science classes and two seventh-grade Science classes for the second semester. She was to encounter more challenges before the end of the school year.

As advised, she reported to the assistant principal of Hiawatha Middle School, to whom she explained that she was still healing with a fractured tailbone, and she would need more sick days for recovery. Conscious and conscientious, Carrie offered to teach every other day for two weeks. "How about coming in Monday, Wednesday, and Friday? Then I can become acquainted with the students and will leave detailed lesson plans for a sub so they will keep up their work?"

"Are you sure you should be here at all?" Was he sincerely concerned, or was he already influenced by tales and wished to postpone the inevitable? He had been assigned to monitor her teaching evaluation.

Carrie, though cognizant of her temporary limitations, assured him she would like to try, so she could get to know the students immediately. What she learned on the very first day was the students, both seventh and eighth graders, were angry. Their teacher whom they were used to had been transferred to an elementary school. Carrie stopped to meet her before her last day. She also lamented leaving, but conceded, "It's just a job!"

The vociferous ones openly opposed this strange new teacher. They influenced some of their colleagues to join in their revolt. Carrie, always successful in gaining class attention, had to take almost a didactic stance to assume class control. She found herself phoning their former teacher for cues and advice. "Pick out the worst troublemakers and phone their parents," she advised. "I had to do that to gain their cooperation at the beginning of the school year, and it did work, but it took some time."

One father answering Carrie's call admitted they were having problems with their child at home. She had been adopted from an Asian organization and they had arranged for counseling, both for them as parents and for their adopted daughter. He decided they would withhold some special privileges until they received a better report of her behavior.

Some students in seventh grade were curious about Carrie's seat cushion. Two watched closely when she had explained the reason she sat on it, and pointed out the injured area on the skeleton in the class. Later, while she was walking away from her desk, curiosity prevailed. Both experimented by sitting on the donut. Amused, Carrie asked, "How does it feel?"

"Cool!" Grinning, they returned to their desks, and their attitude gave Carrie notice that at least she had gained their interest and a beginning cooperation. They did resume their class work with greater attention.

But from the middle school's assistant principal there was no let-up. Having been informed she would be evaluated, he began writing up his observations. Noting the difficulty she had in gaining the first class's attention, his written comments exacerbated them. His written observation focused on her inability to gain the class's attention. He had scrutinized her lesson plans that had taken Carrie the entire previous weekend to prepare, and conceded she was well prepared. Later, at their conference about his observation, Carrie shared the information she had received about one of the class's leading disrupters from her adopted father. He was to write about it in a later evaluation—*She desperately bothers parents about students whom she cannot control.* Other negative statements accompanied these remarks. Carrie realized the harassment begun in the former schools was being continued now, at her present school. Again, her situation needed the attention of the reps in the Teachers' Association. Carrie phoned Shelley. When she finished relating the circumstances under which she had been teaching during these weeks at the middle school, Shelley responded, "Time for a meeting with the principal *to enlighten him,* so let's set a date!"

When Shelley appeared, she listened to all that was said—the complaints in the evaluation reports, which Carrie refused to sign, as well as defensive statements made by the assistant principal. Then she called the principal's attention to the total situation, rampant throughout the district. She focused on Oakton's displacement of many teachers. Carrie's predecessor, whom the students were used to, had been transferred to an elementary class in another school. Students were rebelling at this change. The other science teacher, experienced with middle-school students, had been placed in preschool. A shop teacher, with over eighteen years in the high school, had been transferred to the same middle school as Carrie. He was given classes in Social Studies and seventh-grade math. There were many other misplacements of teachers throughout the system.

The meeting ended without any resolution. Gradually, Carrie found herself gaining a rapport with the students. No other evaluation efforts were conducted. When parent/teacher conferences took place, she was pleasantly surprised at the positive responses from many of the parents. One mother accompanied her daughter and openly complained about her daughter's attitude and behavior reported by another teacher.

"I am truly ashamed of my daughter!" The girl had accused Carrie of being prejudiced, but the teacher who had voiced the complaint to the student's mother was also African–American. This led Carrie to ask the rebellious seventh grader, "Are you going to accuse *him* of being prejudiced?" To this the mother answered, addressing her daughter, "You need to apologize, start behaving in class, and get your lessons done."

Another parent was a principal of an elementary school. His son, in the eighth-grade science class, was always polite, and totally unmoved by disrupting classmates. All his lessons were completed promptly with grades that were respectable. Carrie pointed all this out to his father. When his dad questioned his low test scores, Carrie suggested, "Maybe he needs to bone up a little better for his tests, but his assignments are well done." He thanked Carrie for her close interest in his son, and promised to monitor and encourage him to prepare for future tests.

It was now mid-semester. A note in Carrie's box at the Teachers' room informed her of a meeting to be held with the principal. When she arrived, he informed her that changes in her assignment were to be made the following week. The three science classes held during the forenoon were to be taken over by the science teacher, now returned back from his placement in the preschool classes. Carrie was assigned to three hours in the school's Resource Room. Only the two eighth-grade science classes held in the afternoon would remain as part of her assignment.

She became acquainted with the shop teacher, to whom Shelley had referred earlier, during the meeting with the principal. His classes were right across the hall from Carrie's. She found herself exchanging information with him about their situations. Hers was a placement in middle school science, though her certification was in English, Russian, and History, with secondary education. She had experienced both elementary and middle school teaching in Russian with much success with all ages. But her only science classes in college were Biology and Chemistry. "So I'm filing two grievances on both counts—one for middle school placement when I am certified for secondary and one for the subject placement."

When she learned he had been transferred from his high school shop class after teaching there for eighteen years, and was now placed in seventh-grade math and social studies, Carrie suggested, "You should file a grievance, as well."

Shaking his head, he replied, "No, that's not my style!" But between February and May the man had lost thirty pounds, and at his doctor's advice went on a medical leave for the remainder of the school year. Later, Carrie was informed by another staff member, a friend of the shop teacher, that he had been threatened if he filed a grievance, he would never again return to his former position as high school shop teacher.

Carrie became acquainted with the man hired to substitute for the ailing absent teacher. His substitute had recently returned home from the mission field. It was now about five weeks before the end of the school year. The substitute was only called every two days. Why? So he would not be qualified for receiving any benefits that permanent teachers were contracted to receive. He was facing some of the difficulties subs experience from students who were rebelling at this change in teachers. Henry, as he introduced himself to Carrie, was looking forward to the following fall and was already contracted to be teaching at the Bible School close to Carrie's home. The Bible School occupied the buildings that were formerly owned by Carrie's alma mater. Though Henry's salary would be much lower than that of public school teachers, he was looking forward to more favorable teaching conditions. Students were candidates for pastorates, mission work, and other Christian church staff openings. Many were talented in music. Carrie was impressed by Henry's anticipation. She had no idea what the future held for her. Yet she was determined to help the kids in the Resource Room as much as possible. Matt, always encouraging, had told her, "You can do it, Car, just brighten the corner where you are." She was later able to look back on some very successful results from her teaching experiences there.

There were two in particular. Arriving at the Resource Room one morning, she noted the sad face of Dan, with his Geography book closed. When she asked, "What are you studying today?" his reply was, "Nothing. It's no use. I'm gonna flunk the test anyway!" Ignoring his lament, Carrie proceeded, "Well, let's look at the material for a minute." He opened his book to the chapter assigned.

"Will you read what it says for me?" There were some statistics about the South American country, population, square mileage and size, products produced, and customs of the people in the country.

As the boy read the information, Carrie found herself taking notes to use later. After the student completed reading several pages, Carrie asked him to stop and look at the map. "This is a real place. You might even visit there some day. Now tell me what you think is most important to you about what you have read."

Amazingly, his interest was caught. He looked at the illustrations showing the type of clothing the people were wearing and decided that if he lived there, he would be wearing the same type. He recalled that they produced cocoa and coffee beans, certain plants, and vegetables. The country was much smaller than the United States, with less people, but what they did was important. He loved chocolate.

Feeling confident with this start, Carrie had him continue to read to the end of the chapter. This was Tuesday, and the test would not be until Friday. So, she showed him how to take notes of the important information in the chapter. Then she used his notes to ask questions on the various topics contained. She gave him a pass to come to her room during her planning time to drill him some more. On the following Monday he came to the Resource Room, waving his test paper. He had earned a 94. Smiling, Carrie nodded, exclaiming, "I knew you could do it!"

But the joy for his accomplishment was short-lived. One of the rebels in the Resource Room, maybe envious of his classmate's success, bellowed, "Oh, Danny, she yo' mama?"

Carrie was happy and thankful for the male teacher who was serving for that hour in the Resource Room. Hearing the derogatory remarks, he responded. First, he congratulated Dan for earning his grade, then lit into the young rebel, reminding him that Carrie was there to help with lessons, and she could help him, as well, if he would only cooperate and *settle down*. Gradually, days later, Carrie was able to win this student's confidence when he was ready to accept her help.

The other student Carrie would always remember was Crista. A beautiful child, she had a birthmark in the middle of her forehead. She came to the Resource Room, sat quietly, but did not seem to be working at her lessons. Carrie questioned her. "What are you doing right now?" She shrugged her shoulders, yet didn't say anything at first, but later she explained, "I was sick, so I'm too far behind in Geography, and I lost some of my pages."

"Who is your teacher?" When Crista replied, Carrie went to the teacher's classroom and addressed the situation. "Yes, she's very far behind, and I don't know if I can even pass her." When Carrie explained that Crista was missing some papers, and asked if she could have copies so she could help her each day until she caught up, the teacher expressed surprise. "Are you willing to help her do that?" "Of course, I will." The Geography teacher gladly supplied all missing items, and day by day, Carrie worked with Crista. She also gave her an additional incentive. "When you pass, I'll take you out to lunch." Crista, now encouraged, continued until she completed all the lessons. At the end of the semester, she had raised her grade from failing to a C+. Although the lunch room was closed on the last week of school, when Crista produced her grade report, Carrie gave her two dollars to spend for a lunch wherever she chose. In closure, Carrie told her, "I'm very proud of you."

Finally, at the end of the semester, Carrie was informed of a special meeting she was to attend to bring about closure with her grievances. Several important people were present, an assistant principal in charge of teacher negotiations; the teacher's association rep; and an important member of the school board. The school board member's name was Slavic, one Carrie could translate from the Polish and would always remember—it meant *By Jesus* or *by the way of Jesus.*

Shelley took charge of explaining Carrie's position to the school board member. He listened intently. A union member himself and supportive of employees' rights, he expressed strong disapproval of Carrie's placement. "Why would you assign a talented instructor in Russian and seasoned in Language Arts and place her in science classes? Why remove her from secondary status to the middle school? This does not make sense. I wonder, why am I even here, called upon to discuss this?"

The negotiating assistant superintendent, considered by the teachers to be a real *barracuda,* attempted to explain. At first, he spoke of Carrie's teaching in a complimentary manner. "We had to assign the most experienced person for that position."

"But the most opportunity I had to help students in language and social studies was in the Resource Room, to which I was assigned during the last half of this past semester. Another teacher with far less seniority was given the English position," Carrie defended.

"Yes, and we had a meeting about the threatening evaluating statements attempted during the first half of this semester. Apparently the administrator over Carrie had not been informed of your reasons for placing her in this assignment," were Shelly's pointed remarks.

Then the *barracuda* explained further. "It seems that the mistake of Carrie's placement came about because of an inaccurate assessment of her credentials done by another administrator, Mr. Berkley."

Aha, Carrie thought silently, realizing that *now they're using that man for the 'fall guy.'*

"But we're going to place you in an English position, if we don't reopen the Russian program again. I will consult with Rick on secondary positions open in the fall. Will this meet with your approval?"

Shelley expressed consent. "We will be monitoring all future action in this case."

When Carrie met with Rick to discuss her fall teaching assignment, he gave her the name of a principal at a southeast high school. Carrie phoned him to make an appointment. His secretary took the message with Carrie's home number. The principal returned her call an hour later. When asked her reason for meeting him, he replied, "But I have a good English teacher now, and I want to keep her."

"But I believe I do have more seniority and more years of experience," Carrie countered.

"Doesn't matter, I don't want to change her," he replied.

Had he been talking with two other principals? Carrie wondered.

When Carrie called Rick to report their brief conversation, he gave her the name of the principal at West Side High School. Before attempting to phone him, Carrie decided to confer with Shelley at the Teachers' Association. Shelley admitted that Carrie was in for a challenge. "You certainly are entitled to that first position, but you don't want to face another uphill battle. Try the West Side High School. It might prove better."

It did not prove better. This principal was more polite, but *politely* explained that he felt a strong loyalty to keeping his present English teacher, though she had less seniority than Carrie, but would be retiring in another year. "I feel I owe this to her."

Carrie knew this teacher, if not as a friend, then at least as a friendly acquaintance. She had attended classes with her. Never having been married, after a number of years' work as an office secretary, she decided to return to school and enroll for teacher training. Bewildered by her situation, Carrie confided to the direct supervisor who had monitored her evening Russian classes. Both he and the director were pleased at the number of enrollees, which included the high school students enrolled for credit.

"Look, forget these daytime politics. Bill likes how you teach and he and I both want to invite you into Community Ed. You'll be able to use your creativity to help a lot of people. Why not apply for a transfer?"

And transfer she did. But now, Carrie was looking forward to summer with Matt and "sleeping in" some mornings, after watching a late classic movie in the rec room, one of her favorite spots for *letting go.* Unlike her later sleeping hours, Matt was a morning person. He made their coffee and sometimes brought cereal with sliced banana or turkey bacon and her favorite upside-down egg to her in bed. Often, the tray held a freshly-cut rose from his garden, product of his favorite hobby.

Their summer included a vacation trip to Stratford in Canada, where both enjoyed the theatre. Matt tolerated certain Shakespeare plays for Carrie's sake. Realizing his thoughtfulness, she always tried to include a Gilbert and Sullivan or a contemporary play. He did enjoy Chekhov, and over the years they viewed most of the well-known favorites, two of which Carrie had taught in Lit classes. Carrie usually made reservations from home, before their trip. She tried to include as much theatre as possible in the four days they spent in Stratford. Sometimes, they included tours to Kitchener and St. Mary's or London to see the shops or fairs. Toronto, only about ninety miles away, also beckoned them.

Some summers they visited the Dutch cousins who lived in the suburbs of Toronto for a time. They also made their home in Toronto for a number of years. Cathy was a first cousin to Matt. After surviving the Nazi occupation of the Netherlands during World War II, Cathy's husband wanted to emigrate to the United States. However, the quota was filled for the U.S., so they moved to Canada, instead. Here they built their fortune, lived well, and enjoyed visits from family and friends. Matt and Carrie were their guests a number of times, and were hosted to wonderful hospitality. The cousins always enjoyed seeing each other and shared family updates amid lots of laughter and fun. One particular visit included attending a European-style wedding of their daughter. Unlike their American counterparts, attending the same church, they enjoyed the dancing and fellowship with friends and family as they would have in Europe.

The fall assignment in Community Ed brought about changes in teaching styles for Carrie. Some activities included recruiting students who had not completed high school training. Carrie and her colleagues spent the first two weeks enrolling returning students, eager to earn a high school diploma. Carrie recalled how she and Matt had struggled through college as mature adults with a family, and related well to these adult students. At first, she was assigned to the very same building where Matt had begun teaching full time. Her immediate director was experienced and thoughtfully introduced her to their procedures. Some students were single mothers. Others had physical disabilities. One common factor was that all knew their social security numbers by heart. This was important for identification and proof of attendance. The aim of their education was both completion and eligibility for the job market.

On mornings, driving to the school, Carrie passed the buildings occupied by the Bible School, where her newly-made acquaintance subbing at the middle school was now teaching. These buildings were familiar to Carrie. Formerly, they had been owned by the college that was now her *alma mater,* and she had been enrolled in a number of classes there. She remembered Henry's description of the school. To herself, she muttered, "Boy, I would love to teach at a place like this even if I had to give up my salary for lower pay." It was not really a prayer, but later, Carrie, believing, realized the Lord was listening.

It was about three weeks into the fall school year when a note was found in Carrie's box at the school to which she was assigned. Bill, the director, asked her to stop at his office before arriving at her school the following morning. She wondered at his request.

When she arrived, he gave the reason—"Michigan law allows all young people between ages eighteen and twenty to be given free continuing education. The Bible School has asked us to send them an English teacher. You certainly would qualify, so I made an appointment for you to meet with them this afternoon. If you like them and they like you, you have the job. Of course, we will receive state aid and you will be paid by us at your contracted salary rate."

Astounded, Carrie was nervous. She recalled that one of her Russian students from the Downtown Program told her he planned to enroll at this Bible School. Henry was already teaching there now. When she entered the office of the president, she was met by three people—an instructor in Bible teaching, the registrar, and the president. All three greeted her warmly. She reminded the president she had met him before when he had been one of five successive speakers at her church. The topic was "The Second Coming." He seemed glad that she remembered him. "Oh, yes, that was at the Lutheran Church."

During their conversation, Carrie asked if her former Russian student was now attending here. The registrar and the teacher both knew him. Their conversation ended with setting the time for her arrival—on the following Monday she could begin teaching the morning English classes. The students would be enrolled in Community Ed registration forms. After their meeting, the president closed with a request to see Carrie privately for a few minutes.

His words were interesting to Carrie. "I know you're a Lutheran Christian and I believe you take your faith seriously. Now, there may be a few zealous students who might try to convert you. If they do, just tell them 'I'm here to teach English.' You don't have to feel intimidated by them."

As Carrie drove away to attend the other school, where she would be teaching from noon till two-thirty, she reminisced about her hope. *It was not even a prayer, just a wish, but the Lord heard me. After all the challenges and trials of this past year, what a wonderful opportunity has opened up for me. Thank You, God. To think, God arranged for me to get this job as three-fifths of my assignment, and no decrease in pay. Wait till I tell Matt! Carrie was reminded of the memory she had of Joseph, the son of Jacob in the Bible, and his many challenges. He kept his faith, and in the end, he was rewarded by becoming the Prime Minister of Egypt.*

When Carrie returned to the afternoon classes, she told her immediate director what had happened. "I should tell Bill, he sent me there."

"Use my phone!" Her director punched the keys to Bill's office and handed her the phone.

"I'm glad this worked out," Bill responded. "Now, sign up every student you have on those same forms we used in your other classes. This will help our count for state aid."

On the home front, there loomed another challenge, one that Matt described after Carrie shared her experience. He did express happiness for her and their family both, that all had come about so well. "The Lord is looking out after you. Now there is other news."

Carrie was to enjoy nine successful years of teaching the young adults, as well as a few middle-aged persons who felt called to Christ's ministry. They came from all parts of the United States, as well as from other countries of the world, from Norway, Nigeria, Australia, and Japan, to mention a few. Carrie and Matt both were blessed by their friendships throughout her years there. Their prayers and support during the challenges their family faced were thoughtful and comforting. God's promise to retrieve the years that the locusts have eaten surely had come through.

Carrie would always wonder *why*. Why did God allow her son to become dyslexic? His three sisters were very verbal. She and Matt had done all possible to educate him and help him grow. Sometimes they had to sidestep the obstacles set before them. Not many people understood him. He had his own way of doing things. Now, why this additional challenge in his life, when he had found someone to share it with?

Tim was diagnosed with testicular cancer. Surgery was strongly recommended. It took place on Maundy Thursday. Tim suffered pain for three days. It was not until Easter Sunday evening that relief came for him. To Carrie, Tim's medical experience seemed to parallel with that of the Lord, whose Resurrection took place after his painful scourging, intense human suffering, and death on the cross.

When Tim was released from the hospital and returned home to his wife, they found their situation had changed. No longer were they able to share the intimacy that had bound them together at the beginning. The physicians, having succeeded in removing all vestiges of the cancer, were able to report the positive results to their patient. What neither was able to help with was this personal husband and wife lovemaking the young couple had previously enjoyed during their first year of marriage. Conflicts arose that they could not comprehend or handle.

Several months later, Carrie popped in to visit, bringing a bag of grapes for Timmy. She walked in to find them packing boxes, filling them with clothing and other items. When she inquired, Tim's wife answered, "We're moving. We got a house to rent next door to my folks. It's cheaper, and Tim will be closer to his job. It's too hard on him having to drive round trip thirty miles every day. And now that we're moving, him and me are getting along much better."

Matt was more receptive to the change than Carrie. "They have made this decision. Let them go. They need to live their own lives." And he set about to run a rental ad in the local paper. Two young women, fresh out of college, answered and moved in shortly. Carrie was thankful for her husband's care of their family needs and support during her time of challenges. Yet their move did not help the young couple. The months that followed revealed a lack of willingness for Tim's wife to live up to the promise she had made at their marriage, and again, the words she spoke when learning of his inability to father a child. "So, we'll adopt!"

Nine months after Maria IV passed away, the phone call came. Matt answered.

"Dad, will you come and get me, Tammie wants us to separate."

And Matt brought his son home.

Chapter XII

All Things Work Together for Good

Time brings about changes. Not only are individuals affected, but whole communities and nations. It is interesting that even enemies learn to tolerate each other for various reasons. After the intense struggle against the spread of communism in Viet Nam and elsewhere in the Seventies, the Eighties brought about reactionary forces from individuals on both sides. Responsible persons took action in various ways. There were visits to each other's countries. Open communication took place whenever possible. Leadership in both the Soviet Union and the United States became aware of the great expense and danger of the competitive nuclear arms race.

Listening to a speaker at an assembly of students at the University of Michigan, broadcast on her kitchen radio, Carrie took in his comments with great interest. After all, the study of Russian language and culture had been her strong academic interest for a number of years. The speaker, a retired naval officer, was urging his listeners to phone the White House to protest the continued nuclear arms build-up. When question time arrived, one student asked him, "Do you trust the Russians?"

"Yes, I trust the Russians. The Russian people love their children just as we Americans love ours, and they want to raise them in a world of peace, without the threat of annihilation."

The speaker repeated his advice to all listeners, those with ears to their radios, as well as to his student audience, to phone the White House, offering the direct phone number.

"Address the United States president and voice your protest toward continuing this nuclear arms race." Carrie was rejoicing at this encouragement from a mature military retiree. She recalled the great sacrifices the Russian allies experienced during the Second World War, the loss of over 20 million people, as well as suffering major destruction to their homeland. Their price was great for the victory that was achieved. Now, Carrie felt gratified for her academic goals in teaching Russian, in spite of meeting numerous challenges.

Carrie had been teaching Russian language and culture for more than two decades. Although after nine years, the Downtown School had closed the regular high school program, the evening classes in Community Education flourished. The director welcomed the enrollment of high school students who wanted to continue Russian studies and expanded the attendance time to two evenings per week to allow them to earn credits for graduation. Adults studied alongside the youngsters. Some were businessmen, affiliated with firms doing business with the Soviet Union. There were a few teachers planning to teach English in Russia. Some planned to travel and signed up for tours being offered.

Probably the most interesting student of all was a woman accompanied by two friends. During their third lesson, she surprised Carrie with her reading and careful pronunciation of the language. When Carrie complimented and questioned her, she revealed her history. She had been separated from her family in the Ukraine during World War II. The invading Nazis captured her and sent her to Germany to labor on a farm in Germany. Fortunately, the family there was kind to her. After the war, she was given refuge in the United States where she enrolled in a Christian college. She used her teaching degree on the mission field for a number of years. Now retired, she planned to return to visit a sister who was still alive in the Ukraine. Her two friends and classmates, who had enrolled in the class with her, volunteered to accompany her to her homeland.

A friend of Carrie's had taken the initiative to form an appendage locally to an organization called the Peace Links. Peace Links, founded by a senator's wife, gained a following of members who opposed the Reagan nuclear arms build-up. Gathering a group of interested women, the organization was able to arrange for visitors from the Soviet Union. Carrie and Matt hosted two of the women who were in leadership positions in the Soviet Union. The third visitor was from Lithuania and hosted by another Peace Link. Their main focus was to share their concerns about the mounting arms race and the need for individuals from both countries to establish friendships, and learn about each other's hopes and dreams for peace in the world. It was a challenging trip for the visitors as they had to come to the U.S. from Canada. At that time, during the Carter Administration, their plane was not allowed to land in the United States.

Russian women visited with Americans in Carrie and Matt's home as guests of Peace Links. (Left to right) Two Soviet visitors, Chairperson Annette Remsburg of Peace Links, a third Soviet visitor, and two members of Peace Links.

The three-day visit was filled with activity. It began with a welcome meeting with Peace Links members at the airport on a Saturday morning. Registration for a workshop, starting with a luncheon and followed by two sessions, filled four hours of the afternoon. The workshop topics included Everyday life in the Soviet Union; historical background as key to understanding; woman to woman, across international borders and involving ourselves, contributing to Peace. The facilitators included two professors of political science, instructors at the local college where the sessions were being held. Dinner was held with hosts of the visitors, followed by a performance of the town's symphony orchestra.

On Sunday morning, the Soviet visitors would spend time with their hosts. The two being hosted by Carrie and Matt accompanied them to their church service. Carrie had arranged for a special Russian hymn to be sung in their honor—the tune was composed by Alex F. Lvov, 1799–1870. The focus was a prayerful plea for peace authored by two writers, one writing the first two stanzas, and the

In October 1985, a Soviet Women's Committee delegation visited the USA at the invitation of the American organization "Peace Links Women Against Nuclear War."

second adding on the third and fourth. Words of the first and fourth follow the plea throughout the hymn, titled *God the Omnipotent:*

Great God the Omnipotent, King Who ordaineth

Give to us peace in our time, O Lord

God the all-wise By the fire of Thy chast'ning

Earth shall to freedom and truth be restored

Through the thick darkness Thy kingdom is hast'ning

Thou wilt give peace in Thy time O Lord.

The Russian visitors recognized the tune and liked the words in the hymn. They realized its complement to their mission.

The afternoon included a tour of the city. Everyone from Europe wants to visit Lake Michigan. That was next on the agenda, and after that, a visit to the neighboring towns of Holland and Grand Haven. Dinner was hosted by the Methodist Church in Holland.

Departure took place early the next morning for Minneapolis,

Russians on a peace mission are, from left, Yeta Renszer,
Vera Soboleva, and Antonina Khripkova.

where other Peace Links members planned to continue hosting the Soviet visitors.

On the following year, several Eastern Orthodox clergy men from the USSR, sponsored by a Congregational church, came to visit. They were hopeful to make friends with other Christian clergy here. Carrie was approached to attend the meeting being held to introduce the visiting priest and two deacons. After hesitating, she was persuaded to attend. However, no one briefed her as to why she was invited. As the meeting was to take place, Carrie was offered a chair at the front of the conference room, seated next to the three visiting clergy. Expectations of her were to translate the statements made by the priest and his accompanying deacon. It was assumed that because one is familiar with a language, one should be able to translate into English for the visiting audience. Carrie had never been in such a challenging position. Translators are at a disadvantage if they are not familiar with the person's voice. Carrie's rescuer was the other deacon who helped out because he was familiar with English. A couple of times he was able to offer a correct word before Carrie had translated it. Later, she encountered the pastor's wife, who had invited Carrie to the conference.

(From left) Hieromonk Irinarkh Gresin, Archimandrite Tiran Gurghesian, and Archpriest Sergly Suzaltsev.

"I'm afraid I did not understand I would be expected to translate. I'm a teacher of *beginning* Russian, and not a trained translator, as was expected."

Her host was apologetic. She explained that she had not been told this would be expected of Carrie. Added to Carrie's discomfort was the remark made by the photographer who had observed Carrie's grope for words—"When you're unsure what to say, you should fake it!" Out of character for Carrie!

The evening and the following day proved much more enjoyable. Dinner was hosted for all at the Catholic convent. The boys choir, led by their very talented director, sang a hymn that Carrie remembered was part of their Sunday morning liturgy at the first church she and Matt attended in the early years of their marriage:

All glory be to Thee most high, to Thee all adoration

In grace and truth thou drawest nigh to offer us salvation,

Thou showest Thy good will to men

And peace shall reign on earth again

We praise Thy name forever.

Later, the English-speaking member of the Russian clergy approached Carrie. He was greatly impressed by the singing of the boys' choir and questioned Carrie, "Is this how you gain the interest of your young people, by having them sing?"

Of course, Carrie knew that the Communist regime would not have encouraged or even allowed young people to attend church or sing praises to the Lord. She merely shrugged her shoulder in response, not wanting to remind the priest of their homeland's political situation. Soon after, she was to realize how much attitudes toward religion had been changing; the religious faith of Soviet citizens, under the political leadership of Mikhail Gorbachev, had become more freely expressed. A succeedingly-elected president, Medvedev, had publicly announced his Orthodox faith. He did explain this was a very private choice.

On the next morning, there was another gathering, allowing the local clergy to meet again with the Russian visitors. Carrie had copies of side by side Russian/English New Testaments to give their visitors. Gifts from Russia were received. Carrie was given a *matryoshka*, the doll containing several progressively smaller dolls inside her. Breakfast was served and a small prayer service took place before the visitors had to depart for home. Before they left, it was announced that one of the American clergy was celebrating a birthday that day. The Russian priest took this opportunity to sing the birthday song, *Mnogo let,* thus creating a rather happy ending to a successful visit. It opened a new era for both countries to have visitors come and express their hopes for peaceful relationships and freedom of expression.

However, whatever the lack of certain rights and privileges Russian people experienced under the Communist yoke, there were a number among their citizens who spoke up for human rights and opposed the restrictions imposed upon them by the Communist regime. There was the writer, Alexander Solzhenitsyn, who bravely wrote, criticizing Stalin's administration and certain political followers who tried to prevent free thinking. There were *Samizdat' writers.* One very brave and distinguished spokesman had expressed his views already in the seventies. Both Carrie and Matt continued to observe these spokesmen who dared to oppose the system under which they were forced to exist. There had been one important voice they were to appreciate and acknowledge together as the free western world was watching.

Matt, Carrie's wonderful support, shared information he had read in the book, *Sakharov Speaks,* written by the world-renowned Soviet physicist, Andrei Sakharov, and published in 1974. Added to his reading, Matt had collected a number of articles which he placed in his copy of Sakharov's book. The physicist endured many hardships for his openness under the Communist regime. He publicly championed human rights. For this, he acquired a following. The Communist government removed him from Moscow, the intellectual haven, and forced him to live in Gorki. When it was announced that Sakharov was to receive the 1975 Nobel Peace Prize, the Soviet government would not allow him to leave the country and travel to Norway to receive it. However, his wife, who was in Italy for medical treatment, was able to attend the ceremony and accept her husband's award. Present were King Olav and other members of the Norwegian royal family, who watched as Yelena Sakharov received the prize money, gold medal, and diploma from Aase Lionaes, the chairwoman of the Norwegian parliamentary committee, which nominated Sakharov for his fight for human rights in the Soviet Union.

The persecution of Sakharov's family members was to continue into the eighties. When their daughter-in-law, Liza Alekseyeva, applied for a visa to travel to the United States in order to join her husband, a graduate student at Brandeis University, she was refused. Finally, after Sakharov and his wife had been on a hunger strike reported to the entire outside world, she was granted permission by the KGB to travel to the U.S. Prior to her departure, she was allowed to visit the Sakharovs in Gorki. Sakharov was also refused attendance in courtrooms where other dissidents were being tried for anti-Soviet statements. The western world was watching. It was the hope of many observers that changes would take place. But let us now consider the changes in the lives of our hero and heroine.

The eighties brought changes in the lives of Matt and Carrie's family, or rather, in their children's families. Durinda, who was left a widow with the death of Chad, was now remarried to Bud. Less than a year later, they had a son, whom they named after his great-grandfather, Anton. Wren gave birth to a daughter, whom she named after her dear childhood caretaker, Johanna. Wren's cousin, Christine, gave her the nickname, Joey— that the family adopted. Even more meaningful to Carrie was a new awareness that arose between her and her father, Anton. It came about quite unexpectedly, during a week's visit Anton made in his daughter's home. Now, at age eighty-seven, Anton had become a widower for a second time in his life. Father and daughter spoke to each other with a new openness, an openness that had ceased to continue in Carrie's early childhood, after Anton's second marriage—ceased after developing a special father/daughter relationship, with the evening bedtime stories and songs of her earlier childhood.

Matt drove through a flooded Chicago late that summer, when he and Carrie took Anton with them to visit at their home in Michigan. He drove on the higher road past O'Hare Airport to avoid more deep flooding, driving southward, through Indiana, toward Michigan. Anton seemed to enjoy visiting. He had the double opportunity to visit with his granddaughter, Anna, who was visiting at the home of her parents during this same time. They even got to experience an escapade together while they were at home. Their hosts were absent, doing errands, and when the two walked outdoors, the door was accidentally locked. Neither could budge it. What to do? They noticed that the second-floor bedroom window facing the north was wide open. Anton did not hesitate. He promptly removed the ladder from the garage, and placing it right beneath the open window, climbed it and entered into the house through that window. Anna, who had helped by holding the ladder to prevent shakiness, quickly met him by the locked door. Quite a feat for an eighty-seven-year-old!

Learning of the episode when she and Matt returned home, Carrie began to scold her dad, reminding him of the danger. But Anton boldly defended his action—"I wanted to do it, so if I wanted to do it, I did it!"

Later that evening, father and daughter entered into conversation. Anton found himself questioning Carrie. "You left all of us, you left us. Why did you leave us?"

Carrie recalled the events of that Sunday morning. She had a childhood tiff with her younger sister, for which she was given a harsh beating by Maria II. Although Anton was present, he merely watched silently. Maria II decided Carrie was not worthy enough to attend church with the rest of the family, so off they all went, leaving Carrie home alone, crying. It was then that Carrie made up her mind to change living conditions. She packed a few clothes in two brown grocery bags, checked her purse for carfare, and finding all doors locked, did remember she could escape by opening the bedroom window that led to the front porch. At its end was the top of the stairway going down to the yard; a few steps to the alleyway, and beyond a block or two, was the road where she could board the streetcar to the home of her Aunt Mary.

Now for the first time in many years, she felt free to be candid. After all, this was her dad, with whom she was once very close. He was the person who taught her so much in his native language—the stories, the songs, the very speech that was the heritage he had bestowed on her. In her adult life it had proven to be an intangible gift.

"You don't know why I left, Dad? I got tired of being beaten up."

Anton remained silent as he studied her face. He walked away without a word.

A day or two later, when Anton was already packed and waiting for Matt to announce the time he would be leaving to take his father-in-law home to Chicago, Anton quietly approached Carrie. His words were simple, but they seemed to be from his heart—"Karolina," he addressed her in the native language, followed in his simple English, "if I was a *bad boy,* will you forgive me?"

At that moment, Carrie was unsure whether her father was referring to the ladder climbing incident or the hurts of the past. She merely nodded. Later, when she was relating her father's words to Matt, he suggested that her father was asking her forgiveness for the mistakes of the past.

The eighties had brought about a number of changes in the family for Matt and Carrie. After much attempt on the part of Tim's parents to bring about a reconciliation with his wife, the two separated. The pastor/counselor meeting with the couple for several months, was unable to bring about the progress he and the parents hoped for. Their marriage had ended in divorce.

Tim bought a home with extra sleeping quarters and was able to rent them to lodgers. It proved to be a learning experience for Tim. Tenants varied in values. Some failed at rent payments and had to be asked to leave. Then for a long period of time, he had two stable tenants who appreciated living in a home rather than an apartment. Tim found himself a second job and began establishing a bank account. Dates were few and far between. It would be almost a decade before he became involved in a serious relationship again. However, he was to enjoy doing things with his dad. One adventure took place in the spring of '89. Tim was able to arrange for vacation time to accompany Matt for a trip to Texas. Matt had already retired from his teaching job. The volunteer work that involved much of his time did allow him freedom to join his son for this special trip. They were to tour both southern Texas and the bordering area of Mexico. Tim had long wanted to return to Texas and enjoy, not only the sights around the southwest border, but also tour some of Juarez and taste genuine Mexican gourmet.

Although Carrie was still teaching, she was able to use her spring vacation time, as well as add several days' leave of absence to fulfill a long-time dream—travel to Russia. It began on a Monday morning, when the limousine pulled up in the driveway. Carrie's friend, CeeCee, had already arrived earlier, when her husband, supporting his adventurous wife, brought her to Carrie's. CeeCee, with eight other adult ed students, as well as two spouses, formed the group who together would be touring Russia. The first stop was the airport in Detroit. There was a several-hour wait for the plane that would take the group to Frankfurt. From there, another plane would transport them to Leningrad. Extra special for Carrie was that in Leningrad she would be met upon arrival by her cousin's son, Zdenek, from Czechoslovakia. He had been studying engineering in Moscow. When Carrie wrote his mom, Eva, and described the details of her forthcoming trip to Russia, Eva arranged for her son to meet Carrie at the airport in Leningrad.

When their flight brought them to Frankfurt, they boarded the plane for Leningrad. The plane was almost empty. Other than Carrie's group, the only travelers consisted of a musical band. It seemed they had a contract to play American jazz for a club in Leningrad. The genre was welcome to Russians, especially the young. Many of them enjoyed American music, as well as customs. The band played a number of pieces that gave entertainment to their fellow travelers.

It was still daylight when the plane landed in Leningrad Airport. Zdenek was waiting for Carrie, approaching her with a bouquet of flowers. Second cousins. Children of moms who were first cousins. Carrie had not seen Zdenek since he was a little boy, ten years earlier. Now he was grown, studying to become an engineer, and engaged to be married soon. After completing his tour in Leningrad, he would be returning by train to Czechoslovakia, where he would attend his wedding ceremony.

Most of Carrie's group passed without much note at the airport. It was only Carrie and one other member of her group who were required to have their luggage opened and examined. Two items attracted the attention of the examiner—copies of side-by-side Russian/English New Testaments printed by the Slavic Gospel Association and copies of the *Christian History* magazine, featuring the article describing Russia's Thousand Year Anniversary of Christianity. The examining guard also opened the envelope containing the wedding card and gift of U.S. dollars for Zdenek and his bride. Was this gift considered illegal? Zdenek, standing by Carrie's side, explained Carrie was his family member and the gift was for him and his bride. The guard accepted his explanation. Eager to be friendly and open, Carrie offered the guard a New Testament and a copy of the magazine. The guard accepted both. Opening the magazine, he smiled at the photographed painting of Vladimir and his people involved in a joint baptism a millennium ago.

The bus had been waiting for the group to board. Present was the tour guide, who had been assigned to lead and direct Carrie's group. She accompanied them to the hotel *Pribaltiyskaya,* where their accommodations awaited them. Their guide introduced herself as Gilda. Speaking impeccable English, she advised them to plan for breakfast at 8:00 a.m., and to be ready to board the tour bus at nine. When Zdenek announced he would be accompanying Carrie's group, the guide nodded, already alerted that a student would accompany the group. He then left the group to spend the night at a students' hostel. Their names had already been registered and the maître d' gave each pair their room numbers. CeeCee, who was Carrie's roommate, commented on the comfortable beds and quilts. Also, being aware and practical, she expressed great approval of the water-saving flush toilet in their private bathroom.

Was it commonly accepted jet-lag or the excitement of finally arriving in Russia that prevented Carrie from sleeping soundly this first night? When it was time to waken and get ready for the day, her body wanted to tuck in and sleep. But this would be a first tour of this wonderful city and hot coffee with breakfast should fix things.

The bus took them everywhere in Leningrad. Everything Carrie had studied and learned about vicariously now came alive. Peter the Great wanted his city (then named St. Petersburg) to be outstanding, with canals like those he saw in Holland, where he went to personally learn ship building. Carrie viewed the various waterways, canals, and bridges as if all these sites were magic. Zdenek's status as a student allowed him to travel with the group without pay, under an arrangement made by the Russian government. Throughout the four days that Zdenek accompanied them, they toured and visited many historical sites. Each left a significant impression upon Carrie.

After their bus tour of the city, they visited the Tsar's village and the summer palace. Now, this village had been renamed Pushkin. The palace that had been badly damaged by Nazi planes was completely restored. For a number of years after the close of World War II, a group of art students working to earn graduate degrees, rebuilt and refinished the interior to its original settings. The damaged furnishings had been replaced in their very same original styles and sizes. The dedication to restore and preserve was incredible.

There were many other important sites to visit. Among them was the cemetery where Russian poets and musicians were buried. There was the naval port where the son of Peter the Great had been held prisoner before his untimely death, and the Hermitage, to which Carrie traveled with second-cousin Zdenek, and his colleague. Although they had been forbidden to take photos, both awaited the times when the two forbidding elderly women employed as *watch dogs* were not looking, and snapped the desired photos, at risk of being scolded or threatened to have their cameras confiscated. They did receive a scolding after being caught taking the first snapshot. Carrie felt a sense of guilt, when she realized they were trying to photograph a few pictures of her choice, to oblige her as their guest.

CeeCee repeatedly tried phoning one of the Peace Links visitors at her office, hoping they could meet for lunch and visit, but was not successful. It seemed she called at the wrong times, in between bus stops. However, she was successful in contacting their friend, Zina, whom they had met during her visit in the U.S. Zina was happy to see them and invited them all for dinner, including young Zdenek. The apartment building was very drab, but the inside of Zina's apartment was tastefully decorated, European-style and light. What a lovely evening, to be at home with a friend after touring, eating out and residing at a hotel which was really a *substitute home*. The visitors got to meet Zina's husband, who did know some English. Zina served a very delicious dinner, chicken Russian/European style. Although there was no formal dining room, the group ate around a low table, oval-shaped, and large enough to accommodate all. Both Zina and her husband were now retired, so after dinner, they discussed some of their activities and shared photos of their visits, including some Zina had brought back from the U.S. Their conversation did not dote on politics. This visit was pure friendship. When it was time to leave, Zina called a taxi to return them to their hotel. Carrie and Zina exchanged gifts and Carrie gave her a copy of the English/Russian New Testament.

Another delightful visit took place at the *Pribaltiyskaya*. Somehow, Carrie met a young woman in the lounge. She was from Georgia. What brought her here? She and her husband were newlyweds and were registered in the honeymoon suite. Carrie spoke with her in Russian, but learned her new acquaintance also knew English. As they chatted, Carrie asked about her wedding. Had they married in a *Pravoslavny tserkov*? When she nodded, Carrie told her she had something to give her. They went to the floor where Carrie and CeeCee were staying, the same floor where the honeymoon suite was located. She waited as Carrie fetched a copy of the English/Russian New Testament. How excited she was to receive it! Carrie was reminded that, with the advent of President Gorbachev, worship and religion were no longer forbidden. Her new friend invited Carrie, with CeeCee and Zdenek, to their suite after relating her experience to her new husband, for they were used to caution with new people, especially foreigners. They served tea, and pastries and chocolates, and she gave Carrie several gifts from Georgia, a scarf, and pin, and bracelet. They exchanged addresses. They were able to exchange Christmas greetings and her card had an enclosed note, inviting Carrie and her husband to visit them in Georgia. Although they were not able to travel to Georgia, for a long time they corresponded.

Later, when Zdenek spoke of their meeting, he commented that their hosts were *good Georgians,* in a manner that made Carrie wonder if propaganda may have given him reason to believe that Georgians were *bad people.* Anyway, she was happy to have made a new friend from a foreign country. There would be other opportunities to make new friends and acquaintances as they traveled through the Soviet Union.

One of the requests Carrie made when making her reservation to tour the Soviet Union was to visit a school. Somehow, this did not appear on the list given the tour guide. When Carrie asked her about the request, she was surprised and did not think this was possible. Both CeeCee and Carrie expressed deep disappointment, for this had been a major goal for visiting Russia. Some of the members on the trip were not interested, but several others joined Carrie in expressing their interest in seeing a school. The tour guide was successful in arranging the visit at an English-speaking school, School 1234. The alternative for those not interested in touring the school was a visit at a shopping mall during that time.

The students were happy to see their American visitors. One student presented Carrie with a large photo of President Gorbachev. Later, after visiting several classrooms with students of various grade levels, the visitors were treated to watching a portion of a play, presented in English. Although the actors spoke with accents, their gestures and facial expressions brought out the humor of *Father Knows Best.* Carrie noticed that the eighth grader, named Dennis, who was their tour-guide and interpreter, spoke English without an accent. Questioning him, she learned his father had been sent to the U.S. for four years to serve with the United Nation,s so he had learned to speak English at an American school in New York.

The students in the upper classes presented parts from the plays *Sleeping Beauty* and *Little Red Riding Hood.* They sang American songs in English—"Old MacDonald," "Farmer in the Dell," and "Clementine." Before the close of their visit, the American visitors were led into the library and served tea and Russian pastry prepared by the eighth graders.

When the tourists who had selected to go to the shopping mall joined the school visitors and learned of their experience, they expressed regrets that they had not chosen to visit the school. However, all were greatly interested in their excursion on the following day—the tour of St. Isaac's Cathedral.

Although this structure had been pronounced a museum under the Communist administration, the very beautiful works of art depicting many biblical scenes were on display throughout the cathedral. St. Isaac's Cathedral is the largest cathedral in Russia. Its huge interior can accommodate 14,000 worshippers. Designed by Frenchman Auguste de Montferrand, it was built between 1818 and 1858. As Carrie listened to these details, she couldn't help wondering, recalling the defeat of Napoleon's invasion a few years before the building of St. Isaac's was planned, why was a French architect selected to design and raise this temple? Had there been a motive to indirectly announce the Russian victory over the French invasion? For the French invasion had proved a failure. The Tsar, the aristocracy, and a majority of the citizens had departed before the French military arrived at Moscow, and Napoleon was left without anyone to negotiate at the Russian capitol.

Napoleon's army was not prepared for Russia's fierce winter. Turning back, after the realization that nothing had been gained by their invasion, Napoleon's soldiers were forced to retreat. As Carrie noted from her history studies, the men froze and died; their horses slipped and fell, dying; their vehicles could not be moved; and most of their equipment had to be abandoned. Towards the end, discipline broke down and the army dissolved into a horde of individual fugitives. They were harassed by Russian irregulars along the way, as they picked their way by foot over ice and snow, mostly in the dark for days were short. Of the 611,000 who entered Russia, 400,000 died of battle casualties, exposure, and starvation. 100,000 were taken prisoner. Thus ended the existence of Napoleon's Grand Army.

After leaving his army in Russia in December 1812, Napoleon rushed back to Paris in just thirteen days by sleigh and coach. He raised a new army in France in the early months of 1813. Untrained and unsteady, this army was smashed in October at the battle of Leipzig, which the Germans called the Battle of the Nations. This was the greatest battle in number of men ever fought, prior to the twentieth century. In spite of all this experience with the French, it was only five years later that a French architect had been chosen to build this beautiful cathedral. Now, there was so much to see and absorb as the visitors toured this religious facility.

The exterior is decorated with sculptures, 112 red granite columns, and is topped by a massive gilded dome. Inside the mosaic icons, gold mosaics, and stone decorations are stunning. The iconostasis has columns of malachite and lapis lazuli. Above the altar is a large stained-glass window, depicting the Resurrection of Christ. Carrie noted particularly that throughout, the artwork displayed many biblical scenes—Jesus surrounded by His disciples at the Last Supper; the Judas' kiss to identify Jesus to his captors; the torturous floggings; aid given by Simon of Cyrene, to carry His cross when His weak body had forced Jesus down to the ground; and finally, the picture depicting the Ascension, with Jesus' arms raised to Heaven. Carrie's thoughts evolved to Russia's twentieth-century attitude toward religion. In the thirties, the Soviets had turned this church into a museum of atheism. In current times, services are held in the side chapel. The main auditorium is only used for special services, perhaps for Christmas and Easter. Yet the entire experience assured Carrie and the other visitors that the Orthodox faith had prevailed in spite of Bolshevism.

On the fourth day, changes were announced to take place for the tourists. Carrie would be saying farewell to Zdenek, who was boarding a train to take him back to Czechoslovakia and his marriage ceremony. The tourist group would leave for Moscow by plane. On the fifth morning, their bus took them to the Leningrad Airport, where they were served their lunch. The food was fabulous. Homemade vegetable soup and the entrée, *filet mignon,* much tastier than Carrie could ever recall having in her life. She found herself chatting with the ladies in Russian, complimenting them on their cooking. *Ako varila moja babushka.* This is how my grandmother cooked. She found all of them to be friendly.

But the plane! The group was escorted on one that they were told had been constructed before World War II. Drinking water was poured from a pitcher into glasses for those who wanted it. There were seat belts, but none of the amenities one might expect on an

American plane. Carrie was thankful when they landed safely in Moscow where a bus awaited their arrival.

The group was taken to the Cosmos Hotel. Within a very short walking distance was the Economic Exhibit Park. This did not capture Carrie's interest, but she did enjoy their bus tour of Moscow. They passed the KGB headquarters, paused to watch the changing of the guards, and saw Lenin's Tomb, the Kremlin, and St. Basil's Cathedral near Red Square. They were given two hours to shop at the G. U. M. On display was the huge bell with the crack in it. They made a stop at Cathedral Square with its gold-domed churches. The guard explained that each of the churches was destined for a different purpose—one was for funerals, another for marriages, and another for everyday worship.

The service at the Cosmos Hotel differed from the hotel in Leningrad. Breakfast was served buffet style in a very large dining room. Guests could choose from a large variety of foods, including salmon and baked Russian pastries. Carrie noticed a number of the participants at breakfast were from other countries, including a few Americans, doing business in Moscow. She ventured into conversation with one from New Jersey, who seemed happy to meet with an American teacher of Russian. Later that evening, Carrie and CeeCee were treated to a unique adventure that resulted from a contact made in the United States, some time prior to their trip. The man had phoned Carrie, asking her to contact a journalist friend, who promised to send Russian souvenir items and other imported pins and jewelry to him in exchange for some special services he had given him while visiting in the States, in Michigan, only about fifty miles from Carrie and Matt's home. When Carrie phoned the man, he made an appointment to meet with her in the lobby at their hotel. He could be identified by carrying a copy of *Time* magazine, and he heartily agreed to have CeeCee accompany them.

The hour was late, about ten o'clock, when they met. However, he did not have the items with him, but arranged to have his wife meet them for breakfast on Saturday morning, four days later, and bring them to take home with Carrie. However, he did offer to drive them around the city to do some sightseeing that was not included on their trip. He took them to Pushkin's home, the home where

Tolstoy stayed when residing in Moscow, and several other historic spots. It was a cold, wet, snowy night and at one point his car was temporarily stuck, but fortunately, he was able to exercise a bit of muscle and moved it. He invited Carrie and CeeCee to have a late cup of tea at his apartment. Both his wife and son were asleep. He had an assignment for the following day. He was to accompany President Gorbachev to China. Carrie expressed concern, for it was past 1:00 a.m. when he returned them to their hotel.

"I'm used to it; it's okay," he assured her. "Thank you for seeing my wife on Saturday, and helping me take care of this obligation."

The reason for the delay until Saturday was that CeeCee and Carrie were to take a bus trip to the Golden Triangle, and tour the towns of Vladimir and Suzdal for the following three days.

En route to their destination, Carrie would recall in future memories the beautiful folksy artwork on the rural homes they viewed as their bus passed through the Russian countryside. Even more reminiscent was the human interaction and friendship shown repeatedly by the Russian citizens. Here in Suzdal, as they were eating dinner, Carrie declared to CeeCee, "I'm tired of this trade-off of night and day, walking around on tours half-asleep and being awake at night time; I'm going to sleep tonight!" And she ordered a *koniak*, which did indeed do its duty. But alas, there was a negative result!

It was well past midnight, when sound asleep, Carrie was awakened by CeeCee. "Carrie, please wake up, you're snoring so loud that I can't sleep!"

Apologetic, she turned around to her other side, which she hoped would lower any sounds, and hopefully, would assist her in returning to her slumber. The rest of the night did offer her sleep, much lighter than the deep soundness she was experiencing before her roommate's cry for relief, but still better than she had experienced on all the previous nights on their trip.

The entire group was given free time the following afternoon. Suzdal was a small town and it was easy to walk around the center with its few quaint shops and sights without the crowds that gathered in the larger cities. Carrie strolled by herself, away from the group. When she stopped at a small dry goods store, she saw some things that captured her fancy. After observing several items on display, she decided to purchase an embroidered apron. She paid the owner in Russian cash. After they completed the transaction, he opened a drawer behind the counter and handed his American customer a small souvenir, peculiar to his region. He nodded as Carrie thanked him in Russian, *Bolshoye spaseeba!* He seemed to want somehow to extend a welcome to this American visiting his country.

They were to learn there was a beauty salon located in their motel. Carrie felt the need for a fresh hairdo and shampoo, and given directions from the desk clerk, approached the hairdresser. When observing her hair, which revealed a unique tasteful style, Carrie answered the hairdresser, when asked how she preferred to have her own hair done, saying to her in Russian, "*Samo jak vashe volosy.*" The same as your hair. Nodding, the hairdresser pointed to the sink, which Carrie had to stand in front of and bend enough to get shampooed. Later, combed out and ready to leave, after paying the clerk in Russian funds, she offered her hairdresser a choice. Would she prefer a tip in Russian money or an American dollar— "a souvenir"? The young woman happily pointed to the American dollar.

When Carrie returned to join her roommate, a new Russian acquaintance was waiting with her to meet Carrie. CeeCee had already informed him that Carrie taught Russian to schoolchildren in their home in west Michigan. The man awaiting her arrival shook Carrie's hand and greeted her in English. He wanted to know more about her reason for visiting his country. He was also interested in learning what had led Carrie to teach the Russian language. Her reply included some of her life's history. Carrie found herself telling about her parents, their childhood in Czechoslovakia, and her early exposure to their language, growing up in a bilingual home, and her discovery of the many same words in both of their languages. Her interest in teaching Russian was to acquaint American children to develop a familiarity with not only the language, but Russian history and culture.

"I want our countries to get to know each other, and to live together peacefully. So does my friend here, so that's why we came to visit your country, along with some of the adult students in my class."

"Aha, you are like missionaries," his words reflected both surprise and approval.

They conversed for quite some time, until CeeCee reminded Carrie it was time to eat dinner at the cafeteria. They both asked their guest to join them. However, he politely refused, explaining a family awaited him. But when he learned they would be boarding the bus to return them to Moscow after breakfast in the morning, he offered to join them for a brief visit before they departed. He had never traveled far from his home in Suzdal, but he was a writer who had written a book about his native town and he wanted to bring a copy to give to Carrie.

And so, he did. He also gave a copy of his book, titled *Suzdal*, to CeeCee. They visited until it was time for the visitors to board the bus that would carry them away from their newfound friend. As she began to board the steps at the door of their bus, his words reached Carrie, though they already had said their farewells—"Karolina," he called out in Russian, with such heartfelt emphasis that transmitted a type of bonding that declared a kinship of two persons; though newly-met, it was something built so preciously that words could not explain it. Yet they both knew what their hopes and dreams wanted for their countries, for the world, and for all of humanity— *peace and friendship.* Added to their acquaintance with the couple from Georgia they had met in Leningrad, Carrie felt all of her efforts in teaching Russian were worthwhile.

After their return to Moscow on Saturday morning as they had planned, Carrie and CeeCee met with the wife of their earlier nocturnal host for breakfast. It was a pleasant new acquaintance. As her husband had previously advised them, there was a large package to be transported by Carrie and delivered to the American friend in western Michigan. Contents included a variety of pins and souvenirs from Russia. There was also a special gift for Carrie given in gratitude for her assistance in delivery.

That evening, the group attended their last visit to the theater in

Russia. The play was *Romanda*, that Carrie had seen previously, when the Russian actors performed in Manhattan a few years prior. She had hoped they would see *Swan Lake*, but for that performance Carrie had to wait for a future time.

The flight home from Moscow brought a surprise—the Peace Links visitor, Vera, whom CeeCee was unable to contact earlier in Russia, was on their plane, again to visit in the U.S. They met as friends, ready to update each other on current events in their lives.

Another fellow traveler was a doctor who was attempting to persuade an elderly Russian lady to use her seatbelt, which she vocally refused to buckle. Viewing his plight, Carrie approached her seat, and mustered her best Russian, with a dominant *obyazatel'naw*— absolutely required—grabbed her seat belt, and buckled it before the passenger had time to protest, but she did not undo it. Her brief conversation revealed she was to visit family members in the U.S. What Carrie did not yet know was that during her first week home she was invited to the church who had sponsored the visit of the Russian doctor. Carrie and he were surprised to meet again, recalling their initial meeting on their flight from Moscow. What a pleasant surprise for them both!

How wonderful, Carrie thought. It appeared Americans and Russians are using opportunities to get to know each other.

Now, it was April of '89. The remainder of the school year passed smoothly. In early summer, Matt and Carrie were to celebrate their fortieth wedding anniversary, as well as the birth of a new granddaughter. Summer seemed to melt away rapidly. Both loved being together. Matt tended the roses he had planted, lavishing a fresh one, together with the morning cup of coffee he brought to Carrie, who usually slept an hour or two later than he. They both realized it was okay that their physical systems had related differently to the clock. Matt, who followed Ben Franklin's *early to bed and early to rise* adage, accepted his wife's night-owl journaling, or viewing one of Turner's classics. *Mrs. Miniver*, and other films bringing back memories of World War II, such as *Casablanca*, had always held her interest.

The fall began with Matt's last year of teaching in the city's school system. Teachers willing to retire were offered a financial bonus. Matt hoped to fulfill a long-hoped-for volunteering position in administration with the retirees' organization. Now, there would be an opportunity. Carrie was to continue teaching for two more years before joining Matt in retirement. They planned to travel to the southwest in the winters to visit with daughter Anna and her family. Every drive across the country gave opportunity to tour a historic spot. In Kansas, there was the Truman Library and the home of Harry and Bess, reminders of life and home furnishings that brought back memories of their childhood years. In Texas, they toured the Johnson ranch and museum. Sometimes, they would arrange to visit friends or family members along the way. There were first and second cousins in Mississippi and Iowa; Matt's sister and husband, with two nephews and close friends in Corpus Christi. What fun it was to fulfill visiting desires during travels westward.

Christmas in '89 proved to be a happy time. So much had happened that would change their lives forever. Matt and Carrie reminisced as they awaited the New Year. Carrie's long-hoped-for trip to Russia was fulfilled. Matt and Tim, meanwhile, visited family and friends in Texas and Mexico. Wren gave them a new granddaughter in June, a delightful child for all the family to enjoy. Their home would become her second home for many long visits with her grandparents throughout the future years. For Tim, a new friendship mellowed into a romance; a diamond at Christmas and a promise for a June wedding in the new year. After ten years of being alone, with

Tim and his new bride were married in June 1990.

memories of an unsuccessful marriage, Tim was happy to have Gracie, this new woman in his life. Durinda's marriage to Bud seemed stable. Now, in addition to her daughter, Sheila, they had a son, Anton, named after his great-grandfather. Bud has begun a business of his own, working as a chimney sweep. Durinda, who had gained much proficiency with her computer, assisted her husband with bookkeeping, business calls, and appointments. Anna and her husband were living in Ohio with their two children, daughter Elizabeth and son John. Many travels to visit them were to take place for Matt and Carrie.

Much had happened since the birth of Wren, more than two decades before—the expansion of their family with marriages and new births added. During the summer of '89, Matt and Carrie did celebrate their fortieth wedding anniversary. The difficulties they had encountered more than a decade before had been overcome, resolved, no longer in existence. Carrie treasured Matt's Christmas gift to her—a white gold bracelet—and wore it always. But it was the note that accompanied this jewelry that touched her heart. It expressed Matt's feelings—"To Carrie, Christmas '89 With Love & Devotion, Dutchie." Carrie wondered, *Why did Matt sign this with his long-ago, commonly-heard nickname in their early acquaintance, now seldom used, instead of his formal name? Did this result from a reminiscence of their early romantic years?* Carrie recalled the words the actor stated to his lover in the film she had viewed—"This kind of *certainty* comes just once in a lifetime." Carrie believed that she had indeed experienced this same kind of *certainty;* but unlike the experience of that to which the actor referred, she knew she had never felt the need for anyone else in her life except Matt—Matt, the country boy from Michigan, who became the loving husband to her, the young maiden from Chicago. It had to be an act of Providence that had drawn them together.

One must believe, *All things do work together for Good.*

www.ingramcontent.com/pod-product-compliance
Lightning Source LLC
Chambersburg PA
CBHW071830020726
47502CB00004B/1299